Becoming Stardust

STUART FABE

Becoming Stardust

Copyright 2015 by Stuart A. Fabe

All Rights Reserved

No part of this publication may be reproduced, stored in a retrieval system or transmitted, in any form or by any means — electronic, mechanical, photocopying, recording or otherwise — without prior written permission from the publisher, except for the inclusion of brief quotations in a review.

For information about this title or to order other books and/or electronic media, contact the publisher:

Stuart A. Fabe
Greencastle, Indiana
stuartfabe@gmail.com

ISBN: 978-0-6925098-3-8

Printed in the United States

Dedicated to

My Handsome Twin Brother

JEFFREY BLOCK FABE

We Stick Together!

Chapter 1

THE FIRST TIME I REMEMBER seeing Judge Thaddeus Nathan behaving like a mere mortal, he was looking at a Hubble telescope image of the Milky Way on his home computer.

He apparently hadn't heard me knock on the front door of his house, nor my approach to the doorway of his study. In the subdued light, I could see a solitary tear flow down his cheek and the visage of a man who had endured great personal loss. A small framed photo of his late wife, Ellie, sat on his desk near a short glass filled with an amber-colored liquid. He seemed deeply adrift in his thoughts; his murmurings softly broadcast to a different place. Sensing that I had intruded on his personal space, I quietly backed out of the entrance hall and returned to his front porch.

My name is Wade; Wade Benjamin Henry to be exact, and I am eighteen years old. My mom and I live across the road from Judge Nathan, six miles north of the town of Someday, Indiana. My dad died violently about a year ago, and Mrs. Nathan followed a few days later. Both deaths sent shockwaves through our small college town, and our local officials are still trying to figure out how such brutality could occur within our community. My mom and I have grown much closer to the Judge since then, but they are both reluctant to offer more details with me about our shared tragedies than the media has reported.

Now, I cup my eyes and peer through his screen door and rap on its wooden frame.

"I'm coming; hold your horses," said the Judge in a voice that was firm but weighted with a bit of weariness.

A few moments later he appeared at the door with a handkerchief dabbing at his face and a warm smile when he saw me standing there.

Judge Thaddeus Nathan is a legend in our town. Though not tall in stature, standing at about 5'8", his bearing is patrician, and he radiates refinement; plus he commands a rapier-like wit. People respect; some even revere the Judge. His silver hair, though combed, isn't quite as well-kept as when Mrs. Nathan was alive. In truth, with his beloved Ellie being gone, it was clear that Thad, as his few close friends called him, was showing his nearly 70 years of age… reasonably fit and trim, but a little slower in his movement; a little less enthusiastic in his manner and speech.

"Well there you are, young Sirius, if it isn't that shining star come to brighten up my night sky."

He laughed and patted me on the shoulder as he stepped out to join me on the front porch. In addition to his judicial responsibilities, the Judge had also been an avid astronomer for much of his adult life, and he is forever using celestial terms to describe things. He derives particular amusement at giving me ever-changing starry nicknames. Most of the time I don't have a clue who or what he's referring to, but they make him smile, so I go along.

"Hi Judge, my mom got home from work a few minutes ago and wanted me to see if you'd like to join us for supper.

My mom is probably the greatest mom around, and despite her still being very sad about my dad being gone, she has made it her mission in life to look after me and a small cluster of friends, including the Judge, and to make sure that our family is secure and well-regarded.

I know she loves me very much and that she mourns for her old full-time job of being a wife and mother. Sadly, the wife part is gone, and to my occasional frustration, she has doubled-down on the mothering part. Like I said, I know my mom really loves me, but man, sometimes it feels like she's got me surrounded."

"Well, I sure don't want to be a bother," Thaddeus said, "but if you'll give me a few minutes to put some things away and freshen up, I'd be delighted to enjoy one of your mom's home cooked meals and hear about your heroic achievements at school. See you in a bit, okay.

And, we've got a great, clear sky tonight," Thaddeus called out. "You might want to look at the southern sky. Mighty Orion and Canis Major, Taurus and Gemini are all moving westerly and will be gone when spring fully arrives. Those 10×50 binoculars I loaned you should do nicely. There's a lot to be learned from stories about the stars, and you know we'll all join them someday; so you might as well get to know the neighborhood."

As I walked across the road to our yard, I looked up and tried to imagine how we would ever be up there with the stars. We live in the country outside of town, and the light pollution is minimal; so there's a lot of stars to see if I only remember to do it. Tonight the sky is inky dark, with no moonrise yet, and with the crisp spring air, the stars light up the sky like a cosmic jeweler spreading loose diamonds onto a black felt pad.

I really don't know the night sky very well, but the Judge and I have looked through binoculars together on a few occasions, and I've marveled at his knowledge and his enthusiasm in showing me things.

The Judge told me once, "We're all becoming stardust, my young stellar friend, and that's okay." I'm not exactly sure what that means, but I decided it was something worth trying to comprehend.

A few moments later, my mom called to me outside, "I could use a little help, Wade, if you want to eat anytime soon."

My mom's name is Cassie, a name that the Judge states is short for Cassiopeia, one of his favorite constellations. Mom insists her real name is Cassandra, to which the Judge declares "no problem" since he has a different yarn from classical mythology to share about that name too.

"Evening Cassie, thanks for the dinner invitation," the Judge says as he enters the kitchen, it's awfully good of you to include me, though I feel a little guilty since all I brought is this avocado and some grapes to use up before they get too mushy."

"Thanks Thad," Mom replied. The avocado and grapes will go nicely in the salad which you and Wade could make if you want to help."

The Judge and Wade got right to it, and in characteristic fashion, the Judge called Wade's attention to the avocado's elliptical shape and said it was like orbits in our solar system, with the big pit at the center being the sun, and the grapes like planets orbiting it.

"Hey Wade, did I ever tell you about the time I rode on a comet and saw our beautiful, blue planet from space?"

While Judge Nathan is a man of extraordinary legal expertise, who has established a remarkable career serving the judicial needs of Prindle County, he also has a very vivid imagination and a remarkable gift for telling stories. He often enjoys regaling folks with fanciful tales that contain nuggets of truth. At times it was a challenge for Wade to glean fact from fiction, but this was also the Judge's creative way to help Wade learn to think for himself.

"No, Judge, I don't think so." And I got ready to hear another classic Thaddeus Nathan whopper. He went right into telling his story.

"Well, it was like this," Thaddeus began, "I was in my court-room hearing a vehicular homicide case. The defense attorney was a young public defender named Kenny Clifton, and he drew the unfortunate assignment of representing a particularly nasty fellow named Curly Algol who was no stranger to my courtroom."

"I recall that I was deep in thought considering who was the bigger doofus in the courtroom; the defendant who claimed that running that fella down with a stolen car was justifiable homicide, or his dimwit attorney who actually believed him."

"Well, I guess I grew weary listening to the defense counsel's baloney and must've nodded off, because I soon dreamed I had been swept up by this frozen, blazing ball of ice and I could see the Earth far below. As the dream progressed, I rode this comet and viewed my surroundings with awe and humility.

I saw mighty Jupiter rise high in the east, shadowed by Castor and Pollux, with Regulus and Algieba a little further east. The stars went on forever; old friends that I've viewed for years, but now radiating a certain sentience that brought me a focused clarity of thought and peace of mind. I could somehow see more clearly into the nature of things."

"The defense attorney droned on with his closing arguments, stating that his client had gotten confused in the parking lot and had gotten into the wrong vehicle. He couldn't find his keys so he decided to just hot wire it."

"About that time, attorney Clifton stated the vehicle's real owner stepped out of a shop and saw my client in his car. A heated exchange ensued; the car's engine roared to life; and the car's owner stepped in front of the car to block it's exit.

Fearing that the car's owner would physically harm my client, Mr. Algol threw the Buick in gear and gunned it crunching the owner under the vehicle. Clearly, this is a case of self-defense.

The defense attorney Clifton was oblivious to my tempo-rary lack of mental presence on terra firma, the Judge admitted.

Unfortunately for me, I eventually re-joined the here and now taking place in my courtroom and had to listen to the rest of the horse hockey being slung.

'… and that your honor, and you good folks in the jury, is why my poor client, Curly Algol, ran over that feller with that borrowed Buick.' The defense rested.

The unsympathetic silence that ensued was deafening. Even the prosecutor was bewildered by the line of pure unadulterated nonsense he had just heard.

I instructed the jury to retire and do their civic duty. Fifteen minutes later, my bailiff, Jeff Block, announced that the jury had made a decision. Privately, my first reaction was 'what took em so long'?!

The jury foreman was Frosty Gosport, who owned the hardware store south of town. "Thad, I mean your honor, we the jury find the defendant, Curly Algol, guilty as hell on all counts."

With that, the courtroom erupted and that model citizen, Curly, charged the Judge's bench threatening to get him and all his kin one of these days. Mr. Algol didn't get very far, before security got him wrapped up, but Curly was pretty clear that he was not a happy feller and spit out his vitriolic intentions for revenge."

The Judge recalled that this man had appeared before him previously as a juvenile, and that he had remanded him to the juvenile detention facility for a brutal assault on a young girl at school.

The Judge continued his story, "I sat there calmly taking it all in, still feeling the bliss from my comet ride, and then judiciously set the sentencing for the following week. Curly Algol was one dangerous animal, and I had no intentions of having him walk among the good folks of Someday, Indiana for a long, long time."

"See you next week, Mr. Algol," the Judge said. "Until then, enjoy your accommodations, courtesy of our fine correctional system." With a loud rap of his gavel, Judge Nathan declared "Court is adjourned."

Curly was still slobbering his anger at the Judge; swearing "This ain't over, you high and mighty mother fuck!"

Defense counsel, Kenny Clifton, quietly stuffed papers into his briefcase and beat a hasty retreat out the side door, still trying to figure out how the Court had so badly misjudged his poor misunderstood client.

A week later, with a new public defender at his side, Curly Algol got what was coming to him; a life sentence in the Federal Correctional Center in Russellville forty miles away. Adios Curly!

"Well, as it turned out, Mr. Algol was a lot sharper than our transport guards," the Judge continued. "While being loaded for transport to Russellville, he overpowered two of them and got their keys."

"Mildred McGuffy saw Curly shed his shackles, kick a guard in the face and hightail it down Jackson street. The other officer managed to get a shot off with his service revolver, but the bullet went far wide. Curly had managed to get away and was on the lam for three days. It was not one of our police department's finest episodes."

"Sheriff Noble Penrod thought that Curly Algol was long gone from Prindle County, but that was wishful thinking. No one knew exactly where he'd been for three days."

"Someone swore they'd seen him as far south as Spencer, and another person said they saw him over by Rockville. A third said they saw Curly in Danvillle. Nothing was ever confirmed."

"Finally, the police caught a lucky break when Deputy Cat Newkirk saw someone at the rear of the abandoned Monon restaurant and decided to go investigate. She called for backup and several officers surrounded the surly and snarling escapee at the Monon. He surrendered peaceably enough because he had no choice. With five deputies in two vehicles this time, he was taken directly to Russellville to begin his life sentence."

"However, those three days that Curly was on the run were very tragic days for everyone in Someday, Indiana. It was during that time that Ben and Ellie's tragic murders occurred. Unfortunately, no solid evidence came to light connecting them with Curly Algol."

"The police thought he was the most likely suspect, of course, and they questioned him for hours. Curly Algol swore he was hiding the entire time at the old railroad depot north of town before sneaking back to the Monon restaurant to steal food."

In the end, Curly was going away forever, so maybe it didn't matter if he was convicted of these murders, but the full truth had not yet come out. It was an open wound, and the Judge and Cassie and Wade wanted justice and closure.

The Judge was preparing to go on, but Cassie interrupted him.

"Okay Thaddeus," Cassie chimed in, "that's enough courtroom drama for now. Let's please try to remember that we have an impressionable child present."

Impressionable child… if there's one phrase an eighteen year old guy doesn't want to hear, that may be it.

"Mom, I'm eighteen years old; I'm grown up!"

"Not to me you're not," she protested, "And apparently not to some of your teachers, according to the phone call I got from school today."

Thaddeus Nathan grew very quiet. He thought he'd probably crossed a line discussing this case; no matter how he tried to make light of it. Fact was, he was still grieving tremendously, and talking about it helped him cope sometimes. He realized he shouldn't have gone on about this in front of Wade. Cassie too.

"Sorry Cassiopeia, I still have trouble believing any of this happened to us, and I guess being a Judge for 30 years can also help a fella feel a little entitled to talk. I just get a little full of myself sometimes. Mea culpa, I'm very sorry."

Cassie's tasty meal and the friendly company made for a delightful evening. The Judge asked Cassie about her work in the college's development office, and she talked about the long hours their staff had to work to prepare for launching the school's largest fundraising campaign ever.

Someday, Indiana was blessed to be home to Kissinger College, a private college founded in 1849, with its highly-ranked liberal arts and sciences degree programs. Their crown jewels are diverse: the School of Music, under the visionary leadership of Dean Michael Hatfield, is considered to be among the best in higher education anywhere in the country.

Another jewel is their Von Timm Observatory which is lovingly cared for by Lyndon Tweedy, Chairman of the Department of Astrophysics. Other college departments are outstanding as well, but these programs shine in particular and garner financial support from many alums.

When Cassie's husband, Ben, was murdered, she and Wade benefitted from the life insurance policy he had through work as Executive Director of the Kissinger College's Stanley Institute for Ethics, but it wasn't enough to cover their living expenses and send Wade off to college soon. So, she went looking for work and was fortunate to find a position researching and preparing foundation grant applications to major charitable and corporate foundations.

The University's fundraising goal included a specific goal of $80 million to be raised from charitable and corporate foundations; so there was a lot of pressure to perform and to secure major grants.

Cassie was a natural at grantsmanship. Prior to having Wade, she had graduated from Princeton near the top of her class with a degree in political science, and went off to Cambridge University in England for an advanced degree in international relations. She still smiles when she recalls her subsequent years working at the State Department. It was pretty intense work, with some even more intense individuals, but it was often fulfilling.

After a few years of traveling from one global conundrum to another, she decided that she wanted more in her personal life.

Then, she met Ben Henry, fell in love and they began a family. Their own little happy constellation of three.

"Sorry guys," Cassie said, "I guess I got a little carried away talking about my work. The success of this campaign is going to benefit many academic programs and campus life in general, and it's not easy to leave the work at the office. Plus, we have a lot of heavy-hitters on Kissinger's Board, and a number of major prospective donors, who are politely, but definitely, breathing down our necks to see if we are well organized, and if the financial goals are well conceived."

"I'm sure you and your colleagues will do just fine," the Judge offered, "but I certainly understand the pressure you must be feeling. I got a phone call from Lyndon Tweedy a few days ago wanting to meet and discuss the Observatory's objectives. I guess there's a price for my infatuation with the stars, and it will come in the form of a campaign pledge to support Kissinger's Astrophysics Department. So, I'll do my part to help too."

"Thank you, Thad, I didn't mean for my ramblings about work to be a solicitation for support, but I'm sure Lyndon will be very pleased that you'll participate. He regards you as an highly competent amateur astronomer, which is high praise coming from Lyndon."

"So young Rigel", as the Judge selected yet another star name from his celestial bag of tricks, "how are your studies coming along?"

"Fine" came Wade's one-word reply. Not to be deterred, the Judge ventured another approach.

"Fine is nice, but I want details, young sir. What are you studying in Latin these days or History, Geography, Biology, Algebra? A few more details please!"

"I don't know why I have to take Latin," Wade complained. "It's a dead language. You can't have a conversation with anyone, and it's all about people and stuff that happened a really long time ago."

Wade actually was smart enough to know that his comments were silly, but of late he had grown less interested with his studies and seemed at a growing loss for direction and purpose.

He really missed his dad, and his mom was gone a lot for work. He understood why she was gone, but gone is gone, and the young boy part of him wanted his old family life back. Graduation was just around the corner, and he knew he'd be going to Duke in late August. So, high school was now less important to him.

He had spent many hours training for his cross country races. Wade loved testing his running skills against the terrain and against his competitors. Sometimes he felt like a deer running with the wind. He felt carefree. Then, he'd think about his dad again and sorrow would creep into his legs and slow him to a walk. Adulthood had come up on him fast, and no matter how bright and talented Wade Henry was, he was paying a heavy price for admission.

"You know, poor old Latin can't catch a break," the Judge playfully lamented. "When I was around your age, we all said the same thing. Then a funny thing happened. Almost everywhere I looked, I saw and heard Latin. It was in the English language, and you might as well throw in French, Spanish, and Italian. It's words are in medicine, science and law and art, not to mention a little thing called religion."

"I came to think that Latin was kinda like the universe; it's all around us, but we rarely take the time to examine its influences on our daily lives. Maybe that's why the ancient Greeks and Romans conferred the constellations with Latin names; so we mere mortals would always remember." "I know that appreciating Latin can be a challenge, Wade, but try to give it a little time to sink in," the Judge encouraged.

Chapter 2

WITH DINNER OVER and the dishes washed and put away, the Judge was preparing to head back home when Cassie touched Thaddeus' elbow.

"Got a sec, Thad, I have something legal I'd like to discuss with you."

"Sure Cassiopeia." "Wade, why don't you head outside with the binocs and see if you can spot the Great Orion Nebula and the Andromeda Galaxy. I'll be along in a few minutes."

He waited for a few moments for Wade to leave the kitchen and then the Judge asked, "What's up, Cassie, you have a legal problem?"

"No, I have a kid problem," she confided. I just said that so Wade would go out of earshot. And besides, my name is Cassandra, not Cassiopeia."

"Now, now", the Judge calmed. "Why don't you tell me what's going on?"

"I'm biased, of course, but you know Wade is a very special kid," Cassie started, "but I am becoming very concerned about his studies and his overall attitude. His school counselor, Dr. Benedicts, said a couple of his teachers have found him daydreaming in class, not finishing homework assignments and not involving himself in class discussions like he's usually done.

Worse though are the heated arguments he's getting into with some of his classmates. Heck, Wade doesn't even show interest in girls anymore which is definitely not like him. He's just not himself these days. Sometimes he gives me terse, one-syllable answers, and I just don't know what to do. I try to talk with him, but he insists everything's okay and to stop bugging him. And, of course he runs a whole lot! He's like a deer that's unclear of which direction to run."

The Judge listened attentively, as was his style, and he tried to ascertain from Cassie's testimony what was going on with Wade.

"Cassie, are you sure it's not just a tough phase he's still going through? His dad's gone. You're tied up with major work responsibilities. He's thinking about college and a career and that often befuddles even the brightest of kids. And, he's probably still coming to grips with his dad's murder and the fact that the police never arrested the guy."

"I know, I know. I keep telling myself that Wade just needs some time to heal, but I'm not so sure, Thad. His SAT scores were really good and his grades have been excellent up until recently, and we sent applications to several premier colleges.

He's already been accepted at Duke early admissions, Cassie added, and Wade has told them he wants to be a Blue Devil, but I really worry that my not being home more is adding to the problem. He needs more supervision, and I feel like I'm failing him."

"I understand your concern, Cassie, why don't I plan on spending a little more time with him after school and try to get him to open up a bit more. He's a delightful young man, but he's been through a lot for someone his age. I'd like to help if I can."

"Thank you, Thaddeus. Wade really looks up to you, and any guidance you can give either of us would be deeply appreciated."

"Hey Judge, c'mon out," Wade called from outside. "I can see some really great things with these new Oberwerk binoculars. I can't believe I can see the Orion Nebula with them, and the Andromeda Galaxy is really visible instead of a blur."

The Judge promptly obeyed, and he and Wade spent the next hour training their optics on different parts of the sky, each excited at what they were seeing, and each enjoying the other's company. The early spring constellations provided an excellent sky map to finding alpha and beta stars and locating deep sky Messier objects.

"Well Wade, I think I've had enough fun for one night. It's time for this old jurist to call it a day."

"Okay, thanks Judge, but I think I'll just hang out a little longer. I feel like I'm starting to get the hang of this and putting the binoculars on the tripod sure helps a lot."

They parted company and agreed to do it again on the next clear night.

Back in his study, Thaddeus Nathan settled into his favorite chair and selected a recording by classical guitarist, Ana Vidovic. He looked around at the room's comfortable surroundings, and he felt very much at home with his contemporary Danish furniture and his soft leather sofas. He looked at several of the colorful prints on the walls and lingered on objects that he and Ellie had collected on various trips. His eyes fell on Ellie's photograph.

"Oh Darlin', I swear we'll find the bastard who did this to you and Ben, and if I get him before the police do, the legal system won't have to fret about due process."

For over thirty years Judge Nathan was a faithful servant of the law. He believed in it; he championed it, but when it came to exacting justice for his wife's death and the murder of Ben Henry, he privately nursed a double standard that he hoped would end in one more death.

Cassie was unaware of how much pressure he had put on the authorities to find the killer. Thaddeus brought in the FBI and even hired a private investigator to dig up any leads they could. So far, nothing significant had surfaced.

The Judge emptied the remains of his glass, and poured himself a fresh tumbler of Glenmorangie Scotch. He stared deeply into the amber liquid; then peered back and forth between it and Ellie's picture. Minutes passed without him stirring; lost in thought about his loss, the only woman he ever loved ripped away from him by some ugly human being.

"I swear, Ellie, it's not ending like this. Justice will be served!"

Before long, with his belly full from Cassie's meal and the Scotch warming him, the Judge drifted off to sleep and dreams swept him away.

In his first dream, he felt himself being carried away by the same fiery, icy comet that propelled him from his courtroom some weeks ago. It was a pleasant experience. He felt safe and secure as if he belonged up here as much as anything or anyone else. He marveled at the celestial sights he could see far above the Earth's atmosphere. The nebular gases and dust created a backdrop filled with infinite colors and dimensions. The Moon and planets hung in the vast void of space like a cosmic billiards table. Such are the images that our dreams create.

"Is this heaven?" he wondered. "Is this truly where we are all destined to go?"

The constellation, Orion, greeted him; sending Betelgeuse, Bellatrix, Schaim, and Rigel as its ambassadors. Thaddeus had long ago fallen under the allure of the Orion constellation; both for its grandeur and the legends told for millennia about the great hunter. Orion was his beacon; his champion. Though the rule of law had guided his career, the Judge felt a special kinship with Orion, not as a hunter for game, but as a hunter for justice.

And then the dream shifted, and he and Ellie were by the sea. Ah, their trip to Cinque Terra in Italy; their rooms in Vernazza and Monterossa al Mare overlooking the Ligurian Sea. He had never known such happiness, riding the trains with Ellie, shopping for mementoes, hiking the paths connecting the five villages.

His love for Ellie had grown ever stronger throughout the decades, and even though they couldn't have children, Thaddeus, never felt that his life was missing anything as long as he had Ellie by his side. She was his true North Star.

Thaddeus then awoke with a start. His dreams soon vanished to wherever dreams go, and in his mind the celestial skies darkened; the nebular grandeur was gone; the romance of Italy vaporized; the music of the spheres grew silent, replaced by a steely buzz like a high tension wire.

Thaddeus was now fully awake and his thoughts re-played what he had been told of the tragic scene that had occurred on the road by his home. He pictured the lights strobing from police cars. Radios squawking. Wade's father, Ben Henry, lying in the Judge's front yard, mortally wounded by a knife-wielding maniac. A lot of blood.

Spencer Greenlee's home was the only other house near this part of Brick Chapel Road, and Thaddeus remembered Spencer's statement to the responding officers about how he had been working outside clearing brush when heard a terrible commotion and looked over at Thaddeus and Ellie's home. He had seen Ben Henry rushing across the road to offer assistance because something horrific sounded like it was occurring inside the Judge's house.

Thaddeus recalled Spencer's exact words: "A moment later a loud, angry man comes running from the Nathans' house and attacks Ben as he approached the steps. Poor Ben didn't stand a chance. This crazy guy just leaped from the house and attacked him, hollering something about revenge. Ben didn't even have time to defend himself.

It was awful," Spencer shuddered. "I immediately pulled out my cell phone and called 911. Two police cruisers arrived within 15 minutes and a life squad followed a few minutes later. Nothing could be done for Ben. He suffered deep stab wounds to his head and arms, with a finishing slash across the throat."

And then Spencer had said that the intruder leered briefly at him and was gone. He apparently only caught a brief glimpse of him as the assailant jumped in an old pickup truck and sped away.

Judge Nathan quietly wept under the crushing sadness of the heartbreak that had occurred.

Thaddeus now sat stone still in his study trying to stop the flood of horrifying thoughts about the attacks, but the recollection of Spencer Greenlee's words haunted the Judge more.

"I didn't know what to do," Spencer had admitted, "but I had to see if Ellie was okay, and to try and find the Judge while waiting for Sheriff Penrod and the ambulance. I ran to the Nathans' home and called for Ellie as I entered the house. I immediately saw her laying very still at the foot of the steps leading upstairs.

I didn't see any blood," Spencer had reported, "but I couldn't tell if she were alive or dead. She already showed some nasty bruises around her face and neck and her nose appeared to be fractured. I noticed two of the spindles from the bannister had been broken loose and thought that she had probably been thrown by the intruder from the top of the stairs to the entry hall below. The paramedics arrived a few minutes later and prepared her for transit to Prindle County Hospital."

Thaddeus recalled that he had been in his chambers that day when the tragedy occurred and was immediately alerted by Sheriff Noble Penrod that there was a serious problem at his house. With a police escort, he arrived home as the paramedics were securing Ellie Nathan in the ambulance. He rode with her to the hospital and stayed with her for two days, never leaving her side except when surgery was required to stem the internal bleeding. Ellie never opened her eyes again and died a day later, with the Judge by her side.

In the days that followed, the police came up with no plausible leads. The perpetrator had simply vanished. Spencer Greenlee's description of the assailant offered little help.

"The killer was medium height, with either dark hair or wearing a dark cap, with bluejeans and a medium length dark coat. No distinguishing characteristics. No facial hair; no glasses. That was about it… except the disturbing leer."

Judge Nathan's court docket was cleared, and a circuit judge arrived to hear outstanding cases. Aside from unproductive meetings with Sheriff Penrod to try to determine the identity and motive of the intruder, Thaddeus Nathan remained at home and declined attempts by friends to pay condolence calls.

Cassie and Wade Henry were in total shock. How could something so heinous happen to Ben and Ellie? Thankfully, Cassie and Wade had been at the Mall getting Wade some new clothes for college when the attacks occurred. No telling how much more carnage would've resulted had they been home.

Ben Henry had no known enemies and was universally liked. His direction of the Stanley Institute for Ethics had become an international model for the studies of humanism. Ben had devoted much of his adult life to creating environments where people could come together; discuss various points of view on pressing issues such as race, gender, and income inequality… and the criminal justice system.

Ben and Thaddeus had become close friends, often debating the nature of man and society's role in guiding behavior. Ben believed deeply that if we could bring diverse people together and air differences of opinion, that positive resolutions could result. With a long, serrated blade, the perpetrator put a messy end to that theory.

Weeks passed and the good people of Someday, Indiana tried to put the worst tragedy in the town's history behind them. Spring had finally returned, and with its arrival, folks were heading outdoors to mow lawns, tend gardens, and finally get aerobic exercise aside from hauling firewood and shoveling snow.

To everyone's dismay, Judge Thaddeus Nathan retired from the bench which created another emotional hole in the town's fabric. He had been Someday, Indiana's conscience and its arbiter of justice for thirty years. Now, he had simply lost interest in the job and wanted to be left alone.

Chapter 3

THE BROWN UPS TRUCK rumbled down Brick Chapel Road. Quentin Harp, the driver, knew the road well and navigated the intermittent stretches of gravel and pavement like a pro. He pulled into Thaddeus Nathan's driveway and came to a stop with a cloud of dust cycloning after him. Thaddeus had heard the UPS truck coming from a good half mile away. He knew it would be Quentin, which was fine because he actually enjoyed the young fella's laid back but professional manner.

"Howdy, Judge, how you doing this fine, super fine first day of May?" Quentin grinned.

"If you're delivering what I hope you're delivering, my day could be mighty fine indeed." Thaddeus offered.

"A couple of the boxes are pretty darn big, but I think we can easily handle them together if you're willing to help."

"Of course," the Judge immediately replied and then leaped into action.

The Honorable Judge Thaddeus Nathan usually maintained a certain dignified persona; a very accomplished and well-informed man, thoughtful and comfortable in his own skin. Right now he was feeling about as excited as he could remember being for a long while. He knew what good old Quentin and he were safely hauling inside his spacious study. This was like Christmas morning!

"Wow, Judge, whatever it is, I sure hope you don't have to move it too often," Quentin exclaimed.

"Once I get everything put together properly, it should be fairly manageable, but that's all I'm going to tell you right now, Quentin. The next time you have a delivery for me or the Henrys, stop by and I'll show you some interesting things, okay?!"

"Sure enough! I like a little intrigue as much as the next guy. Have fun, and I'll see you next time then." And in characteristic fashion Quentin sprayed a little road gravel as his brown truck created a new cloud of chalky dust. Then he was gone.

Thaddeus' study was his refuge these days. Throughout his entire life, he had spent innumerable hours at a desk whether in public school growing up in Cincinnati, Ohio, or at Harvard for his undergraduate education or law school at the University of Virginia; and certainly for more than thirty years in his chambers as a Judge.

His home study was a very comfortable and personal space that nurtured academic inquiry and judicial thought. It was also a space for relaxation without much thought. Thaddeus's study was indeed his treasured haven, and he spent many hours alone here.

But Thaddeus wasn't a total recluse. He certainly enjoyed his time with Wade and Cassie. It had a safe, familial feel to it, and that gave heartwarming relief to all three of them, given the gaping wounds they still bore.

And the Judge had begun seeing a few select, long-time friends for coffee and occasionally drinks and dinner, but he was reluctant to get too close to anyone in particular, and he really wasn't interested in amorous relationships at this point in his life. Besides he still loved Ellie.

Judge Thaddeus Nathan was a realist, and he knew that he would never fully recover from losing Ellie. He also knew that he had to continue living and growing as a human being. Ellie would not have wanted it any other way. So, Thaddeus found himself leaving one phase of abject grief to another phase of grief that at least allowed him to live his life with a little bit of enthusiasm.

He reached for his boxcutter, ready to dive into the boxes that Quentin had delivered, when he heard Wade call to him from just inside the front door.

"Back here; you're just in time," the Judge called out. "Come see what I just got."

"Holy cow! It looks like Christmas morning with all of these boxes, Judge. I heard Quentin pull into your driveway and saw you toting all this stuff inside. So, I decided to invite myself in to see what kind of mischief you were getting into."

Together they started in on the first large box that had 'fragile' marked on it. Before long they had packing material scattered everywhere, with a huge pair of binoculars resting on the floor beside them. "Whoa, Wade exclaimed, I've never seen binoculars this big. You'll be able to see forever with these."

"Young Wade, allow me to introduce you to the Oberwerk 45 degree 100 mm binocular telescope with a Jarrah hardwood tripod and a smooth forked mount. Pretty impressive, huh?! You can see a long, long way with this scope; not as far as a telescope, of course, but the optics are really fine and will show incredible views of the lunar surface. Wait till you see the details of the craters and mares. Help me get them on the tripod, okay?"

"They are incredible," Wade gushed. "They remind me of the scopes they have at national parks so you can see things way off in the distance. Wow, I really can't believe how large they are. Good thing you got the heavy duty tripod. Sweet!"

"Yeah, they're pretty special", the Judge beamed. "I debated about getting them for a long time because they're fairly pricey, but I thought it was finally time to breathe some fresh life into my aging bones with some new toys. I think Ellie would've been happy for me too."

"What's in the other big box?" Wade asked with growing excitement.

"Ah, Mr. Henry, that is something that I thought we might use together too," the Judge suggested. With eager hands, Wade and Thaddeus gently coaxed the large optical tube assembly out of the box and its protective womb of styrofoam and plastic.

"Behold!", the Judge declared dramatically, "the Celestron 8" Edge HD Telescope on a computerized Advanced VX mount! For the past few weeks I've been researching which telescopes would best meet my night sky viewing goals, and I finally settled on this. Granted there are much more powerful telescopes on the market, but from reviews that I've read, the best telescope to choose is the one that you'll use most often, and many of the more powerful scopes are just too heavy to be hauling out each time you want to view the stars."

"So, I decided that portability was a key factor for me. This 8" Schmidt-Cassegrain style telescope should be very suitable. I can just grab it and go; plus with the computerized Go To mount, I'll be able to use my iPhone App to have the scope slew to whatever object I want to view. Eventually, I thought it would be fun to try my hand at astrophotography, and this scope will be a good way to get started. I can even use my Canon EOS 5Ti. The sky's the limit, right?!"

Wade was enthralled with the binoculars and telescope that the Judge had purchased and also very happy to see that Thaddeus was eager to expand his comfort level in working with very sophisticated optical and digital technologies. Wade always marveled at the curiosity that the Judge had for many things, especially in nature, but he also was a scholar, certainly when it came to Law.

His interests were very broad indeed. He once told Wade that curiosity was the most valuable of all human traits because without it, humankind would still be living in caves.

Wade and the Judge spent the next couple of hours getting acquainted with both the new binoculars and the telescope; getting the Celestron polar-aligned and making sure everything in the box got put in its proper position. It was a great bonding experience and around 10:30 PM Cassie came across the road to see what these two guys were up to. She was delighted to see them poised over the new devices; reading excerpts from manuals to each other and pouring over star maps to decide which celestial objects to view in the nights to come.

"Wade, it's probably time to head back home," Cassie advised. "You've got school tomorrow, and even though you've already been accepted into college, you need to close out your high school career with a strong academic finish."

"I know, Mom. I just think this stuff is really awesome, and well, time just kinda slipped away. I'm coming," Wade said.

Cassie smiled as she left her two astronomers to carefully put the devices away. She was pleased to see Wade and Thad working closely together, and even happier to see that for the first time in a long while that they were actually showing signs of emerging from the sadness and depression each had shown since losing Ben and Ellie.

"I'll see you tomorrow, Wade. We have a very big universe to explore together," Thaddeus declared.

After Wade left and Thaddeus hauled the packing contents to the trash shed, he settled back into his study and proudly beamed at his new purchases. He turned his music system off and the lamps; then for a while just quietly sat in the dark room and stared out his window to the night sky above.

"Well Ellie, where shall I go from here? Where indeed?!"

Chapter 4

CURLY ALGOL HATED being locked up. Well sure, anyone would, but for Curly the prospect of being confined in prison for the rest of his life made him even crazier than he already was.

Ironically, Curly's road to lawlessness wasn't born from a total lack of family resources. Not that his family was wealthy by any means, but his dad, Herman, owned about 500 acres of crop land and farmed another 1,500 acres of corn and beans in neighbors' fields. Financially, they were okay. Everyone worked; everyone ate. Sunday was the Lord's day.

Nor was Curly's path to prison created by an absence of a caring family. His parents and sister were usually too busy doing endless chores for any of them to dote on one another, but they were a family, and they got along well enough.

No, Curly's meteoric rise to ignominy, characterized by aggressive, mean, hateful behavior came for one reason only. Curly Algol was just plain fuckin' nuts!

Even early in his life Curly didn't communicate the way a normal child should. His remarks and answers to questions often made little sense, and he really didn't follow instructions very well. He seemed agitated a lot, like he had the heebie jeebies. And, his facial expressions were unusual to say the least. Worst of all was this heavy-lidded leer he glued on people, usually accompanied by an unholy smirk.

His parents had met with the school counselor and old Doc Finley when Curly was five years old and entering school. Everyone knew something wasn't quite right with little Curly.

Simply put, Curly wasn't playing nicely with the other children. He hurt a couple of kids. Doc Finley, one of Prindle County's few medical doctors who didn't also practice veterinary medicine, had termed him "learning disabled", but that was about as far as it went. Just a general diagnosis; no treatment plan; no medication; just an educated guess. Small town medicine; limited resources. Not the first time; not the last.

And then, around the time Curly turned thirteen, his behavior began to get pretty scary. His sister, Luella, caught him staring at her when she was in the shower. "It's that look he's got on his face. His leer creeps me out," she moaned. "I told mama, and she said not to worry about it". 'Curly's just being a boy,' her mama, Abigail, said. 'Just ignore him'."

But that was all small potatoes compared to the troubling pattern of events that followed. It's not unusual for kids raised in the country to wander the woods and streams in search of entertainment, and Curly's idea of amusement was in setting snares to capture unwitting rabbits, birds, squirrels frogs, turtles. He became good at it. The troubling part was the way he abused his catch. He reveled in skinning them; even if still marginally alive. He had a special place in the trash shed where he kept his trophies, and he got keenly excited whenever he visited them.

Shoplifting at stores in town became routine, and more than one shop owner had told Curly's parents that he was not welcome in their stores without proper supervision. Curly's parents tried repeatedly to help him understand the error of his ways, but Curly just leered vacantly. Most embarrassing was when Reverend Snoot caught young Curly stealing cash from the collection box.

"Stealing is an abomination," the Reverend directed at Curly. Curly dropped the cash, gave him the finger and ran away.

Fights at school became routine. Actually "fights" doesn't exactly define what they were. Out of nowhere Curly would rush up on some unsuspecting kid and beat him senseless, sometimes with his fists; sometimes with whatever was in reach. More than one kid required stitches and another had a serious concussion.

After the first such episode, Curly's dad promised he would take swift action and that things like this wouldn't occur again. That didn't last long though, and when little Becky Talbot had her left eye severely damaged by a menacing Curly Algol, the police and courts took over. At age fifteen Curly was shipped off to the State's Juvenile Correctional Center adjacent to the Federal prison in Russellville. A year later Curly was released, unrepentant and un-rehabilitated. He was sixteen and not little anymore.

When Curly arrived back home, he refused to ever go back to school, not that the school wanted him, and he defied requests and orders that his parents put to him. He just leered at them and went back to watching television.

The final straw came when Curly put a knife up to his sister Luella's throat and ripped her blouse off so he could play with her "fun things". If it hadn't been for Curly's mom intervening, no telling how far Curly would've gone. He punched his mother in the jaw, fracturing a denture and kicked her in the ribs as she went down.

He bent over his sister and said, "Where do you want it, in your mouth, your hootchie or your ass?"

The poor girl sobbed pitifully and Curly's mom was cowering in the corner. When he heard his dad's tractor pull into the barnyard, brave Curly leered at both of the battered women, told them he'd be back and ran out the back door. The police put out an APB, but Curly had vanished. "Good riddance to bad trash", the whole town agreed.

So a year later now, after being convicted of vehicular homicide by Judge Thaddeus Nathan, Curly Algol sat in his prison cell at the federal penitentiary in Russellville. He spent mind-numbing hours in this cell with his cellmate, Nerf McCabe, another model citizen. Each tried to outdo the other, bragging about their atavistic exploits.

Convicted of homicide for running over that guy whose car he stole, Curly decided his choices were to either break out or die in jail. He knew there had to be a way out of this dump of a prison, and he made it his mission to do just that.

To make matters worse, while inside prison Curly learned from media reports that the man he'd killed on Thaddeus Nathan's front lawn was not the Judge, but a neighbor. He'd killed Nathan's wife when he threw her down those stairs, but he had unfinished business with that high and mighty judge who put him in this pit.

He knew those murders had never been solved, and it was his dirty little secret that he had only bragged about to Nerf. He had a lot of time to think about a lot of stuff. Getting out! Pay back! Covering his tracks with Nerf! He drooled and leered with delight.

That great American, Nerf McCabe, who had been convicted of multiple assaults, burglaries and murder, figured he had nothing to lose, so he agreed to go along with Curly's escape plan which was wacko enough that it just might work.

Chapter 5

THE DAYS LEADING UP TO Wade's high school graduation were passing quickly. His academic career at North Prindle High School had been pretty remarkable for a kid raised in the country. But this came as no surprise to most because Ben and Cassie Henry were regarded by many as being special folks in their own right. They valued education highly and made sure that Wade, despite living in the middle of rural Indiana, was exposed to a broad variety of academic and extra-curricular activities. Having Kissinger College nearby certainly helped.

Wade excelled academically, with a special penchant for advanced placement sciences, especially physics and chemistry. But he also had a very artistic side evidenced by his penchant for creative writing and his colorful photographs that won him several ribbons at the Prindle County Fair.

Additionally, Wade Henry was a National Merit Scholar; a member of the Prindle Community Foundation's Youth Philanthropy Committee; and a fine student athlete. Cross Country was his sport of choice; something he valued as a means of staying physically fit and also for coping with the sadness of losing his dad.

Almost everyday Wade would make time to go for a run; often early in the morning before classes; sometimes later in the evening under the stars. He treasured the time alone because it gave him his own private space to process so many emotions that were flooding him.

The sound of his breathing and his footfalls on the grass transported him away. Breathe in; breathe out. He ran the hills and valleys near his home. He ran the fields and through orchards. He ran the country roads and through covered bridges. And then he returned home, usually refreshed and ready for whatever came next.

Despite his achievements, Cassie continued to be very concerned about her son. She sensed that he was adrift with his future directions. On the one hand Cassie understood that Wade was still a young man with a wide open landscape ahead of him. On the other hand she knew how important it was for her son to be focused on his future. Despite his acceptance at Duke, she hoped that he had a better handle on what he wanted to major in once he got there. If only her husband, Ben, were here to help guide Wade. She knew how much he missed his dad. She tried her best to be a good mom, but it was hard. She missed Ben too.

"Wade," his mom called, "why don't you see if Thaddeus would like to join us for your graduation dinner."

"I'll go over to ask him; then I need to go for a little run. I'll be back in thirty minutes, okay." Wade answered.

Tonight's dinner was actually the only graduation celebration that Wade wanted to have; just the three of them. The graduation ceremony itself had been a very upbeat, positive affair, and Wade Benjamin Henry's name was read several times for high achievement with this course or that school club. He had enjoyed a very successful high school career, and he appreciated the attention he received. With the ceremony over now, he just wanted to be at home with his mom and the Judge.

These dinners for the three of them had become a welcome ritual, and Cassie relished them because she knew that when Wade went off to college , there would be fewer and fewer.

Plus, her work responsibilities in the Development Office at Kissinger College were growing. With each successful foundation grant application she obtained, the College's capital campaign's leadership looked for her to produce even more. Her work was challenging, but she understood the grant writing process, and the successes propelled her onward. The quiet dinners at home were Cassie's way of trying to maintain some semblance of family life. But it was difficult.

A few minutes later the Judge rapped on the back door. "Good evening, Cassiopeia, how're you doing?" Thaddeus said as he entered the kitchen. "Whatever you're preparing sure smells good. Reminds me of Ellie's cooking."

"Now Thaddeus, for the umteenth time, my name is Cassandra; not Cassiopeia, and we're having kidney bean and kale soup with some potatoes and a multigrain baguette. Here; why don't you put the bread in the oven at 350 degrees, and it should be done by the time Wade gets back from his run." Thaddeus dutifully complied.

"Thad, I could sure use some friendly advice about Wade too," Cassie sighed. "Try as I might, I don't feel like I'm juggling my obligations at work and his needs very well at all. He still doesn't have a job for the summer, and he isn't talking about Duke with the kind of enthusiasm I was expecting. He runs cross country even more than he did before, and he seems to talk less at home. I know he's not your responsibility, but I could sure use some help."

Thaddeus looked Cassie in her sad eyes and said, "Of course, Cassie, and I'm proud to say that I feel responsibility for him too. You're both like family to me. He's a very special young man, and he's my friend. You and Ben did a wonderful job raising him. I think he can have a very bright future in whatever endeavor he chooses, but I've sensed what you're describing too, and I think you're right that we should pay close attention to his behavior. And, there's something I'm thinking about that may be helpful too. You'd have to agree, of course. I'm confident that among the three of us we can figure this out."

"Thank you Thaddeus! I really appreciate your caring for him as much as you do. Your support is really special to both of us. Now, I'm obviously really curious about your suggestion for Wade. Care to share now?"

Just then Wade arrived at the kitchen door and was greeted by the embracing aroma of baking bread. He saw the Judge stirring the large pot of soup and reading a book entitled "Aboriginal Astronomy". Wade smiled because it seemed that the Judge's interests were always evolving, always expanding, and usually unusual. He could safely say he never knew anyone who was interested in Australian Aborigine astronomy. So of course, the Judge would be!

"Ah young sir, did you have a good run? You certainly are a road warrior, even with the cross country season over."

And nodding towards his book, Thaddeus said, "Oh, and did you know that the Greeks didn't invent astronomy? Several thousand years earlier, Australia's Aborigines peered at the night sky, using its mysteries to understand and live in harmony with the nature."

"Uh no, I wasn't aware…" Wade replied. Cassie was busily preparing the rest of the dinner but enjoyed listening to Wade and Thaddeus discuss a subject that she also found surprisingly interesting. Like Wade, she also marveled at the Judge's breadth of knowledge and his keen curiosity; plus his skill in telling a tale.

Thaddeus continued his story, "When an Aborigine boy gets to be about your age, he goes on a 'walkabout' alone through the Australian bush. It is a rite of passage leading to manhood that can last as long as six months. The boy would often trace the paths of their ancestors in the wilderness, following their 'song lines', trying to imitate their acts of heroism. The stars and constellations became the boy's guides. It's a great book. You're welcome to borrow it, and I would really enjoy getting your impressions afterwards."

"Thanks, Judge, I've always been fascinated by Australia and someday I'd like to go. I think it's a book I'd enjoy. Sometimes when I'm out running I feel like I am alone in the wilderness and that feeling is strangely comforting to me. It's good to know there's an ancient tradition of going alone into nature to find one's path."

They enjoyed Cassie's dinner, and there was a very natural quiet warmth that enveloped them all. Cassie talked a little bit about the current foundation grant applications she was working on. In areas of specific academic disciplines, she worked closely with the deans of those departments. When it came to grants to support "campus life", she worked with many individuals, from board members and major donors to engineers to finance staff and faculty. It was an impressive scope of work, populated with many diverse people.

Wade smiled more and enjoyed recounting stories about some of his classmates, and how he'd miss several of them once they all went in different directions for college. He even talked a little about what he thought he would like to do professionally. Wade knew that he wanted to have a career that helped guide public policy for positive change. He was also mature enough to understand that good ideas without funding behind them, are ideas often left behind. Wade's dad had set the bar very high when it came to ethics. His mom's current work, and what he knew of her previous career in the State Department, certainly got his attention. Wade believed in the direction he wanted to go, but he still hurt too.

Cassie caught Thaddeus' eye and said, "why don't you guys continue your conversation. I have a very early meeting in the morning with our campaign cabinet, and I need to hit the sack." Hugs all around. "G'night gentlemen!"

"It's actually getting a little late for me too, Wade. I think I'll call it a day too."

Wade said "good night" and then walked into the family room and plopped onto the sofa with the book Thaddeus had given him. What knowledge of the night sky did the Aborigines possess, he wondered. He leafed through the book looking at images of primitive, dark-skinned peoples and reading about their interpretations of the constellations. Wade knew that even over the last five millennia, very little had changed in the appearance of the heavens. People come and people go. The stars go on for billions of years, eventually becoming stardust themselves.

Chapter 6

THE CELLBLOCKS AT THE Russellville Correctional Center were eerily quiet, deathly still; aside from the whistling snores and occasional sobs that pierced the night. The lights on Cell Block C were turned low but still provided enough light for the guards to see. No fewer than a dozen men convicted of murder were housed here. Most of the them would never see freedom again.

It was nearly 2:30 AM and Curly Algol stared at the ceiling above his upper bunk in the cell he shared with Nerf McCabe. He had been awake for several hours now trying to figure a way out of this dump. He swore he'd get that high and mighty prick of a judge who sent him here. But how to break out? That was the question.

He was familiar with the daily workings of the prison by now. His life, along with the other inmates, was regimented to the second. Meals were at 8:00 AM, Noon and 6:00 PM. He was allotted an hour of exercise time mid-afternoon in the prison's main yard; then back into his cell. He was deemed too much of a security risk to be given a job at the prison, a privilege he had yet to earn.

"Hey Nerf, wake up", he commanded. Nerf stirred a little; then Curly tossed his pillow at him to get him fully alert.

"Wha, what, what's going on?" Nerf mumbled. "Is it time for breakfast?"

"No, it's not time for breakfast, you freaking faggot, we got to make some plans!"

Nerf tried to go back to sleep , but Curly jumped off his bunk and squatted on the floor close to Nerf so the guards wouldn't hear. Curly leered at him in the dim light. Nerf moaned, "Go away."

"What time does that dairy truck come to the prison each day?" Curly asked.

"I dunno exactly, but usually around the time the guards are leading us back to our cells after exercise time. What are you thinking about?" Nerf was now fully awake.

"I'm thinking about getting us out of this fuckin' rat hole, and I need to know if you're with me or not cuz once the action starts there won't be any going back. Just follow my lead and be ready, hear me?!"

"Sure", Nerf nodded expectantly.

The morning passed in its typical mind-numbing way. Curly and Nerf joined the rest of the prison population for breakfast which was usually the same; oatmeal, eggs, potatoes, canned fruit, grits, and toast. No breakfast meat, no fresh fruit, no pancakes. Despite its mediocrity, breakfast was actually a highlight of the day. It generally went downhill from there.

Back in their cell, Curly withdrew within himself. He needed the quiet space to really focus. He had to try to be clever and not hold anything back… be ruthless, hit the enemy hard and get away fast.

"Ah, a diversion! Yeah Nerf, we need to create us a little diversion," Curly stated, and his smirk grew into a vile sneer. He had an escape plan, and Nerf had a role to play.

"Hey Nerf, listen up now!" Curly barked, and then proceeded to tell him his plan. Nerf wasn't convinced it would work, and he was not wild about his role in the plan, but anything was better than sitting in a prison cell with Curly Algol as your roomie.

Exercise time in the large prison yard was exactly one hour mid-afternoon, right around the time of a shift change for the guards. The prison yard measured approximately fifty by seventy-five yards and was surrounded on all sides by an eighteen foot wall that was topped by razor wire.

Beyond this wall was another tall chainlink fence that was electrified. During the history of the Russellville Correctional Center, several inmates had attempted their escapes. Virtually none cleared the high wall, but one inmate actually managed to climb some ivy on the wall only to have his ass fried when he encountered the electrified fence.

Curly knew that scaling the wall was not a viable option, and armed guards were posted by the two massive doors that were situated in the east and west walls. After lunch, Curly and Nerf were led outside with the rest of the inmates for their hour of exercise in the yard.

Exercise was a euphemism for what actually occurred during that hour. There were those few inmates who exercised constantly, both to kill time, and to also stay physically fit to fend off attacks by other inmates. The majority just gathered in clusters of six to twelve men, usually by race, nationality or ideology. The Blacks stuck together, as did the Hispanics, the Neo-Nazi white supremacists, and finally a cluster of very tough-looking Asians. Of course there were plenty of guys like Curly and Nerf; ignorant, white, pissed off and mean.

Curly and Nerf eyed the positions of the various groups and the guards. They heard the dairy truck pull into the secure space by the loading dock, just outside the east wall. Curly nudged Nerf to walk across the exercise yard to the group of Hispanics. Curly's plan was in motion.

Curly's brilliant plan was for Nerf to hurl insults about the smallest Mexican's mother and then punch him in the jaw. Curly told Nerf that he would take care of the rest of the plan after that.

Dumb-ass Nerf sidled up to Ernesto Diaz and hollered, "Hey wetback, yo mama sure enjoyed it when I rammed my little white dickie into her. She moaned like a cow in heat." Senor Diaz did not speak English well, but he understood when someone was insulting his madre. His compadres looked at Nerf like he had just arrived from the Moon and then made sure that Ernesto understood the gravity of the insult.

All along, Curly's plan included Nerf getting the shit kicked out of him; maybe even killed. Nerf was clueless. He watched with giddiness as little Ernesto stared at Nerf trying to understand why this nasty Gringo had been loco enough to cast aspersions on his mother's character. With preternatural speed, Ernesto slammed his fist into Nerf's nose, with a geyser of tissue, snot and blood erupting on the wall behind them.

Curly guffawed with amusement at Nerf's unenviable predicament as the rest of the Mexicans joined Ernesto's assault and began kicking and slamming Nerf into a barely recognizable bloody pulp. Curly's strategy was proceeding as he'd planned.

"Sorry, Nerf, you were just expendable," Curly chuckled to himself.

The guards were in the middle of their 3:00 PM shift change when the hullabaloo occurred, and it took a few moments for them to understand that a small riot was in progress.

The guard standing near Curly put his riot shotgun down to shout orders for dispersal in his bullhorn. Other guards rushed to the site of the melee, and during their attempt to secure the scene and determine Nerf's status, Curly elbowed the nearby guard in the solar plexus, kneed him in the nuts and grabbed his shotgun.

Like they say in war, all strategies go out the window when the first shot is fired. Curly fired a blast at the guard, blowing off his right hand and transforming the bullhorn into a twisted hunk of shredded plastic and metal. Curly followed with another shotgun blast that nearly cut a young guard in half who was attempting to block the door through the east wall. Everyone in the exercise yard hit the ground.

Curly grabbed the door keys from the wounded guard who was bleeding profusely and clearly in shock. Confusion reigned. Guards were streaming in through the west door. Sirens were blaring and men were hollering everywhere. All the inmates were still flat on the ground, and the Mexicans stepped several yards away from Nerf's bloody form and crouched low like the others.

"C'mon asshole, you're coming with me," Curly shouted at the wounded guard. Curly had the poor guy by the hair and was dragging him through the east wall door. It was a struggle because the poor guard could barely walk and was becoming dead weight for Curly.

Curly saw the dairy supply truck and quickened his steps. The truck driver made the mistake of coming into view at the rear of the truck, and Curly fired another shotgun blast hitting the hapless guy in the abdomen. He went down hard. Curly kicked the driver out of the way, grabbed his truck keys and hurled the mangled guard into the back of the dairy truck.

Gunfire now erupted from all directions. Curly lunged into the driver's seat, turned the ignition and took off toward the main gate. Choosing not to take any chances, Curly just aimed the truck straight for the guard shelter and literally rammed through it, crushing another guard in the process. A few moments later he was gone.

"Be ruthless, hit the enemy hard and get away fast." That was Curly's entire escape strategy. Nothing fancy; nothing guaranteed, and damned if it didn't work.

Chapter 7

WADE AWOKE ON THE SOFA where he'd fallen asleep reading Thaddeus' book. Cassie had quietly left the house for her early meeting at work and had written a note with chores for him. Wade was still waking up, and fragments of the dreams he'd had began returning to him. He sat very still sipping a cup of coffee and tried to resurrect what he could. He closed his eyes and breathed slow, meditative breaths.

He recalled seeing a group of dark-skinned men standing around a teenage boy near a campfire that crackled and sparked, sending glowing embers up to the night sky above. He heard low murmurings from the men and the hypnotic sounds of rattles and a didjeridoo. The scenes began flooding back to him with a realistic clarity.

In his dream, he was the young man, clad in a tanned kangaroo skin covering his torso and loins. The tribal elder looked remarkably like the Judge. Wade's father, Ben, had his hand on his shoulder and spoke to him, pointing into the outback.

It was a Bora; a ceremony in which a young Kippa learns sacred songs, stories and dances, often involving scarification by losing a tooth or part of a finger. They were preparing him for a walkabout and his eventual return to the tribe as a man. It was a rite of passage that all adolescent Aborigine males are expected to make. Above them, the sky was a celestial panorama, featuring the Emu constellation.

The elder spoke to him, "You have come to the age when it is time for you to trace the paths of our ancestors. You must follow their songlines and try to imitate their great deeds. Our people's songlines have been handed down in stories and dance, paintings and songs. You have learned them, and now it is up to you to use this knowledge to travel the land by carefully repeating the words and listening to their rhythms. In so doing, you shall be able to navigate great distances by recognizing landmarks and waterholes. During your walkabout, you must remember to observe and listen to the songs of the land. The paths of our creator beings and our ancestors will be your guides."

In his dreaming, Wade understood the elder's words. He recalled that he felt no fear or hesitation in taking this ritual journey. He looked to the sky and privately asked the Emu constellation, the Canoe in Orion, the Pleiades, the Moon to lead him at night and for the landmarks to guide him by day. He was ready to listen to their rhythms; to recall the heroic deeds of his ancestors; to join his tribe as a man.

A knock on the front door brought Wade to full wakefulness. The fragments from his dreaming left him like smoke on the wind, and he looked up to see the Judge standing on the porch holding yet another, larger book.

"Ah, there you are, Wade, I was hoping to continue our conversation from last night. Did you get a chance to look at the book?", the Judge asked.

"I did," answered Wade. "Great book, and I had the most curious dream last night."

"And what did your dreaming tell you?" Thaddeus asked.

"I'm not entirely sure," Wade confessed, unlike a lot of dreams, this one really stuck with me. My dad was in it, and you were too. You were both encouraging me to go on a walkabout in the wilderness. It was strange because we were in the Australian out-back, and we all looked like Aborigines. I think the combination of losing Dad, and the big changes coming from graduation and leaving mom for college are more stressful for me than I thought. Your voices in the dream were telling me to go out and discover the world beyond what I've experienced. You know, to find my place in it and become a man. Weird huh?!"

Thaddeus looked at Wade with a knowing smile, and said, "Let's sit down, Wade, there's something I've been thinking about suggesting to you and your mom, and now seems like a good time to float it by you. Then if you're agreeable, we can talk to Cassie when she gets home."

Wade and Thaddeus prepared another pot of coffee and slipped two slices of bread in the toaster. While they were waiting for their coffee and toast, Thaddeus sat down at the kitchen table with a world Atlas and opened it to a map of North America.

Wade had been fortunate to travel quite a bit with his parents, mostly in the states but also a grand trip three summers ago with his folks to southern Europe; principally Italy and Greece. Wade recalled that their Mediterranean adventure had taught him that it's a big world out there, and that travel provides a fascinating way to learn about other cultures, other points of view. He really enjoyed the diversity.

"Well sir," Thaddeus began, "you may recall that Ellie and I went to the Canadian Rockies a few years ago. We flew to Calgary, rented a car, and drove north. We stayed briefly in Canmore," which he pointed to on the map, "and then we travelled north to Banff, Lake Louise, along the Columbia Icefield Parkway, past the Athabasca Glacier, and eventually to Jasper and the national park. The scenery was breathtaking. Pristine wilderness; dramatic landscapes. It was one of the best trips we ever took together, and we always promised ourselves that we'd return."

"I do remember", Wade said. "I have the soapstone carving of the fisherman in a kayak by an artist named Muckpah that you brought me from a shop in Jasper."

"So I was wondering", the Judge carefully offered, "if you'd like to join me on what I've been thinking of as a 'watch-about'. Jasper is known for its incredible views of the night skies. Astronomers, both professionals and amateurs alike, come to Jasper every year to star gaze. Many residents and merchants in town turn down their lights to help reduce light pollution, They really get into it. Jasper offers some of the best sky viewing in North America."

Now, I know we'd have to be back in time for you to prepare to go to Duke, but we could take my new telescope and a few pairs of binoculars and see some awesome deep sky objects. And, there's a ton of things to see and do along the way. It could be like our own walkabout with a stargazing twist. A young man and an aging guy off to face the world head on." The Judge waited for Wade's reply.

"Well, how would we get there and how long would we be gone?" Wade asked.

"I thought we'd drive," the Judge said, "take the Toyota Land Cruiser. Heck, it's only four thousand miles roundtrip. We'd share the driving, and you can bring your own music. I figure we'd take a week to get there; spend a week or so touring around and stargazing; and another week to drive home. So, about three weeks; maybe a little longer, depending."

"It's a long haul, the Judge admitted, and we'd obviously be spending a lot of time together, which I think I can handle if you can. I know I'm just springing this on you; so I'll understand if you want to think about it a bit. Then, of course, we'd have to have your mom's blessing. View it as a graduation gift… all expenses paid."

"Wow, are you serious? Let's look at the map. I want to get a feel for where we'd be heading and how we'd get there… and honestly, I just want to think about it a little too. Mom will probably freak, but I think she'll be okay once she realizes that she's still a good mom even if I'm not there for her to dote on".

"Like I said, two thousand miles one way" as Thaddeus pointed to Someday, Indiana on the map. We're situated here an hour southwest of Indianapolis, and here's Jasper, Alberta in the Canadian Rockies." He traced a straight line with his finger through Illinois, Wisconsin, Minnesota, North Dakota, and Montana and then pivoted northwest into Alberta, Canada… "a long way to go, but some of the finest land our continent has to offer. On the return trip I thought we might travel east through the Canadian provinces and drop down to the states through Minnesota. But, no firm plans are necessary, okay. We can just go wherever we please."

Wade was spellbound. It was as if his dream of the Aborigine Bora had somehow mystically created an extension of itself into this waking dream about Jasper. Wade knew this was not possible, of course, but he found it both curiously amusing and transcendentally coincidental. Wade closely studied the map.

Shortly thereafter they heard the sound of a truck rumbling down Brick Chapel road and saw Quentin Harp bring the UPS truck to a stop on the road between their two homes. Thaddeus and Wade went outside to see what he was delivering.

"Greetings Judge, howdy Wade!" he called out. "I got another package for you, Judge. Thank goodness it's not as heavy as the ones I delivered a few days ago."

"Oh thank you, Sir Quentin, that's probably the new knapsacks and duffle bags I bought from Amazon and a couple of new eyepieces I ordered for both the telescope and the binoculars. Come take a look."

Quentin looked at the telescope and big binoculars and whistled his admiration.

"You planning on taking a trip, Judge? I'll be happy to help keep an eye on your place if you are," Quentin offered.

"Thanks Quentin, I'm thinking pretty seriously about it. Might be leaving in a couple of days. Could be gone a month, so sure, I'd like it if you would keep a close eye on things. Heck, you're a single fella, you might even consider staying at my place while I'm gone. Wade here might even join me, and maybe you'd pull a little double duty by watching my place and helping Cassie Henry as needed."

"That's a definite possibility, Judge. You know I rent the little apartment above Maude Archer's garage. Her granddaughter will be a beginning Freshman at Kissinger College this fall, and Maude told me a while back that she'd offered the apartment to her and wants to do a little decorating before she arrives. So, I have to find a new place to live, and bunking at your place would be great and give me some extra time to find the right place of my own. I'm game if you are!"

"Well, let me take care of a few more details, Quentin, and let's touch base tomorrow. Wade and I still need to make certain Cassie is comfortable with our driving all the way to Jasper, Alberta.

But, thank you very much, Quentin. Obviously, I'd want to go over some things with you before we leave, so if you have time tomorrow, why don't you see if you can spend a half hour with me to get a key and discuss watering the garden and mowing the lawn; things like that."

"Sure thing, Judge, I'll be by around 7:00 tomorrow evening, Quentin said, and I hope you know I would be very respectful of your belongings."

"And Wade, I'd be happy to help your mom too. I'm obviously on the road a lot for work, but I'm generally home by 7:00. It'll still be light then, so I can work outside for a couple of hours."

Both Wade and Thaddeus told Quentin how reassuring it was to know he'd be around. After Quentin left, Wade smiled at

Thaddeus and said, "You know this trip idea of yours could be something pretty awesome. And having Quentin around to keep an eye on our homes makes me feel much better about leaving mom. Heck, I wasn't sure what I was going to do this summer anyway. Why don't you come over later this evening, and we'll talk with mom, okay?"

"Sounds like a plan. I'll see you later then," Thaddeus said, and the Judge went inside his house and Wade set off down the road on his daily run.

Chapter 8

CURLY ALGOL'S ESCAPE FROM the Russellville Correctional Center, was bad enough. Killing the prison guard and dairy truck driver made it the worst day in the prison's history. And no one knew the fate of the wounded guard that Curly had dragged with him as a hostage. Given the nature of his injury, no one expected him to live long with a blown off hand. He'd bleed out pretty quickly.

Having lived his entire life in Prindle County, Curly knew a few secret places to hide the truck and hunker down till things calmed a little. He slowed his speed once he got a few miles away from the prison. He didn't want to draw too much attention to himself, although he was sure every cop within a hundred miles would be looking for the dairy truck. He had to ditch the truck and get another vehicle. He also needed to get rid of the guard in back. Dead or alive didn't matter to Curly. He'd bury him alive if he needed to.

Taking back county roads, there was very little traffic, though he passed a couple of farmers on tractors and a brown UPS truck over by the Maple Sugar Camp. He waved to the UPS guy as he passed and maintained his moderate speed. Quentin didn't recognize the dairy truck driver but waved back. Quentin Harp waved to everyone.

Curly drove about another two miles, checking his rearview mirror to make sure he wasn't being followed, then turned into an old field that ran along Big Walnut Creek. He knew the field was part of an abandoned farm because he and his father worked it before the owner died. Now the field was fallow and the farm house empty and deteriorating.

Curly was smart enough to know that the cops would be searching every inch of the county; every farm house, dog house, hen house, out house, shed, shelter and pole barn. He swelled with pride thinking that he was now Public Enemy #1. He grinned at himself in the review mirror. "Fuck em all", he snarled. "You too, Judge Thaddeus Nathan!"

Curly drove past the dilapidated farm house to an area hidden from view until he came to an old wooden barn where the now deceased farmer had kept his tractor and bush hog. He opened the rustic barn doors and pulled the truck into a wide stall. He closed the doors again and dragged the dead guard out the rear door. There was a lot of old hay and straw in the hayloft, so Curly climbed up and began forking it down onto the truck until it was totally covered. An hour later anyone looking inside would just see a huge mound of old hay.

Next he propped the dead guard against the wall and began digging his grave. It was back-breaking work shoveling the hard soil, but Curly kept at it until he'd dug about four feet down. Then he dragged the guard to the edge of the hole and kicked him in. He filled the grave in with soil, covered the gravesite with hay and admired his handiwork.

Now, he began thinking about getting another vehicle and finding something to eat. Then, he could lay low and make plans.

He thought about where he could get a vehicle and then leered and giggled at his own cleverness. He knew where.

After all the physical exertion, Curly found a working hydrant at the rear of the barn used for watering livestock. He drank deeply and watched the sunlight go down through the slats of the barn siding. He surveyed his surroundings again and decided he'd better get some shuteye for a couple of hours before leaving the barn. He crawled deeply into the base of the hay mound, covering himself completely, and fell asleep.

Meanwhile back at the prison, the chaos had been contained and all of the inmates were returned to their cells. The prison was in total lockdown. Several of the guards and inmates were treated for various minor injuries sustained while trying to quell the uprising.

Even several of the veteran guards were having difficulty emotionally dealing with the horrific events that had occurred. It had been a raw, bloody and terrifying day. Nerf McCabe had been rushed to the prison hospital and then from there airlifted to the Indiana University Trauma Center in Indianapolis. He was a mess; barely alive, but he was alive, and twenty-four hours later his vital signs were becoming stable.

Lying in that hospital bed, Nerf looked like he was nearly mummified with gauze dressings and bed linens everywhere except his eyes and mouth. He'd suffered a fractured skull and serious concussion. He had four broken ribs and a compound fracture to his right leg where the Mexicans had stomped him. He had an IV drip mainlining pain meds and antibiotics into his arm. He had a breathing tube in his nose and a tube entering another orifice. The fluid in his catheter bag was a grotesque reddish orange. He was pissing a lot of blood.

When Nerf tried to open his eyes, he saw a blurry nurse standing near his IV pole assuring proper flow. Beyond her were two doctors going over his chart and checking his vitals. And beyond them were two very serious looking men dressed in suits. Either state police or the Feds. He wished he'd been killed in the riot.

And then Nerf began to think about how stupid he'd been to listen to that maniac, Curly Algol. Curly had set him up to be the fall guy, and it had very nearly gotten him killed.

"What was I thinking," Nerf said to himself. He shuddered and cried softly. The little sobs racked his broken ribs with pain and he moaned softly. He swore he'd make that asshole Curly pay for his treachery. He had stories to tell. Stories that might even help him cut a deal. He tried to move in bed, but he saw he was handcuffed to the bedrail. He also noticed that his right leg couldn't move. He sobbed out loud. The nurse leaned over to check on Nerf and informed the doctors that the patient was now conscious.

Chapter 9

"WHOA, YOU'RE KIDDING," Cassie yelped when Wade asked her if it would be okay for the Judge and him to drive to Jasper, Alberta and maybe be gone for a month.

She sputtered and stammered and could only shake her head and say, "I don't know about this."

She looked at Thaddeus who was sporting an amused smile and said, "Can we please start at the beginning? What exactly is it you two want to do, and Judge, please feel free to dive in here any time you want!"

Wade was more than happy to have the Judge take the witness stand in front of his mother.

"Well Cassiopeia, it's like this", and he proceeded to calmly recount all of the things that he and Wade had discussed. How they'd pack up the Land Cruiser, drive to Jasper, probably stop along the way at Glacier National Park in Montana, do some hiking, fishing and a lot of stargazing and then return home. Simple. He said it was his graduation gift to Wade, and when they got home in June, it would still be more than a month before Wade had to report for freshman orientation at Duke. Cassie stood there thinking about his proposition.

"Cassie, he continued, I know we're really catching you by surprise with this, and especially the short notice on when we'd be leaving. Fact is, I need to be back also in about a month to settle some final matters with Ellie's estate and a few other personal estate issues. Then, I may have some other travel plans in August that I'd need to prepare for also. That's why I'm sorta pushing our leaving."

"Cassandra," the Judge began again, "We've all been through a lot of heartache for a long while now. We've been wounded horribly by Ben and Ellie's murders. No one should ever have to endure what we have, and yet we've managed to come through. Honestly, I don't know what I would've done if I didn't have you and Wade in my life. You're my family now. And I know how hard you work to strike a healthy balance between your responsibilities at the college and your home life with Wade. You're a terrific mom, but I know it's been very hard."

Thaddeus went on, "This trip is something that can be a terrific adventure that maybe gives us all a little time to put some of the tragedy behind us, and to learn to look forward again. I hope you know that I would never let anything happen to Wade. And believe me, I'm not just doing this for your son. I need to go and find myself again, come to terms with my own future, and retirement without Ellie."

Cassie sighed and looked at Wade. "And you sir, anything else you care to add?"

"I love you, Mom. The more that I've thought about this, the more I've realized that this trip is not just something I want to do. I need to do it. High school is over. College is on the horizon. We can't fix the past with Dad, but at least I can try to be the person that you and he have always wanted me to be. I sense that this trip will help me get there. It's like a two-man walkabout, you know, like the Aborigines." Cassie closed her eyes and nodded that she understood.

"And besides, we'll have our cell phones with us, and I'll call you everyday. And, Quentin, the UPS guy, is going to be staying at the Judge's place and said he'd be happy to help you with anything you need like cutting the grass, burning the trash, watering the garden."

Cassie laughed. She knew how much Wade wanted to go, and she couldn't think of anyone she'd entrust her son to more than the Judge.

They all stayed up late that night, drank some wine, and talked about all manner of different topics… the Judge's life with Ellie, his career on the bench, his interest in astronomy, his community volunteer work. Cassie brought them up to speed about the Kissinger College fundraising campaign. She told some outrageously funny stories about a few board members and some of the more colorful members of faculty. She wept just a little when she talked about Ben. Wade talked about the colleges a few of his friends would be attending . He said he was okay that his high school career had come to an end, and he admitted that going to Duke still seemed far enough away that it didn't feel quite real to him yet. He knew he was leaving his childhood behind, and it was time. Traveling to Canada with the Judge would be his gateway to adulthood.

As the evening progressed, virtually all of Cassie's anxiety about their trip vanished, and she became more comfortable with the idea. Deep down she was very grateful to Thaddeus for suggesting it. And so it was agreed. They'd go.

The next day came and as promised, Quentin arrived promptly at the Judge's house at 7:00 PM. Like always, Thaddeus and Wade heard his truck rumbling down Brick Chapel Road a half mile away.

Like always, Quentin pulled the truck to a stop with a cyclone of road dust trailing behind him.

"Greetings gents," Quentin exclaimed. "Did you hear the big news about Russellville?" Thaddeus' ears immediately perked up.

"They had a jailbreak; first ever," Quentin reported. "Apparently an inmate killed a guard and a civilian and then escaped in a dairy truck. His accomplice got the snot kicked out of him by a bunch of Mexicans and is in the trauma center in Indy."

"Oh no, I had not heard," the Judge said. "When we're finished going over things for your stay here, I'll give the Sheriff a call and see what's going on."

Thaddeus knew how serious this was. He'd sent many of those inmates there himself. Only hardened career criminals went to Russellville. Most never left.

Both Wade and Thaddeus gave Quentin a list of things they wanted him to routinely do at each of their homes. Thaddeus gave him a door key and the code to his security system. Both of them gave Quentin their cell phone numbers and email addresses, and Cassie's too, so there shouldn't be any reason why they couldn't reach each other if need be. Wade and Thaddeus would be leaving tomorrow afternoon, and that worked perfectly with Quentin's schedule.

After Quentin left, Wade said, "Hey Judge, I don't know that I've really thanked you enough for this trip. I'm looking forward to it a lot, and well, you know, thanks. I think mom will be fine too. She's a strong, can-do woman!"

Then with a more somber tone he asked," Are you concerned about the Russellville prison break? I remember going there once on a field trip for school. It was meant to shove reality in our faces and show us that this was not the kind of place you ever wanted to be. Sure worked for me!"

"I'm certain it's nothing to worry about, Wade," but something in the Judge's voice wasn't entirely convincing. "I'll call Sheriff Penrod in a bit."

They spent the next several minutes making lists of personal things they needed to take. They wanted to travel light, but a month is a long time to be gone, and they wanted to be prepared for different weather. Then they started packing the Land Cruiser with their astronomy gear and other essentials like photography equipment, fishing tackle, a good first aid kit and a cooler. Wade went home and brought over his tackle box with a nice spinning outfit his dad helped him pick out for his last birthday. He carefully packed the 10 × 50 Oberwerk binoculars and the tripod the Judge had loaned him. Their excitement grew.

"So, why don't we call it a night and finish packing tomorrow morning." the Judge said. "I want to put a hold on the mail, send an email to folks in Jasper to reserve our cabin, and stop by the sporting goods store to pick up a few supplies. Anything you need for me to pick up for you?" Wade said he was good to go.

Thaddeus and Wade said goodnight at about 9:00, and the Judge entered his study through the outside door. He walked around the spacious room looking at various books and artifacts; occasionally stopping to connect with something he treasured. He turned around and Ellie's picture was smiling at him. Her beauty still took his breath away. Thaddeus sighed deeply and shook his head in disbelief that she was gone. He walked over to his credenza, poured himself a glass of Glenmorangie scotch and selected a Tad Robinson CD. The lights were low; the mood wistful.

He sat quietly in his study listening to music for about thirty minutes and was about to call Sheriff Noble Penrod when his phone rang. "Hello, this is Thaddeus Nathan," he said evenly.

"Thad." came Sheriff Penrod's familiar voice, "Sorry to bother you at home so late, Judge, but there's some stuff going down that I thought you better know about."

"Let me guess, Noble, it's about Russellville," the Judge intuited.

"Yeah, I wanted to come out and see you personally, but everything's in turmoil with us looking for the escapee. I'm juggling a lot of inter-agency law enforcement egos right now and trying to find a homicidal maniac at the same time. Since Russellville is a federal prison, the FBI and folks from the Bureau of Prisons are here, and it's quite a scene.

Anyway," he continued, "come to find out that the main perpetrator in all this murder and mayhem is our old pal, Curly Algol."

A shudder went through the Judge as he recalled what a sorry excuse for a human being Mr. Algol was. He also remembered he had sentenced this waste of skin to the Russellville Correctional Center, for life.

Thaddeus exhaled loudly. "Not exactly good news, Sheriff, any idea if he's still in the county or if he's bolted?"

"We set up road blocks at all of the primary and secondary roads heading out of Prindle County," Noble Penrod said, "But as you know there are a lot of roads to cover and since Curly's lived here his entire life, he undoubtedly knows his way around these parts better than most of us. Truth is he could be holed up anywhere. We talked to his parents, but they haven't see or heard from him. Nor do they want to. They're just as scared of him as everyone else."

"Thanks for letting me know, Noble, and I'd appreciate your keeping me informed. Although I'm not on the bench anymore, Prindle County is my home, and I put that SOB Algol away. At this point he's got nothing to lose by killing more folks."

"And just so you know," Thaddeus continued, "I'll be leaving town tomorrow afternoon for about a month. Wade Henry and I are driving to the Canadian Rockies. Quentin Harp, our UPS driver, will be staying at my house while I'm gone. He's also going to be helping out Cassie Henry while we're away too."

"Well, hope you guys have a great trip," Sheriff Penrod exclaimed. "I have to admit that I'm mighty envious. You'll have beautiful scenery and hopefully no serial killers. I'll keep you posted on anything else we learn, okay." They hung up.

Thaddeus stared at nothing in particular and took a sip of his scotch. The thought of Curly Algol being on the loose was very unsettling. He was glad he was leaving the county.

Chapter 10

CURLY ALGOL AWOKE a few hours later around 3:00 AM. In the dark he was initially confused by all of the stuff clinging to him until his nostrils reminded him it was hay. He lay very still recalling the fortuitous events of the last twenty four hours. He was free! No more jail. No more listening to that nitwit Nerf McCabe. No more being caged like an animal. He lay very still for a few more minutes listening for any sound beside his own breathing. He heard nothing.

Quietly Curly climbed out of the hay mound and carefully replaced hay to cover his lair. In the dim light he found some old coveralls hanging on a nail. He pulled off his prison garb, wadded it tightly and buried it in the hay mound too; then slipped into the coveralls. He noticed an old glass Ball jar, washed it out at the hydrant and filled it with drinking water. Not as good as a canteen, but it was better than going without water.

He looked around some more for anything useful and found a rusty hatchet that felt firm in his hand. He then grabbed a length of bailing twine and tied it around his waist. There was nothing else he could use.

Curly stood inside the barn door listening for any sound outside. Again, he heard nothing. He slipped through the door and re-attached the hook and eye closure. It had been many months since Curly Algol had stood outside with the dark sky above. He smelled the night air, stared at the stars, exhaled a primitive grunt and started walking. He figured it would take him about two hours to reach his destination before sunup.

At this time of morning there were no vehicles on County Road 200 N. so Curly just walked down the middle of the road. He figured he'd see or hear any car coming long before it got to him, and there were plenty of bushes and ditches to hide if need be. He walked around the old cemetery and headed north on County Road 50 W.

He walked past the old Arnold homestead and was within a mile of his destination. He knew the area very well. Curly left the road and began walking through a newly planted bean field until he came to the locust grove near his parents' house. He squatted low, drank from his Ball jar and watched the house for any activity. It was about 5:30 AM, and he knew his folks, Herman and Abigail, and his sister, Luella, would be up soon. Before long, he saw a light come on in the kitchen and saw Abigail in her old housecoat put the coffee on to brew and began preparing breakfast. A few minutes later Luella joined her in the kitchen, and Herman came out the backdoor to do a few chores in the barn before breakfast. Curly waited for his father to step inside the barn, and then he bolted for their rear bedroom window and sneaked inside.

No one could ever accuse Curly Algol of being the sentimental type, but for a brief moment he was glad to be back home. It was where he'd grown up and where he'd learned all about farming. His parents were good people who tried to give Curly and Luella as good an upbringing as they knew how to.

Unfortunately, Curly truly was fucking nuts and his sentimentality evaporated pretty quickly when he heard the women's voices in the kitchen. He grabbed his father's 12 gauge Remington shotgun that he kept propped in the corner. It was loaded. He quietly began walking down the hall.

Luella was talking with her mother when she saw her go deathly still. It was like the blood had drained from her face. Luella turned and briefly saw her dear, sweet brother Curly before the butt of the shotgun thwacked her in the forehead and she went down in a heap.

"Howdy Ma, what's for breakfast?" Curly giggled. "Are you happy to see me?

I told you I'd be back."

"What are you doing here? How'd you get out of prison? We all thought we were rid of you." Abigail said.

"Now Ma, is that any way to talk to your baby boy who you haven't seen for a long time?" She just stared at Curly and dropped to the floor to help Luella who was slowly regaining consciousness.

With one hand on the shotgun, Curly grabbed a loaf of bread from the kitchen counter and began gnawing on it. "Good grub, Ma, better than they got over Russellville way." She just stared at him.

"I reckon Dad will be in soon, and we can have ourselves a little family reunion," Curly said.

Abigail helped Luella sit up, but when she saw Curly again, she let loose with a blood-curdling scream. Curly smacked her in the head again with the butt of the shotgun, and she plopped over on her mother who began screaming uncontrollably. Curly knew the jig was up and saw Herman racing across the barnyard to see what on earth all the commotion was about.

"Howdy Pa, you're just in time for breakfast," Curly announced as Herman reached the kitchen door.

"You!" was about all that Curly's dad could utter, and when he saw Luella passed out on the floor and his wife sobbing, he roared,

"You sorry excuse for a man. Get out of here!" He lunged toward Curly, and a deafening shotgun blast propelled old Herman back through the kitchen door and on to the porch. He twitched; then went still. Adios Dad.

His mother, Abigail, flew into a frenzy, grabbed the bread knife and slashed at Curly's shoulder but didn't pierce the rugged coveralls.

"After everything your father and I did for you, this is how you repay us," she bellowed in rage.

"Now Ma, you shouldn't oughta done that. You could've hurt me with that knife."

His mother ran at her thankless child with the knife again, but Curl pulled the trigger and a pink mist splattered all over the kitchen wall. A bloody stump was all that remained where her head used to be. Luella was catatonic; not even a whimper.

"C'mon Sissie!" Curly said to his older sister. "No use crying over spilled milk, I mean blood."

He grabbed Luella by the hair and dragged her outside and tied her tight with the bailing twine and ripped a length of duct tape he'd gotten from the kitchen cabinet and stretched it across her mouth. She lay in the yard bound and gagged and wet herself.

Daylight was coming which actually worked to Curly's advantage. He rummaged through the house and retrieved some of his father's clothing and more shotgun shells. He loaded up some food in a sack and grabbed a thermos which he filled with water. He found his dad's bottle of Old Grand Dad and his wallet containing $44 in cash. Abigail's wallet had $12 and an expired Visa card. He went back outside. Luella lay in the wet grass frozen in shock.

Curly grabbed the keys to his father's old F-150 and filled the truck with gas from five-gallon cans they kept for the tractor. Next, he dragged Herman's lifeless body back inside the kitchen and placed it next to Abigail's headless corpse. He thought for a moment about the best way to cover his tracks. With a swift motion, he kicked the propane conduit away from the gas stove. Propane fumes began to rapidly fill the kitchen. Curly went outside and hefted Luella into the truck and made sure her bindings were secure.

"Now for one final touch," he said to himself. With another blast of the Remington, he ignited the propane, and the house exploded into a ball of flame. He figured nothing would be left of his Ma and Pa for the cops to find.

The Algol farmhouse was several miles away from its nearest neighbor, and with the morning sun rising, he thought no one would hear or see the fire in the distance. He took one final look at his latest piece of demonic handiwork and steered down the dirt driveway to the road. Luella stared straight ahead. Numb.

So, Curly had achieved a couple of his goals at his family's expense. He'd gotten another vehicle, some food and water, a little cash and whiskey, and he had Luella as a hostage. Now, he had to decide what he wanted to do next; stay in Prindle County or vamoose. He also had to decide what he wanted to do with his dear old sister, and there was still some unfinished business with that high and mighty Judge Thaddeus Nathan. One thing was certain; he would never go back to prison again.

Now, he had to find another place to hole up and get some rest. He reached over and squeezed Luella's left breast… maybe have a little fun too. He leered at her and drooled.

Chapter 11

THE NEXT MORNING brought a beautiful sunny day. Thaddeus rose early, made coffee and leisurely finished going through his mail and paying a few bills. He sat on his patio just outside his study and waved to Cassie who was preparing to leave for work. Cassie walked across the road to see the Judge and asked one final time.

"Now you're sure about this trip, Thaddeus? Dealing with a teenage boy 24/7 can be a bit trying at times, and I want you two to still be friends at the end of this trip."

"We'll be just fine, Cassie, so stop fretting, okay?" The Judge knew he had a few of his own idiosyncrasies, and he expected Wade might get a little weary of his quirky jokes and his infatuation with astronomy. He had confidence they'd make it work.

"We'll be leaving about Noon," he said, "And Quentin should be here about 7:00 or so. You have a great time while we're gone, Cassie, and please don't fret."

"Plus, you can always call us, Cassie, although cell service might be a little spotty in some of the places we'll be, but we'll all keep in touch. I'm leaving another note for Quentin too. In case something needs to be repaired at either of our places, I'm telling him to just get things at the hardware store and put it on my household account. I'll be heading to town in a bit to put a hold on my mail, and I'll stop by the hardware store to tell them that Quentin can charge things."

Cassie gave Thaddeus a warm hug and fought back a little tear.

"Now, you guys take good care of yourselves and each other. And, don't you dare make me come up to Canada to get you out any jams." She cried a little more and gave Thaddeus another hug.

"I already said goodbye to Wade, so I guess that's it, for now." Fearing that she would cry again, Cassie walked to her car and drove away.

When Thaddeus returned from his trip to town, Wade was sitting in his patio with earbuds listening to a song and viewing his iPad. He was all packed for the trip and had his knapsack and gear resting by the garage.

"Ah, there you are," the Judge said, "I see you are ready and raring to go. Let's do a final check of things we'll need like our passports and cash, then go over our itinerary again. I gassed up the Land Cruiser in town, got fresh batteries for our flashlights and packed some snacks and drinks in the cooler. So, if you're ready to begin our watch-about, my friend, let's hit the road. Why don't you drive the first leg, okay." And so their adventure began.

They drove about a mile down Brick Chapel Road, waving to Spencer Greenlee as they passed his home. The pavement was rough and potholed as it usually is after Spring freezes and thaws, but Thaddeus figured they might see far worse in the Canadian wilds before they returned to Prindle County in a month.

Wade turned left on to US-231 and headed north toward Crawfordsville and Lafayette. In an hour they were through West Lafayette and veered left onto I-65 North towards Chicago.

"What say we stop in Merrillville for a late lunch," the Judge offered, "and then take I-90/94 through Chicago toward Minneapolis? Hopefully the Chicagoland traffic won't be as heavy as it can be. From there, it's pretty much northwest till we get to Fargo, North Dakota. We'll stop somewhere before then though."

Wade grinned with excitement. He had never driven this direction before, and it was a thrilling experience for him being on the road with the Judge, and not having Mom supervising his comings and goings.

After lunch Thaddeus took over driving duty and they continued into Wisconsin until it started to get dark.

"Look Judge," Wade exclaimed and pointed to the very bright, distant planet. "Venus is so bright. Isn't it the second brightest object in the night sky after the Moon?"

"Right you are, young Galileo, she's a dazzler! Named for the Roman goddess of love and beauty. Since ancient times Venus has been called the "morning star" often rising in the morning before the sun or the "evening star", often appearing at dusk. We are viewing Venus as the evening star now. Beautiful."

"But remember," Thaddeus continued, "Venus is a most inhospitable place. It wasn't known until about 1960 that its surface temperature of 860 degrees would be too hot for human life. Plus, the planet is shrouded by a thick glowing layer of clouds raining sulphuric acid down below. Hardly a vacation spot," he mused.

"I guess it's like a lot of things," Wade suggested, "something can appear rare and beautiful on the surface, but often upon closer examination, it's core is less than attractive. All things, I guess: planets, objects… people."

"Ah, I'm traveling with a philosopher," Thaddeus exclaimed. Nice to have an enlightened companion! I'll have to stay on my toes, eh."

"Esse quam videri" Wade blurted out, and he began to laugh at one of the Latin verses he remembered from school.

"Wow," the Judge exclaimed, "and I thought you didn't appreciate your years of taking a "dead language" in school. What does it mean?"

"Esse quam videri. It means 'to be rather than to seem'." He laughed at how tickled his Latin teacher, Mr. Hoffheim, would be that he remembered something.

"So," Wade continued, "beautiful Venus is actually very unpleasant when you really get to know her… ergo, 'to be rather than to seem".

The Judge was impressed and gave Wade an impressive nod.

They drove on in relative quiet for a long while, shuffling between each of their musical CDs. They each talked a little about how their musical tastes weren't limited to just one genre, but they found it amusing that few of their favorite genres overlapped.

Yes, they both enjoyed some Jazz, but not the cool Jazz Thaddeus loves. Yes, some country vocalists are fine as long as they're not too twangy. Definitely Rock n Roll, but miles apart on volume and heavy metal. Surprisingly, they both really appreciated most Classical music, but not Opera. It had been a good day, a positive start to the journey."

"Well, Wade", the Judge started, and Wade looked at him surprised he hadn't been called by some star's name. "How about we find a place to eat, crash and get an early start in the morning?"

"How early?", Wade asked.

"Oh, say 7:00 AM", Thaddeus said.

"How about 8:00 AM, and I promise not to be grumpy," Wade proposed.

"Deal!", said the Judge, "let's eat at this Panera in Eau Claire. Okay with you? And by the way, I was prepared to go to 9:00 if you'd pressed it." Both laughed.

After a relaxed dinner, Wade and Thaddeus walked to an adjacent motel that Thaddeus called earlier to reserve two rooms. They stood outside in the parking lot looking up at the night sky. Orion stood tall above them with Canis Major to its lower left and Taurus poised to its upper right. Wade and Thaddeus stood admiring their celestial display.

They took several minutes getting their bearings and Thaddeus pointed out the constellation Cancer to Wade, with Hydra's head below. They stood silently for a few minutes more and then headed toward their respective rooms; travel weary but happy to be on the road.

"You should call your mom before it gets too late, Wade," the Judge called out. "You know she'll be waiting up for your call. I'll see you around 8:00 AM."

Inside his room Thaddeus sat on the edge of his bed following the news on CNN and looking at Mapquest on his iPhone to confirm tomorrow's driving directions. The phone rang as he was holding it, and he instantly recognized its source from his caller ID.

"Evening Sheriff Penrod. What's going on, Noble?" the Judge asked.

"Well Thaddeus, I wish I could say this is a social call, but I have some information to share with you, and I'm afraid you're not going to like it very well."

Thaddeus Nathan sat stone still on the bed, all color draining from his face as the Sheriff shared the disturbing news. A combination of grief and rage consumed the Judge. He was relieved Wade was in another room.

They finally knew for sure who had murdered Ellie and Ben.

Chapter 12

CURLY WAS DEFINITELY bat-shit crazy, but he was also a fairly crafty sonovabitch. He still knew Prindle County very well, even though he had been incarcerated for the past year. He drove his father's F-150 down a secluded country road and located the old abandoned mill near Monocah Creek.

He used the truck to punch through the old iron gate across the access road and stopped at the rear of the mill. From the looks of things, no one had been around for quite some time. Luella was still bound; so Curl hefted his sister out of the truck, kicked open a feeble wooden door and dropped her inside the old structure. Birds flew away and rodents scurried across the rotting planks.

"We'll bunk here tonight", he told her, but his sister just stared and didn't utter a word. Curly ate some of the food he had taken from his parents' house and offered some to his sister. She didn't respond. "Okay, more for me then," he said.

"Now you do as I say, Sissie Luella, and you may just get to see the sun come up."

After eating his snack, Curly sat down next to Luella and put his hand on her thigh. He giggled like a pimply-faced adolescent and lifted her dress for a peek. Luella began to shake uncontrollably. After all the carnage she'd witnessed at her home, she had broken down mentally. She was a shell. Her spirit was nearly gone.

"Mama", she whimpered. "Mama!" she sobbed a little louder, but bound as she was, she couldn't fend off Curly's advances.

"C'mon now Luella, I ain't never had any hootchie, and well, being in prison and all, I just wasn't able to score any. But, seeing how you and I are alone here, and since ma and pa will never know, I don't see how it would hurt nothing."

He played with the hem of her skirt some more, and she moaned "mama" once more and went catatonic. Then, smelly, nasty old Curly had his way with his sister.

Around sunrise the next morning, Curly packed the truck with the shotgun and his meager belongings. He couldn't tell if Luella was alive or dead. He shook her shoulder, and she moved slightly. She had wet and soiled herself during the night, and she was bruised and battered.

Curly barked, "C'mon get up Luella," and then he remembered she was still bound and could barely move. "I got stuff we need to do", and he hefted her over his shoulder and deposited her in the truck. "Girl, you smell stinky," he said. "I ought to leave you here for the rats, but I'm not finished with you yet. You do as I say now; let's go!"

Curly walked down the access road a bit to see if he could hear anyone coming. Aside from a chilly northeast wind, it was dead quiet. He got back in the truck and turned it toward Brick Chapel Road.

Quentin lounged aristocratically on Thaddeus' patio drinking a cup of freshly brewed coffee. He'd have to get ready for work in a little while, but he wanted to enjoy his delightful surroundings. Quentin always enjoyed the Judge's wit and wisdom, and he really admired the homestead Thaddeus and Ellie had made.

He had never really been inside the Judge's home before, except to drop off packages just inside the studio door during inclement weather. Quentin had walked around when he arrived the evening before, admiring the Judge's library of books and music, appreciating the contemporary Danish furniture and colorful art glass and sculpture situated with a simple elegance.

Quentin whistled a soft note of amazement. He saw the Judge's graduation diplomas: Bachelor's degree from Harvard University and his Law degree from the University of Virginia. He saw a framed letter of congratulations from Supreme Court Justice Earl Warren. Quentin's respect for the Judge grew even more, and he recognized that Thaddeus had entrusted a very special place for him to enjoy and protect. Quentin was humbled and felt grateful for the opportunity to stay here. Enjoy and protect.

As Quentin was finishing his coffee, he heard a truck slowly coming down Brick Chapel Road. He rose and saw a youngish couple riding in an old Ford F-150 pickup. It was faded teal in color and looked to be about a 1994. Quentin walked over to the gate and cast a wave to the truck's occupants when they got about forty feet away. The truck slowed to a halt with the woman in the passenger seat putting down her window.

"Now you better remember, Luella, what I told you exactly to say if we saw anyone. You fuck this up and the last sound you hear will be this shotgun blowing you in half… and I'll kill this fucker here too. You remember!" he barked.

At this point Luella truly wished she would die. In her mind she was already dead. Her lunatic brother had murdered her parents and had ravished her. She was beyond despondent, but she did not want be involved in one more senseless death. She would do what she had to do to stay alive and to save this guy, if possible. And so, she went along with Curly's script.

"Excuse me sir," she managed to say, "excuse me we're looking for Judge Thaddeus Nathan's house. Our families were friends a long time ago, and we just wanted to pay our respects as we're passing through town."

Something seemed a little odd to Quentin. He couldn't see the driver's face, but the girl looked vaguely familiar. She wasn't on his UPS route because he would've remembered her, but he thought he knew her from somewhere.

"Why yes, Ma'am," Quentin said brightly, "this is the Judge's residence, but if you're looking for him, you're a little too late. I'm Quentin; staying at the Judge's house for a while. Anything I can help you with," Quentin offered?"

"Oh no," Luella replied, "no we just wanted to see the Judge, and I suppose we'll just have to stop back some other time. Any idea when the Judge will be back?"

"That's hard to tell. Three weeks anyway; probably a month. He left midday yesterday with a neighbor heading northwest towards Jasper, Canada. Said he wanted to drive his new black Land Cruiser to see cities like Fargo, and Bismarck and Billings before heading towards Calgary and Jasper."

Quentin bit his lip. He didn't know why he shared so much information with new people. He knew better than to yack a lot to strangers, but he was just an outgoing feller, and these folks said their families go back a ways. Quentin was just trying to be neighborly.

He changed the subject. "Are you all right ma'am? You look a little beat up with that knot on your forehead and all."

"Oh that, I'm alright," her hoarse voice managed. "That darn mule of ours knocked me against the stall when I was mucking it out. It hurts a little, but not too bad."

"Well anyway, Quentin said, do you want to leave your name and phone number with me, and I'll pass it on to the Judge when I email or talk with him next."

"Oh thank you, but no, we sorta wanted it to be a surprise," Luella said. "We're the Hutchinsons from over Huntington way. I'll drop him a letter in a few days. We've got to go now. You've been very helpful, and you take care now, okay?" With that, Curly put the truck in gear and steadily pulled away.

Quentin watched the teal pickup pull away and wondered what the hell that was all about. The girl looked a little familiar and pretty banged up too. He never saw the guy's face, and he couldn't determine if that was intentional. And, the truck looked oddly familiar, but not something he saw on his regular route. Teal 1994 Ford F-150. He also thought it was odd that she said to him, "you take care now, okay." Almost like a warning. Weird! He went inside to get ready for work. Puzzled.

Down the road Curly turned to Luella and said, "you done good Sissie. Heck, I almost believed you myself. The Hutchinsons," he laughed. "That clodhopper back there spilled all the beans to us. Now I know where high and mighty Judge Thaddeus Nathan is heading and what he's driving. And, I sure don't want to hang around these parts with all the cops hunting me. Maybe time for us to scoot and have a little adventure of our own. Put one more guy and maybe his buddy in the ground. How's that sound, Luella?"

For the first time since Curly showed up in their kitchen and began the bloodbath, she turned and looked at him, directly in his eyes. She just stared. Dark darts.

"What?" Curly said, "and of course I got to think about what to do with you." She continued her unblinking stare. "Maybe you'd like me to give you another poke," Curly chuckled. Her stare grew even darker. Chilling. Curly backed off.

Quentin got ready to go to work, but he had a nagging feeling about the Hutchinsons. He hadn't seen the man's face. The woman looked awfully beat up. He vaguely remembered her from somewhere, and that truck too. Plus, that "take care of yourself" comment. Something unusual about how she said it, and they just didn't seem like the caliber of people the Judge would associate with. Quentin shrugged it off for now, but a grain of uneasiness remained with him through the day. He'd be sure to let the Judge and Wade know when they communicated next.

Chapter 13

THADDEUS REMAINED SEATED on the bed trying to compose himself and process the highly disturbing information Sheriff Penrod had just given him. He was heart sick with grief all over again, and he thought about the impact the news would have on Wade and Cassie.

According to the Sheriff, Nerf McCabe had recovered adequately from his injuries and was talking to anyone with whom he thought he might be able to strike a deal. He learned very quickly, however, that he wasn't going anywhere except back to prison for a very long time. He was so pissed about Curly's betrayal though that he really didn't care. He wanted Curly to get what was coming to him. Big time!

Sheriff Penrod had recounted Nerf's story to Thaddeus about how Curly had bragged about getting even with the Judge who sentenced him to a life term. Curly had laughed about how he escaped from two guards during transit and got away for three days.

He said Curly went to the Judge's house hoping to find and kill him but had to settle for killing his bitch wife instead. Curly had told Nerf, "I broke in and found her upstairs. She fought real good, and I thought about having my way with her, but she fought like a fucking hellcat; so in the end I just hurled her ass down the staircase. She crashed real hard… didn't move."

Nerf said Curly was especially glad about slashing that guy he thought was the Judge on the front lawn. "Slice and dice" were the words Curly had used. Then, how Curly was mad when he found out in prison that he got the wrong guy. He promised to still make good on his threats. Nerf said all Curly talked about was getting out and getting even with that high and mighty Judge Thaddeus Nathan.

Nerf's story was credible; especially in the context of the neighbor, Spencer Greenlee's earlier testimony. And so, for the first time in over a year, the authorities finally had a solid lead on who killed Ellie and Ben. Curly Algol. The same killer who had just broken out of their federal prison.

The Judge was beyond rage but knew he had to contain his temper for Wade's sake. Thaddeus also thought about Cassie's safety and Quentin's too. Sheriff Penrod said he would drive over to see Cassie personally early in the morning and would inform Quentin to keep his guard up. Thaddeus thought that maybe he and Wade should turn around and head back for home, but the sheriff wasn't sure what that would solve. Enough people were already in harm's way. Thaddeus had to tell Wade about the murderer, but he wanted to try to sleep and talk with him in the morning . He stared at the ceiling for over two hours and finally drifted off. Disturbing dreams populated his fitful sleep.

At 8:00 the next morning Thaddeus Nathan rapped lightly on Wade's room door. Wade immediately opened the door, looking fresh and ebullient.

"I'm ready to go, Judge," Wade exclaimed. "Let's get some breakfast and hit the road. We're burning daylight!"

"Okay, my friend, but first we need to talk."

"Is something wrong?" Wade inquired, "You don't look like you slept well last night."

"I didn't," the Judge softly replied, and he stepped into Wade's motel room and Wade followed him back inside.

"I got a phone call from Sheriff Penrod last night," the Judge began. "It would appear that a man I sent away for life to the Russellville Correctional Center has broken out of prison and killed two, maybe three people in the process."

Wade just stared at him and told the Judge he was sorry to hear this tragic news.

"Wait, there's more," the Judge said. "We now know who killed your dad and Ellie."

Wade said, "I don't understand. Do the police think the guy who broke out of Russellville also murdered dad and Mrs. Nathan?" Tears were forming in his eyes.

The Judge nodded. "They do, and so do I. His name is Curly Algol, and he's a very dangerous man that I sentenced to a life term for vehicular homicide. It occurred right around the same time of the murders. He had appeared before me for other offenses when he was younger, and I'd sent him away to the Juvenile Detention Center near the prison. Clearly, he was not rehabilitated. If anything, prison turned him into a hardened criminal. Like I said, he's a dangerous man!"

Please sit down, Wade, I need to tell you everything the Sheriff told me. He's going to see your mom this morning and tell her everything too. Then we should all talk and decide what we want to do next. I'm very sorry."

Over the past couple of months, the invisible wounds that Thaddeus and the Henrys endured had begun to fade a little. Now the pain and heartbreak came roaring back. They were reminded of the tragedy of their losses once again.

Wade and Thaddeus just sat there; neither one knowing what else to say for a few moments. Finally, Wade said, "I need to go for a run. Can we put off calling mom for a little bit, Judge?"

"That's fine, Wade. Sheriff Penrod is probably on his way to your house now. We should give him time to speak with your mom. He said they'd give us a call afterward. Then we can talk with your mom. You should think about what you want to do too, Wade. If I'm not in my room when you get back, I'll be over at the restaurant getting some coffee." Wade took off.

After Wade left, Thaddeus stared at nothing in particular for several minutes and thought about his life without Ellie. "Oh Ellie, it's so hard without you, he sighed.

Sheriff Noble Penrod drove his patrol car down Brick Chapel rode around 7:30 AM and pulled to a stop in front of Cassie Henry's home. Quentin was again enjoying a morning cup of coffee on the Judge's patio when the sheriff arrived.

"Morning Sheriff, Quentin called out as Noble Penrod exited his vehicle. I haven't seen Cassie yet this morning, but I imagine she's getting ready for work."

A few moments later Cassie Henry stepped outside and walked up to the Sheriff. "Hi Noble," she said in a cautious voice. "To what do we owe the honor of your visit so early in the morning?"

"Morning Cassie," the Sheriff returned. "There are some developments that I want to share with you, and seeing as though Mr. Harp is staying at the Judge's house, it would be good if the three of us talked. I called Thaddeus late last night and talked with him, and we agreed we would call him back after I spoke with you."

"Well," Cassie said nervously, "this sounds rather ominous, Sheriff. Why don't you and Quentin come inside. I still have coffee left, and we can hear what you have to say."

Sheriff Penrod spent the next several minutes telling Cassie and Quentin all that he knew about Curly Algol and Nerf's account of Curly bragging to him in prison about the murders. Cassie sat very still; just listening. Quentin was stunned by what he was hearing.

Quentin told them both, "Something weird happened here yesterday morning. I was going to tell the Judge about it. This young couple pulled up in an old pickup truck and said they were looking for the Judge. Said their name was Hutchinson from Huntington and that their families were friends. The woman looked like she had taken quite a beating, and I never did see the man's face. They just didn't seem like the kind of folks the Nathans would be friends with. And, I think I may have screwed up by telling them where the Judge was heading and what he was driving."

Cassie and the Sheriff looked very concerned, and the Sheriff took a full description of the Hutchinsons and the pickup truck from Quentin. He radioed his dispatcher, Donnabelle Stoner who sent out a BOLO for them. While on the radio Donnabelle informed the Sheriff about a report that she had just received from Deputy Jeff Block and was preparing to alert him when he radioed in.

"Deputy Block, a rookie on the Prindle County police force, was driving in the northern part of the county when he noticed that the view of the Algol house didn't look quite right. With his window down, he also noticed an unusual odor. He drove down their long drive and when he got to the rear of their hill, he saw that the house had burned to the ground. Deputy Berg reported that when he carefully examined the scene on foot, he saw two sets of charred skeletons. Grizzly."

"They were burned beyond recognition, the dispatcher continued, "and Deputy Berg assumed it was Herman and Abigail Algol.

He radioed me immediately and asked that you and a forensics team be notified. That's all we have right now," Donnabelle reported.

"Oh no," Sheriff Penrod breathed, and Cassie and Quentin looked at him waiting for more details. "Well," the Sheriff told them when he signed off with the dispatcher, "It appears that our suspect's home has been burned to the ground and presumably with his parents in it. We'll know more when the forensics unit finishes their initial investigation. This just keeps getting messier by the moment," he sighed. "I had better get over there pretty soon and make sure the scene doesn't get contaminated." Cassie and Quentin looked just as stunned as the sheriff.

"Can we please call Wade and Thaddeus while you're here, Sheriff?, Cassie asked. I want to make certain they're okay, and for us all to be in the loop on this."

Sheriff Penrod nodded agreement, as did Quentin.

Wade had just returned from his run and found the Judge at the restaurant drinking coffee when Cassie's call came through. Their booth was in a quiet corner of the restaurant, and they put the call on speakerphone.

"Wade honey, it's Mom. Are you okay? Sheriff Penrod is here with me and Quentin too. Did the Judge tell you about this Curly Algol person?"

"Yes Mom, he did. I just got back from a run to clear my head, and we were preparing to call you. Do you want me to come home? I will if you want me to."

"Maybe before you decide about that," Sheriff Penrod interjected, "you both need to know that Quentin thinks he spoke with a couple yesterday morning that may have been our suspect and presumably his sister, Luella. They said their name was Hutchinson, from over Huntington way, and that your families go way back."

"Well, that's very curious, Noble, I don't recall any mention of a family named Hutchinson," Thaddeus said. "Got a description?"

Quentin spoke up and said, "Hi Judge, yeah, they were driving an old teal-colored F-150. I didn't catch a plate number. I also didn't get a look at the guy's face, like he was hiding it or something. The woman was just sorta plain looking, with the exception of a monster knot and bruise on her forehead. She seemed distressed and told me to 'take care', kinda like a warning."

"There's more," the Sheriff said. "We put a BOLO for an older teal-colored Ford F-150, with a youngish couple inside. I also just got a report that the Algol house was burned to the ground last night, and that two people are confirmed dead. They were burned beyond recognition, and we're assuming it's Curly's parents. We'll know more when the lab reports come back. The feds will speed things up for us.

So, if indeed these deaths were caused by Curly that would bring his string of murders to eight, and those are the ones we know of," Sheriff Penrod stated. "I think it would be appropriate to describe Mr. Curly Algol as a serial killer. What do you think, Judge?"

For the first time Wade and Cassie heard the Judge cast aside his usual judicial bearing and reply with a raw edge in his voice.

"I think we need to get this bastard, Sheriff, and make sure he goes down hard once and for all. If anyone ever deserved the death penalty, it's Curly Algol. Life in prison is too good for this scum. He needs to die."

The Judge's comments hung in the air. No one offered any disagreement.

Thaddeus continued," Sheriff, I know your manpower is probably already stretched to the breaking point, even with some of the state police and federal agents around. I imagine you'd be hard-pressed to have a few of your officers watch our houses round the clock. So, I'd like to make a suggestion." They all listened.

"Cassie, we don't know what the suspect is likely to do, and we know he's capable of committing heinous crimes, so I suggest that you contact the president's office at Kissinger College and see about getting temporary housing on campus. The students are pretty much gone for the summer, and there should be some vacancies that campus security can keep a close eye on too. This way you'll be safe and be able to continue your work."

"But Thaddeus," Cassie implored. "What about you and Wade? I know that housing wouldn't be a problem and that the college takes its security very seriously, but it sounds like this crazy man knows where you're heading and that he might try to find you and Wade. And what about Quentin? We don't want him in harm's way."

"Of course not," the Judge replied. "What are you up for, Quentin, do you want to see if the College can put you up too?"

"Well, you know, Judge, I never did like someone thinking they could push me around, and I really don't feel like starting now. I told you I would keep a close eye on your place, and that's what I intend to do, if you're game. I think your suggestion for Mrs. Henry to stay at the College is a really good idea. I'm sure I can get some vacation time from work. So, if it's all the same to you, I prefer to stay right here and look after both your homes. And just so you know, I'm not doing this because I'm especially brave. I'm really pissed off too."

"Wade honey," Cassie said, "what do you think we should do?"

Wade was struck by the concern in his mom's voice, but he also felt oddly encouraged because she really wanted his opinion. While on his run a little earlier, he had used his physical exertion to burn off the pain and hatred he was feeling from the information about the killer. He wanted to tear the killer's throat out.

Then, he pictured his dad's face and remembered his warm manner and his teachings, and a certain calmness reached through the pain. He wanted to be there for his mother, for sure, but he couldn't imagine how he could help much by returning home now. He knew his mom would be safe at the college and that her focusing on her work would probably keep her from fretting all the time. He also knew that their cell phones and texts would keep them instantly connected.

Beyond that, Wade felt his watch-about, as the Judge called it, was something he really needed to do… a stepping stone to his future as an adult. The Judge remained silent knowing that this needed to be Wade's decision alone.

"Mom," Wade started, "no one knows what the future may bring. We've certainly learned that, but I feel like we've all been victims long enough. Please don't misunderstand. I want to always be there for you, and I'm scared too, but I want us to continue to lead our lives in a way Dad would've wanted. I have faith that the Sheriff will get this guy, and the only running I want to do is for exercise and not out of fear.

So," Wade continued, "if you're okay with it, and if Quentin and the Judge, and of course the Sheriff, are okay with it, I prefer to finish what the Judge and I originally set out to do… go to Canada, then come home and get ready for Duke."

A little sob caught in Cassie's throat as she realized that her baby boy was becoming a strong and thoughtful young man.

"Well sweetheart," she said, "I just love you so much, and I don't know what's harder; having to deal with a serial killer or watching my son growing into a man." She laughed a little and cried a little at the same time. Wade did too.

The Sheriff said he had better get over to the Algol property to supervise the investigation. He and Cassie and Quentin exchanged contact information, and Noble asked Cassie to confirm her residential status with him once she'd talked with Kissinger's administration. He said his office would coordinate directly with the school's security office to help assure her ongoing protection.

After Sheriff Penrod left, Thaddeus and Wade, Cassie and Quentin remained on the line with their speakerphones. As much as anything they just wanted to hear each other's voices, and to understand each other's comfort levels going forward.

The Judge asked, "Quentin are you sure you still want to stay at my place and watch Cassie's too? You are potentially putting yourself in harm's way. This guy can be bestial, and he's got nothing to lose at this point."

"Judge," Quentin said, "you've entrusted me with your home and property, and I'd like to stay on to finish the job. You and Wade should go. Put some distance between this place and where you're heading. Believe me, I'll be careful."

"Thank you! You're a good man, Quentin Harp," the Judge said. "I'm very grateful for your dedication, and I'll remember this. Cassiopeia, do you have anything else you want to say?"

"How can I possibly say no to something like this when it is so important to Wade. Sure I'd like to have you here, but this is different. Wade, being a parent isn't easy, and your dad and I were unified in our overriding goal to help prepare you for adulthood. I know your dad would be very proud of you, as I am. So, I'm respecting your decision to continue on your watch-about with Thaddeus. Just pay attention to your surroundings and try to stay in cell phone range. I'll see you in a few weeks. I love you very much!"

Before they hung up, Thaddeus made sure Cassie had the name and contact information for the cabin they'd be staying at in Jasper, Alberta. The Chalet Village along the Athabasca River.

He also suggested to Quentin that he look in the sideboard's left drawer in the dining room. I authorize you to use whatever you find there in self defense."

Quentin acknowledged this, and Wade cast a fast glance at his mother to try to divine the cryptic meaning of what the Judge had just said to Quentin.

They said their goodbyes. Quentin would stay at the Judge's home. Cassie would temporarily move to the College. And, Wade and Thaddeus were now preparing for the next leg of their journey.

Chapter 14

THE JUDGE AND WADE decided to stay in the restaurant for breakfast and go over their itinerary. They each sat quietly, thinking about the conversation they'd had with Cassie, Quentin and the sheriff. Bewildering times; a lot of drama.

"Well," the Judge said, "we can either look at life in the past or make plans for the future. I vote for the future. What say we finish up here in Eau Claire and head toward North Dakota?" Wade nodded his agreement.

The drive along I-94 from Eau Claire, Wisconsin was very picturesque. With Wade at the wheel, the Land Cruiser ate up the miles. Road signs displayed town names like Cedar Falls, Menomonie, Woodville and Baldwin. Wade was struck by the thought of so many people across the country he would never know. It was a big world for an eighteen year old kid from central Indiana, and he looked forward to getting much better acquainted with it. He was feeling ready.

They crossed over the scenic St. Croix River which runs north and south and marks the state boundary between Wisconsin and

Minnesota. A little further south, it joins the mighty Mississippi. Thaddeus and Wade stopped for lunch in Afton State Park and talked with a young family from the area that knew good places to fish northwest of Minneapolis / St. Paul. They mentioned the Otter Tail River and Upper Lightning Lake near Fergus Falls. They drove on.

Wade listened to music with his earbuds, and Thaddeus quietly hummed an improvised melody as he drove. Both men needed some private time to process a lot of feelings, and each respected the other's space. Wade would've really enjoyed going for a run, but for now he was satisfied just to be on the road with someone he trusted like the Judge. The highway stretched out before them in a welcoming way.

Once past Minneapolis, I-94 cut through beautiful lake country. It sure didn't look like central Indiana anymore. There was something very special about the north country to Thaddeus. It was the allure of vast pine forests, birch, poplar and maple trees, lakes and streams, lichen-splattered granite, and wildlife. The animals were different than what he was familiar with in Prindle County too, especially the fish. He was glad they had their fishing gear and looked forward to stopping along the way to see if they could lure a smallmouth or a rainbow from their hiding place.

They drove on toward Fergus Falls, and finally Wade returned from his solitary thoughts and he rejoined Thaddeus. "What made you decide you wanted to be a judge?" he asked out of the clear blue.

The question surprised Thaddeus at first because, aside from the sound of the tires on the road, it had been so quiet.

"That's a very good question, Wade. What makes you ask?"

"I was just thinking about all of the different cases you must have heard in your courtroom over the years, and what it must be like to pass judgement on someone," Wade answered. "I don't know how I would act if a criminal like Curly Algol came before me."

"I admit it wasn't always easy," the Judge continued, "but I remained committed to conducting my courtroom with dignity and assuring that all parties involved followed the rule of law. Everyone was innocent until proven guilty, and the attorneys for both sides knew they had to prove their cases before me.

As to how I decided to become a lawyer and then eventually run for judge, that's a story that takes me back to my my youth, when I was about your age now actually." The Judge thought back for a few moments and then began again.

"As I think you know, I was very fortunate to be accepted into Harvard University for my undergraduate education. I wasn't thinking about law school at the time. Basically, I was trying to get a good liberal arts education and then decide what I wanted to do about a graduate degree. I also didn't want to get drafted into the Vietnam war which seemed to go on forever."

"One of the best parts about going to Harvard wasn't just the high quality education I received," Thaddeus continued, "but getting to know many people of diverse backgrounds. My roommate in my junior and senior years was a guy from St. Louis named Dan Brody. Danny was a Jewish fella and probably one of the smartest and most talented people I ever knew. On top of that women just adored him; so it didn't hurt to be Danny's good buddy in that regard too," he laughed.

"We became very close friends and stayed in contact for many years after graduation. He was actually my best man when Ellie and I got married. We were like brothers. Unfortunately, Danny died several years ago from an aneurism, just like that…gone. Very tragic. I still think of him a lot and miss his friendship greatly."

"Since Danny and I came from different religious backgrounds, I was curious about the differences and similarities, and we talked philosophically a lot. Something that I always remembered was his saying that Christianity is a religion centered on faith, and

Judaism is a religion based on social justice. The 'social justice' part impressed me tremendously, and I honestly think that was the beginning of my wanting to explore law as a career."

"Very interesting," Wade said. "Makes me wonder who and what will influence me."

"One thing's for certain, young sir," the Judge professed, "you've already gotten off to a great start thanks to your mom and dad. Funny thing about influences though. You don't always know where they'll come from, or if you'll even realize them at the time."

They drove on for another hour listening to Click and Clack on PBS' Car Talk and really enjoying how brilliant and zany these two brothers are. Wade told the Judge that he regrets that car repair was something he and his dad never did together. Wade said his dad would joke he was the only guy living in the country who didn't know how to work on a car. Thaddeus admitted that he was a member of that very small and inglorious fraternity of automobile dumb-asses too.

It was a good drive, and they were putting some of the earlier unpleasantness about Curly Algol behind them. Wade was feeling more relaxed about leaving his mother in Prindle County, and at the same time he was trying to comprehend why any human being would be as wildly violent as this Curly asshole. The behavior was so bizarre and brazen. Wade had more questions for the Judge.

"So Judge, who else besides Dan Brody influenced you along the way? And as I think about it, you and I have never really discussed religious viewpoints, you know, like God and heaven and such.

My folks," Wade went on, were never really big churchgoers, although we've enjoyed the fellowship at the Unitarian church. I think dad really put his faith in the ethics that religion teaches rather than the religious establishment itself."

"I think I would have to agree," Thaddeus said, although I am generally cautious about discussing religion with most people because many folks hold very strong feelings, and I prefer to tread lightly on the subject. What do you think, Wade?"

"Ah well," Wade began. "I'm not entirely sure. Sometimes I think that if there really is a God, he never would've let good people like Mrs. Nathan and my father get hurt. I'm still angry about it, and I'm not ready to just embrace a religion out of blind loyalty. The biblical stories are fine but mostly fiction, and I prefer to think for myself. So, I guess I'm trying to appreciate the teachings and not get lead astray by established dogma. I hope that makes sense."

The Judge smiled and nodded his understanding. "I concur and while I believe religion helps many people get through the night, I agree with your focus on the teachings rather than the organized religion itself. There are many lessons to be learned and honestly I enjoy looking to the heavens sometimes for understanding. The stories related in the constellations are no less allegorical or instructional than many stories in the bible.

So, pick a subject," the Judge continued… heroism, vanity, hunting, love, monsters, animals… many stories are written in the stars. I personally choose to blend the lessons from those stories with lessons from law and yes, even some from the old and new testaments.

And going back to your question of who played an influential role with me, I'd have to include people like your father who had a very sharp mind and a warm heart. He helped confirm my thinking on a number of subjects, including the nature of man and the need to focus on justice instead of revenge."

The Judge continued, "Above all, though, I would put Ellie at the top of list. She defined goodness to me, and I wanted to live my life in a way that made her proud of me. Little else mattered in comparison.

I hope that someday you can experience a similar kind of partnership and love, Wade. There were other influential people in my life, of course, but it was Ellie above all others. She was my rock and my salvation… my true north."

Chapter 15

CURLY STEERED THE Ford F-150 down Brick Chapel Road and turned right on County Road 400 heading toward the village of Morton. He knew he would have to do some serious driving if he expected to catch up with the Judge and his companion.

"Well Luella," Curly said. "We've had a barrel of laughs, but I guess its time that you and I parted company."

Luella cringed, not knowing whether this meant Curly was about to kill her. He sure hadn't felt much compunction about murdering their parents. Curly pulled the truck over to the side of the road and looked at her. He told her to get out. Luella just sat there, not knowing if her dear brother was about to blast her.

"What're going to do, Curly, kill me in cold blood just like you killed Ma and Pa?"

"Naw," Curly replied. "You've been a good sister all things considered and that poke I gave you felt real good; so just climb on outta here while I'm feeling charitable."

Luella carefully opened the passenger door and slid out of the truck. For a long couple of seconds, Curly and Luella just stared at each other. He figured he would probably never see her again, and she prayed that would be the case. A moment later Curly put the truck in gear and slowly pulled away.

With Curly out of sight, Luella breathed a sigh of relief and looked around for a direction to go. She was alive, but she had no home, no parents, no money, no phone. She was battered and bruised and the clothes she wore reeked. She took off walking the way she'd come, back toward Brick Chapel Road.

If Curly Algol had one dominant trait, aside from being a ruthless killer, it was his ability to fixate on a goal. In this case he was focused on finding and settling the score with that high and mighty Judge Thaddeus Nathan. Yeah sure, he had killed the Judge's wife when he threw her down the staircase, but he wanted the Judge to suffer even more pain, and God help any sumbitch who got in his way.

Curly gassed up the truck in West Lafayette near the Purdue University campus and bought a map. He wanted to rob the gas station attendant because he was running low on dough, but he thought it best to not draw any more attention to himself than necessary; so he got back on the highway. He wasn't sure how he'd find the Judge, but he was determined to try. He had driven all night to make up for the head start his prey had, but he believed he was getting closer as he drove through Eau Claire, Wisconsin.

Despite being tired from driving all night, Curly tried to stay alert and look for any sign of the Judge's black Land Cruiser. He had a sense that Judge Nathan would be taking his sweet time going to Canada, and he knew from that clodhopper he spoke with at the Judge's house that he'd likely be driving through towns like Fargo, Bismarck and Billings which meant he was probably heading west on I-94.

Curly had had plenty of time to think about his life up to this point. Prison sure gave him time to reflect, as if Curly was capable of doing any thinking close to resembling reflection. The drive also gave him ample time to reflect as well. Every once in a while Curly would think back on growing up on his parents' farm. Whenever he thought of something happy that brought the glimmer of a smile to his face, the reality of what he'd done to his parents and Luella came rushing back. He knew he was different from other people even from a young age, but he gave it little or no thought beyond that.

"Fuck em all," he said out loud. "I guess even if I did want to make things right, it's just a little late now," he thought.

His delusional mind made it very easy to place the blame on others. "It's all that Judge's fault. If he hadn't sent me away to reform school when I was just a kid; well I think things would've been different. It's the Judge who's responsible for those guards getting killed and Ma and Pa too. He's got to pay! Now I'm the judge judging the judge." He laughed at his little play on words. "Gonna git you, Judge Thaddeus Nathan, and that shitty kid riding with you too."

Curly decided he needed to get some shuteye. He pulled off the highway at Afton State Park and went into the visitor's center which was virtually deserted. After peeing and vandalizing the candy machine, he walked back toward his truck and saw a young family playing frisbee on the lawn.

He walked over to them and asked the man, "Say, you didn't happen to see a buddy of mine driving a black Lexus Land Cruiser through here did ya? I'm supposed to meet up with him but we got separated, and I don't have his cell number."

"We sure did," the fellow replied, not even an hour ago. They asked for some good places to fish, and we told them where we like to go up around Fergus Falls."

Curly couldn't believe his luck. He tried to contain his enthusiasm and thanked the man as politely as he was capable.

"Oh and by the way," Curly said, "you wouldn't happen to have a few dollars you could spare? My buddy has got our dough, so that's why I'm trying to find him; plus I'm running real low on gas."

The man looked at Curly, and said, "Sorry friend, I'm not in the habit of giving money away to strangers, and I got my family to look after."

"Yessir, you got a right nice Christian-looking family there, mister. Be a shame to see anything bad happen to them. You sure you don't have a few bucks on you to spare? I could be on my way right fast if you did," Curly pressed.

The man looked at Curly and then at his family. He saw that Curly was actually a rather despicable looking character, who also had a rather menacing looking shotgun resting on the rack by the truck's rearview window.

"Well," the fellow said, "I reckon I could give you a little help, if you promise to leave us alone."

"Why sure thing," Curly said as he approached the man.

The frightened feller pulled a small wad of bills out of his pocket and was peeling off a $20 bill when Curly reached over and grabbed the whole wad.

"Hey!" the man shouted, and Curly rammed the palm of his hand into the hapless man's nose and kneed him in the nuts hard. The poor guy went down moaning.

His wife was standing about twenty feet away and saw what had happened. She called out "Norbert!", but Norbert was lying on the ground, sucking wind and clutching his jewels.

"Hey little lady," Curly said. "If you didn't have those little kids with you, I'd be right happy to give you a poke, especially since old lover boy here may not be up to it for a few days."

"Now you get out of here before I call the police," she hollered and pulled her two small children close to her. Her husband lay on the ground still groaning.

Curly just leered at her and said, "Well, maybe some other time then. I gotta go tidy up some loose ends with my friends… hey, that rhymes," he chortled.

He climbed back in the truck and looked down at poor Norbert laying in the grass in a fetal position and said, "Thanks for the donation, you goober!"

Curly then flipped the bird at the older child, put the F-150 in gear and slowly pulled away. "Ignorant goober fuck!" he called out. Then he was gone.

Chapter 16

QUENTIN HAD MADE a morning and evening ritual out of lounging on Judge Nathan's patio furniture. Coffee in the morning; beer in the evening. It was close to sundown, and he was enjoying a cold bottle of Fat Tire beer after a long day in the UPS truck.

Aside from the music coming from the stereo in Judge Nathan's study, it was fairly quiet on Brick Chapel Road. Cassie had safely relocated to secure housing on Kissinger's campus, and the college's security department had been alerted by Sheriff Penrod about Curly Algol and the teal 1994 F-150. Her house was quiet now.

Even the earlier drone from Spencer Greenlee's lawn mower had ceased, and now just the locusts' rhythmic buzzes were the only other sounds to be heard. Quentin reclined on the lounge chair thinking about the tragic developments that had occurred recently and shook his head in disbelief.

Unlike some folks, Quentin Harp hadn't had it especially hard growing up in Prindle County. His father was a factory worker who made decent money, with seniority and benefits, and his mother waited tables at the diner across from the county fairgrounds. They were good, hardworking folks, and they were kind parents to their only child. Quentin had a pretty good upbringing, and he was comfortable setting high standards for himself.

When Quentin graduated from South Prindle High School, he decided he didn't want to go to college; just had had enough of school for a while. He was fortunate to get a job with UPS and had been driving for them the past six years. He took his work seriously, and his supervisors had come to rely on him.

Quentin also felt very proud that Judge Nathan had regarded him well enough to entrust his home to him. He promised himself he would do whatever it took to protect the Judge's and Cassie's properties.

Quentin lay on the patio's lounge chair, still listening to music and occasionally taking a pull on the beer bottle. He was about to get up and prepare some dinner when he noticed a vague form coming down the road, off in the distance. He watched the form for a few more seconds and realized it was coming his way in a shaky, unsteady manner.

When the form was about fifty yards away, he stood up to get a better view. It was the Hutchinson lady who had stopped by before with her brother looking for Judge Nathan. Only now, Quentin knew her real name wasn't Hutchinson and her brother was public enemy #1, Curly Algol. She was alone and was having difficulty walking. He slowly rose to his feet and approached the road. She saw him and collapsed to the ground. Luella lay there in the dirt, unconscious.

"Oh no!" Quentin called out. He looked around for any sign of her crazy brother, jumped the picket fence and quickened his pace to the woman lying in the road.

She was a dusty nasty mess, and she smelled even nastier. He gently touched her shoulder to see if she'd stir, but she didn't. Quentin quickly returned to the house, filled a glass with water and grabbed his cell phone. She was still unconscious when he kneeled back down next to her.

"Hey now," he whispered. He gently touched her shoulder again and repeated, "C'mon now, miss, c'mon back now."

He put a little cool water on his fingertips and gently touched her parched lips. She stirred slightly and her eyes began to flutter. He lightly put a little more water on her dry lips. When she slowly regained consciousness, she was staring right into Quentin's concerned eyes.

"There you are," he said with a cautious smile on his face. "Had me pretty scared there for a minute. Your brother, Curly, isn't around, is he?"

At the mention of Curly's name, Luella physically cringed. Her eyes darted here and there just in case he had returned.

"No, he left me by the side of the road a few hours ago. I've been walking ever since. Said he was going after the Judge somewhere up in Canada."

Quentin's blood went cold for a minute with dread. He'd have to get this woman out of the dirt road and get her stabilized. Then, he'd call the Sheriff first and then Cassie.

"Can you get up, miss, we sure don't want to leave you here in the middle of the road," he suggested. "We can go over to the Judge's house and get you cleaned up."

"I think I can get up," Luella said, and she moved her legs and managed to stand. She rested her hand on Quentin's shoulder and together they walked through Thaddeus' gate and into the house to the bathroom.

After giving her more water to drink and making sure she was okay physically, Quentin said, "Pardon me for saying this, Miss Algol, but you could use a bath. Why don't you take all the time you need, and then put that robe on when you're done. Your clothes aren't really worth keeping at this point. We'll figure out something to do for clothes for you."

As exhausted as Luella was now, she couldn't have argued with him even if she wanted to. Quentin made her promise that she was feeling stable enough to bath without his supervision. She eagerly nodded that she was, and he ran the bath water for her and exited the bathroom.

While she was bathing, Quentin called the Sheriff's office and got the dispatcher, Donnabelle Stoner, on the line. Donnabelle immediately understood the gravity of the situation and said she'd contact the Sheriff directly. He hung up with the dispatcher and called Cassie's cell phone number. He expected that he'd have to leave a voice message and was about to do so when Cassie picked up the phone. She sounded out of breathe.

"Quentin, what's going on," Cassie quickly said. "Is everything okay?"

Quentin proceeded to tell her about Luella's arrival and pitiful condition. At first Cassie wasn't the least bit sympathetic; then as Quentin gave her more details, Cassie's heart softened a bit. "Oh my, this woman's been a victim too."

Quentin told Cassie that he had a phone call into the Sheriff and expected him to either call or show up very soon.

Cassie said, "I have a few things I need to quickly finish up here; then I'll come meet you at home. In the meantime, go over to my house and get some clothing for her to wear. That includes undergarments, Quentin. You'll find panties and a bra and socks in the dresser and jeans, blouses, a belt and shoes in the closet. Put some in a sack and take them back to her. And Quentin, if you tell anyone I let you go through my underwear drawer, you won't have to worry about Curly Algol coming back. Do you hear me?!"

"Yes ma'am," was the only reply she heard. She smiled.

They hung up and Quentin ran across the street to the Henrys' house and let himself in with the key Cassie had previously left hidden for him. He quickly assembled a bag full of clothes for Luella and returned to the Judge's house. He gently knocked on the bathroom door, and a moment later the door opened a crack and Luella peered out at him. Her hair was still wet but combed and her face was puffy and pink from the bath water. She actually looked human and that unpleasant odor, that had clung to her like a dark shroud, was gone.

"Here," he said. "Mrs. Nathan offered these clothes for you to wear until we can get something more your size."

Luella took the clothes and closed the bathroom door again. Quentin went back into the kitchen, and a few minutes later Luella appeared in the doorway wearing Cassie's clothes.

"Why don't you have a seat here," Quentin said, "and I'll fix you some tea and a bite to eat. I only have bread and tuna fish or peanut butter and jelly. Hope that's okay."

She said, "Thank you, I really don't want to be a bother. Peanut butter would be fine. And what is your name again? I'm afraid I forgot it from when we spoke the other day."

"Quentin. "My name's Quentin Harp, and you're Luella Algol, right?"

She nodded yes. "And just so you know, Luella, I called the Sheriff and Mrs. Henry while you were in the bathroom, and they'll both likely be showing up any minute. Now, I don't want you to worry none because they're both very good people, but I'm sure they'll have questions for you, especially Sheriff Penrod."

Again, she nodded that she understood and quietly nibbled on her sandwich and sipped her tea. They talked a little on and off, but it was clear that Luella was beyond weary. Her grief and anger and pain and sorrow weighed like lead.

A few minutes later, Quentin heard the sound of tires on the Thaddeus' gravel driveway, and he saw Sheriff Penrod and a female deputy with a medical kit exit his patrol car. Twenty seconds after that, Cassie Henry pulled to a stop in her driveway. She waved to the Sheriff and came across the road to join them. Quentin meet them on the front porch and opened the door for them to enter.

Chapter 17

"ACCORDING TO WIKIPEDIA," Wade read out loud from his iPad, "Fergus Falls, Minnesota has a population of 13,138 and is the county seat of Otter Tail County. They have several parks and lakes nearby. Why don't we try fishing for bass in the Otter Tail River, then spend the night in town?"

"Sounds good to me," Thaddeus said. "We can pick up fishing licenses at that bait shop we saw coming in to town. We've been sitting in this car for a long time. It'll feel good to get out and walk around a bit; and I imagine you'll want to go for a run before dinner."

An hour later they were standing on the bank of the Otter Tail River at a spot that the bait shop owner told them had deep holes that held some nice-sized smallies. Wade and the Judge decided to try different lures to see if one was more productive than the other. Wade tied on a floating Rapala for surface fishing and Thaddeus decided to tie on a purple plastic worm to jig the deeper holes.

It was a gloriously warm, sunny day, and they found that their spot on the river offered adequate shade. Wade immediately hooked a dandy 14" smallmouth and safely released him back in the river. He quickly followed that up with another smallmouth and was beginning to feel a little cocky.

"Hey Judge," he boasted. "You sure you don't want to change lures. They seem to be hitting on the surface, and besides, no self-respecting bass is gonna want that plastic worm of yours."

"We'll see, young Pisces," Thaddeus replied. "It's a little soon for you to be saying what'll work!" The Judge and Wade smiled at each other and went back to their fishing. Each one was determined to catch the next sizable fish.

Then, Wade tied into another nice bass and tauntingly held it up for the Judge to see. They fished for the next two hours, and as luck would have it, Thaddeus' jigging technique started showing results. First, he landed a large catfish which put up a great fight and must have weighed six pounds.

"Hey Judge, I thought we were fishing for bass; not bottom feeders," Wade taunted. "If you want me to give you a few pointers, I might be able to find a little time between all the fish I'm catching here."

Before long, Wade's words came back to bite him. Thaddeus landed three smallmouth bang, bang, bang, and Wade cast a sideways glance at him to see how he was doing it. The Judge just gave him a little smile and went back to fishing.

Then Thaddeus landed a 16" smallie and Wade muttered, "nice fish." Thaddeus carefully unhooked the beautiful fish and released it back into the river.

Try as he might, Wade didn't land another fish the rest of the afternoon. The Judge, however, caught and released six more smallmouth, the last one measuring 19", a nice smallie in anyone's book.

"Hey Wade," the Judge said as they were putting their fishing tackle back in the Land Cruiser. "Did I ever tell you the story about the old bull and the young bull?"

"Uh no, that might be one of your tall tales that I've missed," Wade said cooly.

"Well sir, it was like this: Seems there was an old bull and young bull standing on a grassy hill looking at a bunch of pretty cows grazing in the valley below. The young bull says, 'hey old-timer what say we run down there and screw us one of those cows?!' The old bull turns to the young whippersnapper and says, 'why don't we just walk down there and screw em' all'?"

Both of them started laughing, mainly because it was the first time Thaddeus had ever told a joke that was even remotely off-color. Wade was a good enough sport to appreciate that the Judge had soundly put him in his place by catching several more fish. They'd had a great afternoon fishing and just being good-natured fishing buddies.

"Vanity of vanities… all is vanity", Ecclesiastes 1:2," the Judge added. "There's a lesson to be learned here, young Aquarius. And speaking of vanity, did I ever tell you the classic myth about Andromeda and Perseus?"

"Well uh maybe," Wade started, but he was too late. Judge Nathan was on a roll!

"Ah," the Judge began, "tis a classic tale of vanity and ultimately heroism. As the story goes Andromeda, the daughter of King Cepheus of Ethiopia and his vain Queen Cassiopeia ran into some serious trouble when Cassiopeia boasted that she was even more beautiful than the Nereids, who were a particularly alluring group of sea nymphs. The Nereids were not amused by Cassiopeia's boastfulness and beseeched Poseidon, the sea god, to punish her.

"Poseidon sent Cetus, a terrible monster, to attack King Cepheus' kingdom. The weak king, Cepheus, was terrified and asked the Oracle of Ammon for his counsel. The oracle said the king must sacrifice his virgin daughter to appease the monster.

Alas, poor daughter Andromeda was chained to a rock and her mother was forced to watch from shore. Seeing Andromeda's plight, Perseus astride the winged-horse, Pegasus, swoops down, waiving Medusa's severed head, and saves her just in the nick of time with the swing of his mighty sword."

"I see," said Wade. "So, you're telling me I shouldn't brag, huh, about fishing and stuff or bad things can happen."

The Judge smiled and nodded, "Not unless you want a sea monster to come after your kids, or unless you have a guy on a flying horse waiting to swoop down and save the day. But you know, that's your call," Thaddeus deadpanned.

They finished packing the Land Cruiser. It had been a great day; two guys on the road, fishing a dandy little river and telling tall tales.

Wade and Thaddeus checked into adjoining rooms in the Fergus Falls Inn and made a reservation for dinner at the motel's restaurant. Wade was anxious to get some exercise so he went off for a run, and Thaddeus phoned Quentin to see how things were going back home.

"Evening Judge, yeah we had a little excitement here earlier today. You'll never guessed who showed up out of nowhere, all battered and messed up. Luella Algol."

"You're kidding," the Judge said seriously. "Curly Algol's sister just showed up?!"

"She was in a pretty bad way, Judge. Apparently, she witnessed Curly murder her parents and burn their house to the ground. Then later he raped her. I brought her inside and got her cleaned up and immediately called Sheriff Penrod and Mrs. Henry. I'm sorry, Judge, I probably shouldn't have brought her into your house, but she really was in a bad way."

"Don't worry about that, Quentin. You did the right thing," the Judge consoled. "Where is she now and what did the Sheriff and Cassie do?"

Quentin said, "The Sheriff came immediately with a lady deputy named Kristi Donovan, and she examined Luella and drove her to the Prindle County Hospital so the doctors could check her out.

I told Sheriff Penrod that if she didn't need to be hospitalized, she was welcome to stay here a while. No funny business, Judge, I mean I won't take advantage of her or nothing. I got some vacation time off from work, and she looks like she needs to heal, both physically and mentally. She seems to have suffered every bit as much as you and Wade and Cassie, you know."

"Quentin, you are a surprising young man. Yeah, that's fine with me. She can stay in the guest room," the Judge said, "and it's got its own bathroom. The bed linens should be clean, and I have some extra cash stashed in that drawer with the handgun. Take it, if you need it. Save your receipts, okay. And if you need any assistance with clothing or feminine things, ask Cassie for help. Wow, you have had a little excitement going on."

"And there's something else," Quentin added, "Luella says her brother is coming after you, all the way to Canada if necessary. I'm really angry with myself for telling them where you're headed and what you're driving. I'm awful sorry for that boneheaded move, Judge."

"Don't beat yourself up about it, Quentin. Forewarned is forearmed. In a way I hope that human scum shows up. Wade and I might be able to save the judicial system a little time and money. Oh well, I don't plan on changing my life just because we have a deranged serial killer after us," the Judge mused.

"You might ask Sheriff Penrod to contact the police in Fargo, Bismarck and Billings and alert them to keep their eyes peeled, okay. We'll be passing through these towns over the next day or so." Quentin agreed and they said goodbye.

Wade ran like the wind! Breathe in, breathe out. One foot in front of the other. Concentration on form and gait. Wade ran on a path along the Otter Tail River. He thought about his mom and wondered how she was doing, Breathe in, breathe out. He thought about his dad and how much he missed him. Breathe in, breathe out. He flashed back to his dream about the Aborigines and the walkabout. He thought about the wilderness around him and the people in his life. He thought about the Judge's lessons, and he thought about going to Duke. High school already felt like a long time ago. He was ready for whatever came his way; or so he hoped.

Wade ran further downstream toward the bait shop where he and the Judge had purchased their fishing licenses. He stopped about fifty yards short of the shop and bent over to massage a cramp that was forming in his calf. As he looked up, he noticed a truck over by the bait shop. It was a faded teal green 1994 Ford F-150 pickup. It had an Indiana license plate. He didn't wait around to see the driver. Breathe in, breathe out. Wade ran like the wind all the way back to the motel and banged on the Judge's door.

Thaddeus opened the door to a sweating and panting Wade Henry. "We gotta get away from here," Wade managed. "I saw the truck. I saw it at the bait shop. We gotta get out of here, now!"

"All right, Wade, now just catch your breath and calm down," the Judge said softly. "Exactly what truck did you see?"

"It was the one we think that Curly Algol asshole is driving," Wade cried. "I didn't wait around to see him, but it's gotta be him."

"Look, I'll hide the Land Cruiser in the garage behind the motel, then we'll talk this over, okay. But I need to tell you, Wade, I'm not running away from this jerk. I certainly don't want to be foolish about this, but I'm 70 years old, and I don't like being angry and afraid and looking over my shoulder. We'll be careful, I promise, but I want us to live our lives on our terms; not his. I want us to be like Orion the hunter; not Lepus the hare. So, that means we get to enjoy our adventure to Jasper as much as possible, and to also have a backup plan if need be. We'll talk more about that later."

The Judge hid his car in an obscure corner of the garage, and when he returned, Wade had regained his composure.

"Sorry about my outburst earlier, Judge. I just freaked thinking that that monster was closing in on us. I feel better now. How about I shower, and then can we get some dinner and talk some more, okay?"

"You bet, the Judge said. "We can make this work, Wade, if we stick together." They looked each other straight in the eyes, extended their hands and shook on it.

Chapter 18

CURLY ALGOL FELT LIKE he was getting closer to settling the score with Judge Thaddeus Nathan, but even he had to admit that his search was like finding a needle in a haystack. On the other hand he figured that he really had nothing to lose by searching. He knew he could never go back to Prindle County, so he might as well go to wherever he thought the Judge was going. He needed an enemy to keep him motivated. Otherwise what's the point in living. He leered at himself in the truck's rearview mirror. Curly also realized that he needed to dump his father's truck which he was sure all the cops were looking for.

"Hell, I should've stolen that goober fuck's car back at the rest stop, but then the cops would've known to look for that vehicle too," he said to himself. He leered at himself again. No, he had to be smart about this and smarter than the cops.

The sign for the bait shop read "Nightcrawlers $5 a dozen." Curly decided to stop in and ask if his "friends" had come through this way. The bait shop owner said he hadn't seen his friends in a black Toyota Land Cruiser which was true enough because the owner never saw the Judge's vehicle, but the shop owner also didn't like the looks of the creepy looking man asking questions. He saw no sense in helping Mr. Creepy out, especially since he didn't look like he was stopping in to buy anything.

"Naw, ain't seen nobody who's driving a black Cruise Lander," Wally Snerd said. "Been here the whole day too so I think I would've seen one. You might try up closer to Fargo."

"Say," Curly said. "You don't know where I can pick up another vehicle cheap do you? My poor truck's outlived its usefulness."

"Naw," came Wally's quick reply, "except maybe over at George's shitty car lot, but you gotta watch ol' George. He's a shifty guy, plus you gotta listen to all of his political rants. Don't know what's worse, George's dumb-ass mouth or the crap he sells on his lot."

"You wouldn't have one you'd be willing to sell cheap, would you?", Curly inquired. I got cash money, and I wouldn't care about transferring title or nothing."

"Naw," Wally said again. "I have me a nice little green Honda Civic that's got low miles and is easy on my pocketbook. Sure didn't get it from George's lot, and I didn't have to listen to his political crap neither. By the way, you gonna buy anything here, or what? Because if you're not…"

Curly just leered at the shop owner and said, "Well sir, I reckon I might as well hit the road then", and as good ol' Curly was turning to leave, his right hand shot out and he grabbed Wally Snerd by the throat and began to squeeze his Adam's apple. Wally squawked and tried to breathe but Curly had him solidly.

"Now then, Mr. Crawler Man, hand over your car keys, and I might let you live."

Wally tried to get away, but Curly was bigger and stronger and meaner. Wally struggled to get his hand in his vest pocket and managed to retrieve the car keys.

"Thank you kindly, Mr. Crawler Man. Sure is getting warm outside. Maybe you'd like to cool off."

Curly palmed Wally hard in the nose like he had done to that man at the rest stop, and Mr. Snerd's eyes rolled back into his head. He dragged the hapless shop owner over to his walk-in freezer and dumped him inside.

"Oh, and here's a little decoration for you." Curly took a large Muskie stick bait and crammed the treble hooks into Wally's forehead. "You look right purdy now!"

Curly went through Wally's billfold and retrieved $56 and then rifled the cash register for the few bucks that were there. He pocketed a bunch of crackers and snacks and a liter bottle of Mountain Dew. Curly then turned the closed sign so it appeared from the outside and turned off the lights. No one else was around. He quickly took the Indiana plates off the F-150 and grabbed his map and his daddy's shotgun and piled into the green Civic. "Nice little ride!" Then he drove away.

And, after that little episode Curly knew there was no point in hanging around town for someone to find Crawler Man Wally all frozen and decked out with fishing accessories. He steered the Civic on to I-94 West and put Fergus Falls, Minnesota in his rearview mirror.

He figured he'd try his luck looking around Fargo a bit; maybe have a "friendly conversation" or two with folks. Maybe jog some memories. He was in no hurry. "Haste makes waste," he chuckled out loud.

And so at this point, unbeknownst to anyone, Curly was now ahead of Wade and Thaddeus on their journey northwest toward Jasper, Canada.

Several hours later, Deputy Kristi Donovan returned to the Judge's house with Luella.

"The doctors at Prindle County Hospital gave Ms. Algol a very thorough examination," Deputy Donovan said, "and despite some dehydration, cuts, contusions, and psychological trauma, she appears to be fairly stable. The rape is another story, and we won't know the results for a little while yet, but in the main, she seems to be okay. But, she's obviously been through a lot."

Quentin said "I'll be sure to look after her, and I'll give Mrs. Henry a call to let her know that Luella is back here." The Deputy left and Quentin led Luella to the guest bedroom where she promptly curled up in a fetal position on the bed.

"Anything else I can do for you miss?" Quentin gently asked. "Otherwise I'll just let you rest, and we can get you something to eat when you wake up."

Luella's eyes met Quentin's, and she said, "Thank you for helping me. I'm just so tired. I just want to sleep."

She closed her eyes, and a few seconds later Luella Algol was in a deep sleep. Quentin watched her for a few moments longer to make sure she was alright, then quietly slipped out of the guest room and closed the door.

Quentin went back out to the patio with a fresh beer and gave Cassie a call and then he phoned Judge Nathan. Cassie promised to stop by the house in the morning to help Luella with some more clothes and to make sure Quentin was comfortable with his new found role as a caregiver. The Judge complimented Quentin on his handling a difficult situation and also let him know the latest with Curly's truck being sighted.

"Looks like the Algol family, or what's left of it, is causing it's share of issues for all of us," the Judge said. "I'm sorry you got dragged into this mess, Quentin, but I'm grateful for your help. Please keep us all informed, okay."

They said they'd touch base tomorrow and then hung up.

Chapter 19

Aﬆer dinner Thaddeus said, "Wade, it's a beautiful clear night, and it's too early for me to go to bed. What say we pull out the binoculars and take a look at the night sky for a while. It'll take our minds off of other things."

Wade thought it was a really good idea, so they retrieved two pair of Oberwerk binoculars from the Land Cruiser, along with tripods, and walked up a grassy hill that gave them an unobstructed view of the sky.

There was very little light pollution, and the moon was a thin waxing crescent. Venus floated like a brilliant jewel a fist-width away to the west. It reminded Thaddeus of the star and crescent that has become associated with Islam. He made a mental note to talk with Wade about that.

The night sky spread out above them in stellar wonder. They both looked heavenward and were speechless at the magnificence of the Milky Way. And they knew that what they saw was just their viewable portion of our Milky Way galaxy, and that our galaxy was just one of hundreds of billions of other galaxies, each containing hundreds of billions of stars and innumerable planets, moons and other satellites.

Finally the Judge broke the silence and softly said, "What did ancient man think when he looked up at all those stars? Even for us several millennia later, to see the Milky Way from our location on its Orion Spur, it's astonishing in its beauty and scope. They say it would take over 100,000 years traveling at the speed of light to go from one end of our galaxy to the next."

Thaddeus just shook his head in amazement. "It's the closest thing to heaven that I can imagine, and we're all destined to remain a part of it even after we've died. We'll all become stardust… saints and sinners, alike… we're all destined to remain a part of this vast wonder."

"Look Wade!" and the Judge pointed upward. "The winter constellations are almost gone now, Thaddeus continued. Orion is still visible in the west and so is Auriga with its alpha star Capella. Andromeda is slipping into the horizon in the northwest and Perseus is following her, just like in the myth."

He pointed to Taurus with its giant red star Aldebaran and to Gemini a little further to the east featuring Castor and Pollux. Sirius and Canis Major were bright to the southeast of Orion, and Leo was easily visible in the southeast with Regulus at its heart and Denebola at the tip of the lion's tail.

It had taken Wade a while to learn to recognize these constellations and the names of their major stars, but under the Judge's tutelage these past months, he was beginning to surprise himself at what he'd learned.

"This is so awesome," Wade exclaimed, as he looked through his binoculars. "I would do anything to get a close up view of the Orion Nebula. Next time let's set up the Celestron telescope, okay?! I think astronomers refer to the nebula as a nursery for newly forming stars. Even with binoculars though it's pretty incredible."

"Ah, you are learning well, young Galileo!" the Judge proclaimed. "We'll definitely do it. When you're finished admiring the Orion Nebula, try to locate the Andromeda galaxy. Cassiopeia points to it. That galaxy is the closest one to ours, and yet it is 2.5 million light years away. That means that the light that we're seeing now has taken 2.5 million years to reach us. It is so enormous though that you can faintly see it even with the naked eye."

They continued to use their binoculars, and from time to time Wade or Thaddeus would summon the other to look at what they were viewing…the Hyades and Pleiades clusters in Taurus, the double stars Mizar and Alcor in Ursa Major. As the evening went on and their eyes adjusted to the growing darkness, they saw even more stars. It was a glorious night for stargazing and sharing stories.

"Why is it that the constellations seem to mostly have Greek and Roman mythology names and so many of the stars have Arabic names," Wade asked.

"Ah Wade, that is an excellent question," Thaddeus replied. "Fact is, many individual stars, especially the brightest ones, have names given to them by ancient cultures. The Australian Aborigines, as you now know, were ancient stargazers as were the Egyptians and many others. Although all of the constellations have Latin names, most all of the stars within constellations have Arabic names because during the Dark Ages in Europe, many European scholars lacked interest in astronomy and science. During this time the Arabs studied Claudius Ptolemy's 2nd century manuscript, the Almagest, which contained the Latin and Greek names for stars. They translated many of those names into Arabic. Interesting, yes?"

"Very interesting!" replied Wade. "I guess with so much of the turmoil in the Arab world being fueled by Islamic extremists, it's hard for me to see the scientific aspects of their culture. And yet, many individuals were and are brilliant people with math and science. Seems like the Arabs were good stewards of astronomical knowledge, and the western world eventually regained its scientific curiosity."

Thaddeus and Wade continued to look through their binoculars for another hour or so. The temperature had just a hint of chillness to it, but there was little wind even on the hilltop.

"Well, what say we pack it in and call it a night?!" Thaddeus suggested We'll definitely find a great place in Montana to pull out the telescope. It's not called 'Big Sky Country' for nothing," he laughed.

The next morning began with sunshine and great promise. Wade went for an early morning run, but definitely not in the direction of the bait shop where he'd seen the teal F-150. He ran along the Otter Tail River and thought about the things that the Judge had shared with him last night. It wasn't just the information that Thaddeus shared but the nurturing and instructive way he communicated with Wade.

Wade found it a little sad that the Judge and Mrs. Nathan had never had children because he thought the Judge would've been a terrific dad. Wade was also sad that his own dad was gone; never coming back. No one could ever take his father's place, but the Judge was about the best surrogate granddad a guy could have.

Wade stopped briefly to catch his breath at the old mill. He watched the flowing river turn the large mill wheel and thought about how life is constantly in motion. Everything and everyone comes and goes... even the stars. Breathe in, breathe out. Wade returned to the path and ran back to meet the Judge.

An hour later they took their gear to the garage and climbed back into Thaddeus' black Land Cruiser. They had only traveled about three miles when they came upon the bait shop, and they both stared in disbelief. There were a half dozen police cars and yellow tape at the entrance to the shop indicating a crime scene. Wade pulled the Land Cruiser to the side of the road, and he and the Judge got out. They also noticed the faded teal 1994 Ford F-150 pickup truck parked under a tree.

"Evening officer," Thaddeus said as he approached a very serious looking state trooper, what's all the commotion about? My name is Judge Thaddeus Nathan from Prindle County, Indiana."

"You're a long way from home, Judge," the trooper stated. "We have what appears to be a homicide, but I'm not at liberty to divulge any information regarding an active investigation. I'm sure you understand," the trooper said officiously.

"I definitely understand, officer, but my companion and I may be able to shed some light on the situation. Why don't you take us to whoever's in command?"

The trooper lifted the yellow crime scene tape and the Judge and Wade ducked under it. They walked up to the entrance to the bait shop and were stopped by another equally serious looking officer who held up his hand for them to stop.

The two troopers spoke briefly, and the second officer went inside the shop. He reappeared a few moments later with an even more serious looking county sheriff.

"I'm Sheriff Rory South. I understand you may be able to help us out here. I hear you're a Judge from Indiana, and who's the young man with you?" the Sheriff asked.

"This is my neighbor and friend, Wade Henry. I'm retired Judge Thaddeus Nathan. We stopped by here yesterday to get our fishing licenses and lures and talked quite a bit with the shop owner. Your deputy mentioned something about a possible homicide. I'd appreciate your sharing anything you can with us, and I'll be happy to tell you who I think may be responsible."

"Well, Judge Nathan, why don't you just tell me what you know first, and then I'll decide what I can share with you. How's that sound," he said in a slightly perturbed voice.

Judge Nathan told Sheriff South everything he could about public enemy #1 Curly Algol, going back to the vehicular homicide conviction that got Curly sentenced to Russellville Prison for life, his escape from the guards during transport to prison, his murderous attacks on his wife and Wade's father; Curly's escape from Russellville, and his chasing after them on their way to Jasper, Canada.

"That's quite a story, Judge, I am very sorry for your losses," Sheriff South said sympathetically. "What we have inside appears to be another homicide. The bait shop owner, Wally Snerd, was found this morning by his wife, Juanita, who came to the shop looking for him when he didn't come home last night. She had a spare key to get into the shop and found Mr. Snerd frozen dead inside the shop's walk-in freezer. It would seem that the killer enjoyed cramming a large Muskie bait to his forehead. It also appeared to be a robbery since we found no money in the cash register and Mr. Snerd's wallet was found empty on the floor."

"Well Sheriff, I think this goes way beyond murder and a simple robbery. By my reckoning, Curly Algol has now murdered at least nine people," the Judge said.

The Sheriff whistled his surprise. Then, Wade told the Sheriff about his seeing the F-150 yesterday afternoon when he passed by the shop during his run. He told the Sheriff that the truck had Indiana license plates yesterday and was identical in description to the vehicle that they believed Curly had stolen after murdering his own father. The Sheriff whistled again.

"Wow, you folks sure don't mess around in Indiana," the Sheriff deadpanned. "We'd appreciate it if you did a better job keeping your serial killers under wraps."

"I know. Me too, Sheriff South," the Judge said solemnly This has just been one tragedy after another, and it may not be over yet."

He gave the Sheriff the phone number for Sheriff Penrod in Prindle County and encouraged him to phone him right away to exchange information. Sheriff South said he would do that as soon as they got poor Wally Snerd tagged and bagged for the coroner.

"Judge Nathan, it would also appear that this Curly Algol maniac is now driving Mr. Snerd's green Honda Civic, Sheriff South said. I doubt he's still in our jurisdiction, but you'll probably want to keep your eyes peeled for it. And, if you get any further information about the whereabouts of this Algol feller, I'd sure appreciate your letting me know ASAP."

The Judge nodded agreement. They all shook hands and Wade and Thaddeus climbed back into the black Land Cruiser and headed to I-94 West toward Fargo.

The Judge was at the wheel and happy to put Fergus Falls, MN behind them.

Thaddeus and Wade looked at each other, and the Judge said, "I suppose this is as good a time as any to discuss the backup plan I mentioned yesterday. Why don't you reach under the console here and pull out the locked case." Wade did as he was told, and Thaddeus handed him two little brass keys. "Keep one for yourself."

Chapter 20

THE NEXT MORNING FOUND Quentin on his favorite lounge chair on Thaddeus' patio enjoying a cup of coffee and watching two mourning doves work on building a nest. The male was walking back and forth a lot bringing twigs while the female instructed him where to place them. It was a rather comical exercise to Quentin who thought the male would be a good UPS driver with all the dutiful deliveries he was making. He sipped his coffee and listened to low music while enjoying the visual entertainment.

At around 8:45 AM, Quentin heard the door to the Judge's study open, and Luella appeared in the doorway dressed in the clothes Cassie had loaned her. She appeared tired, but she had a small smile on her face and seemed to be okay.

"Well there you are," Quentin brightly exclaimed. "I thought you might sleep all day given everything you've been through. How about some coffee and breakfast?"

"Coffee would be fine right now, but I think I'd just like to sit here on the patio for a little while and enjoy the morning. Living in the country, I'm accustomed to waking up early for chores, but it would be nice just to sit quietly and try not to think too much. I miss ma and pa so much, and I can't believe I'll never see them again. I guess I need to speak with the Sheriff's office and the coroner later today about funeral arrangements. It's all like a horrible dream. Right now though, I just want to sit here and feel safe, okay?"

"That's fine, Luella. Just take your time," Quentin said sympathetically. "And, one cup of coffee coming right up, ma'am." He got up and reached for a clean cup and poured.

"Oh, and by the way, I got a text message from Cassie a bit ago. She's going to come over about 11:00 after she goes to the grocery. I know she misses her home, and now that we know Curly is probably in Minnesota, I think she's feeling safer about coming back home." Luella nodded her understanding and took another sip of coffee.

The silence lasted for several minutes, and Quentin quietly pointed to the two mourning doves who were still in nest construction mode. Luella smiled and nodded her approval. Quentin got up to clean the kitchen a bit, and to give Luella some time alone to collect her thoughts. Four minutes later Quentin asked, "Are you ready for a little breakfast now or do you want to wait a little longer? There's no rush, of course." He mentally kicked himself because he didn't want to be too pushy. He was beginning to like having Luella at the house. It made him feel, well, needed.

"How come I never met you before, Quentin?" Luella inquired. "Seems like being in a small town and county like ours, we would've met at the Prindle County Fair or somewhere."

"I wondered that too," said Quentin, "but I think I'm maybe a couple of years older than you, and we went to different high schools; you at North Prindle and me at South. In any event, it's very nice to meet you now," he offered politely.

A few minutes later they were finishing their coffee, and Quentin heard Cassie pull into her driveway. He walked over to the Judge's picket fence and waved to her as she was getting out of the car.

"Let me help you with those groceries, Cassie," and he leaped over the fence and bounded over to her car. "I'll be back in a few minutes," he called over his shoulder to Luella.

"Thanks Quentin, I sure appreciate your help. I see that you also mowed the grass and took care of the trash. I could get used to this kind of help," she winked.

"They call me 'Full Service Quentin', he quipped, and he hefted a large bag of groceries and walked with her to the kitchen door. "It sure is good to have you back, Cassie, especially with Luella here. I'm imagine she'd appreciate having another woman to talk to."

"So, how is she doing, Quentin?" Cassie asked with a concerned tone.

"Near as I can tell," Quentin replied, "she seems to be doing okay, but I am not an expert on women, and I am certainly no expert when it comes to people who have endured what she has been through."

Cassie nodded her understanding. "Why don't you head back over to the Judge's house. I'll be over in about twenty minutes after I've put these groceries away and started a load of laundry. Then, we'll both try to assess how she's getting along and what we want to do from here."

Quentin finished bringing in a final bag of groceries and then went back across the road to join Luella. Luella smiled when he returned and said, "I'm feeling a little hungry now, Quentin, if your offer for breakfast still stands, but I don't want to be any more trouble than I've already been."

"Of course the offer is still good! In fact, I found some frozen waffles and berries in the Judge's freezer earlier this morning. We've even got maple syrup from the maple sugar camp, and I found some Egg Beaters if you're willing to give 'em a try."

Luella said, "Sounds perfect. May I help?" And the two of them went into the kitchen and began preparing enough food so Cassie could join them as well.

Several minutes later Cassie knocked on the kitchen door and came inside to warm aromas of eggs and waffles cooking. She walked over to Luella and the two of them just looked at each other for several seconds, each wanting to try to understand the nature of the other. Cassie reached her hand out and gently pulled Luella toward her. They both began to cry instantly and held on to each other with heartbreaking sobs. Quentin could feel an immense sadness permeate the room. Thirty seconds later Cassie and Luella weakly smiled at each other. They stood apart again, but they knew that their shared experiences at the hands of Curly Algol would make them forever friends.

"Oh gee," Quentin blurted out, "the eggs!" And he immediately removed the skillet from the stove top. It was a perfect segue from the sadness of a few moments ago to a little more relaxed environment. The women smiled at the combination of Quentin's shyness and his determination to be a good host.

Thanks to everyone pitching in, the breakfast turned out very well. Part way through the meal, Luella turned to Cassie, and said, "I don't have adequate words to say how sorry I am that my brother killed Mr. Henry and Mrs. Nathan. She sobbed a little and caught herself when Cassie reached over and lightly touched her forearm. "I'm just so, so sorry that he hurt so many people, even his own family."

"What was it with him Luella?" asked Cassie. I just don't understand how a human being can behave that way."

"It's hard for me to understand too, Mrs. Henry, I just don't. Curly was always, and I mean always, a very strange boy. He was hurtful to other children. He stole things, even from church. Then when he got into puberty, whew, he was downright scary the way he'd look at me and other girls. He would just leer, and he didn't care who saw him doing it. He just didn't care."

Luella continued, "My parents are, I mean were, very caring, hard-working people. They knew Curly was a handful, and they tried to get him help, but there wasn't much to be done. Finally, after a little girl almost lost an eye due to Curly's 'roughhousing', Judge Nathan sent him to the reform school near Russellville. He came out worse, and that was the start of his fixation on getting even with Judge Nathan."

Cassie and Quentin sat there spellbound by Luella's description of Curly Algol's history. "Man!" was about all that Quentin could say. Cassie shook her head as if to will the tragedy of all of this away. They talked a few minutes longer and then they cleaned and put away all of the dishes and pans.

Cassie finally said, "Luella, have you given any thought about where you would like to stay? You obviously can't go home, and I don't know if you have other family in the area. If you're comfortable, you're more than welcome to stay at my place or with Quentin. I'm back home now for good, but I'm still up to my ears with my work at the College. I've been putting in some long hours, and I'm not around a lot; so you'd have your space and Quentin would be across the road. Or, you may choose to stay right here with Mr, Harp. I think Quentin would agree that whatever you decide is fine with us." Quentin nodded yes.

"I can't thank you both enough," Luella said. "For a while there when Curly killed our parents and was holding me hostage, I began to question whether life was worth living anymore. But now," she said quietly, "you're both so kind, and I just want to feel safe." Tears formed in her eyes again but she caught herself. "If it's okay with the two of you, I would just as soon stay here with Quentin until I can get back on my feet again, but I'll work real hard for both of you, you know, helping out with what ever you want. If that's okay."

And so it was agreed that Luella would stay at Judge Nathan's home with Quentin. Cassie told them that she needed to get back to work and would return home later that evening. She also said that Luella should help herself to her clothing and cosmetics in the bathroom cabinet until they could go shopping. It had turned into a very good morning. Very emotional, but healing. Luella was beginning to feel like a phoenix reborn from her ashes. Quentin was pleased to be genuinely appreciated.

Chapter 21

THE DRIVE FROM FERGUS FALLS, Minnesota to Fargo, North Dakota was relatively uneventful; uneventful with the exception of Wade staring at the two Glock G43 9mm pistols in the case that the Judge had handed him. Growing up in the country, Wade was accustomed to hearing gunshots, especially during hunting season, and he knew people who kept handguns either for personal protection or as collectibles. But Wade was more comfortable with shotguns for hunting quail and pheasant. Handguns were a different matter altogether though, and he stared at the two pistols on his lap as if they were alien beings.

"Wow Judge, I had no idea that you carried pistols with you," Wade solemnly said.

"Well, I know it's a different sort of thing from what you might expect of me," the Judge said, "but given the number of unpleasant judgements that I rendered from the bench over the years, it seemed prudent to be prepared for any eventualities. They were given to me as a gift from the Hoosier Judges Association when I retired from the bench. Ellie sure wouldn't have been happy about me having them, but I think she would've understood; especially since she knew that pissed off miscreants could show up unannounced at any time. Lord knows I've received enough death threats over the years. I actually forgot that I own the Glocks, but right now they provide a modicum of reassurance."

"My dad was pretty much against most guns and especially assault rifles, but he understood the need for people to protect themselves living in the country without immediate access to law enforcement. We also went hunting for quail and pheasant at a hunt club over by Rockville a couple of times, and we shot trap at several family reunions. I enjoyed it, and I felt like I learned a skill and a healthy respect for guns.

My dad made it a positive experience," Wade continued, "but also with very serious cautionary words about being too casual with firearms. As an ethicist, we had a lot of conversations about the gun lobby and second amendment rights. He didn't mind the handguns so much as he did the assault rifles which he thought made no sense. Actually none of it made any sense to mom."

"Well, Wade, my opinion on the subject could go on for hours, but that's not something either of us wants to hear. Suffice it to say, sitting on the bench for over thirty years, listening to accounts of tragedies as a result of guns is one thing, and they certainly influenced my thinking that we need some form of gun control. I admit, however, that it is an entirely different thing when you know there is a serial killer on the loose and looking for you. That has definitely changed my thinking about being armed. We'd be foolish not to have protection. When we find an appropriate place, let's pull over and do some target shooting. We should get acquainted with the Glocks, okay."

Wade agreed, and he smiled to himself as he thought about the Judge. Here was Judge Thaddeus Nathan who was widely respected, almost revered, both as a jurist and as a human being, and he was reacting on the Safety level of Maslow's Hierarchy of Needs. Wade appreciated his humanness, and the fact that this seventy year old man didn't plan on taking anyone's shit. That attitude was a little unexpected which was also the reason that Wade smiled. His admiration for the Judge grew.

The two men continued their drive along I-94 West and sailed through Fargo, heading toward Bismarck. The Judge chuckled as they went through Fargo.

"Remember me telling you about my good friend, Danny Brody. He used to tell me great stories about his summers at the boy's camp on the shores of Lake Nebagamon, Wisconsin. Apparently whenever a counselor got fired for some misdeed, the campers were told a fib that the counselor had to go to Fargo. So, if someone got 'Fargoed', it meant he got fired. Even to this day whenever I hear the name Fargo, I always think of Danny's story. Funny what you remember."

They drove on past Valley City and Jamestown, over Pipestem Creek, and decided to stop somewhere for lunch near Bismarck and Mandan along the banks of the mighty Missouri River. Wade pointed to a sign for the Bon Ton diner in West Salem, North Dakota. They found it easily. It was conveniently located next to the county sheriff's office, and they pulled into the gravel lot.

"Let's eat here and gas up the Land Cruiser," the Judge suggested. "Then, I want to stop in the sheriff's office to alert him about our nemesis, Curly Algol, and to see where we can safely do some target practice."

The Bon Ton diner was pretty much what you might expect, good coffee and country-style cooking although not exactly the healthiest fare. They served breakfast twenty-four hours a day which was always something that the Judge enjoyed. They took the map inside and confirmed their GPS route heading west and considered a few destinations along the way that looked fairly entertaining: Salem Sue, the World's Largest Fiberglass Holstein

Cow and the Dakota Dinosaur Museum. Wade couldn't wait to see Salem Sue, and the dinosaurs would be cool too.

Thaddeus and Wade lingered over a tasty breakfast, and Wade said he'd need to go for a run before too long to wear off the calories from his meals and long miles spent sitting in the car. There was a sheriff's deputy sitting at the counter finishing his lunch, and Thaddeus approached him as they were both getting ready to pay.

"Good afternoon, officer," Thaddeus said. "My name's Thaddeus Nathan, and I'm a retired judge from Prindle County, Indiana." Thaddeus showed the deputy his credentials and his photo ID. I'm getting ready to go over and see the Sheriff, and I'd appreciate it if you could give me his name and whether you know if he's in the office right now."

The deputy looked the Judge up and down and then checked out Wade. "Sheriff's name is Chris Bester, and he should be over there now. Beulah Glotzbach is our administrative assistant, and she should be able to help you if he's stepped out."

Wade and Thaddeus thanked him and walked next door to the Sheriff's office. Beulah was a rather rotund affable-looking woman about fifty years old. She peered over the tops of her glasses at the two men who came through the front door and said, "May I help you gentlemen?"

"Yes ma'am," the Judge said. "I presume you're Beulah Glotzbach. My name's Judge Thaddeus Nathan and this young feller is my friend and associate, Wade Henry. We're from Indiana, and we'd like to speak with Sheriff Bester if he has a few minutes." He showed her his credentials as well.

Beulah straightened up in her chair and tried to determine how this stranger would know her name. Then she recalled that her name plate was proudly displayed on the edge of her desk.

"Let me check and see if he's available, your honor. We've had a very hectic morning ever since the convenient store the next county over was robbed, and the store manager got walloped to within an inch of his life." She stood and waddled over to a closed door, knocked and went inside.

Wade cast Thaddeus a quick sideways glance as if to say "I wonder if that was Curly's doing." The Judge nodded back to him, but said nothing further.

They were both thinking the same thing though. A few moments later Beulah returned to her desk and Sheriff Chris Bester strode out of his office door.

"Good morning," he said. "I've got a lot on my plate right now. Why don't you step into my office and tell me how I can help you."

Wade and Thaddeus entered the sheriff's spartan office and took the two seats opposite his desk. Thaddeus reintroduced Wade and himself to Sheriff Bester and showed him his judicial credentials. Thaddeus then proceeded to tell him everything he could about Curly Algol and his path of murder and mayhem ever since he was a child to present day.

"So," the Sheriff said. "You think this Algol nutcase is possibly responsible for the robbery and assault over by Mandan."

"Yes, I do," came the Judge's reply. "I encourage you to speak with Sheriff Rory South in Fergus Falls, Minnesota and Sheriff Noble Penrod in Prindle County, Indiana. We've all been horribly victimized by Mr. Algol, and I think he's hell-bent on tracking Wade and me to Canada, if necessary."

Thaddeus gave Sheriff Bester a description of Mr. Algol and the green Honda Civic he stole from Wally Snerd. The sheriff had Beulah Glotzbach put out an all points bulletin for his small police force. He said he would also contact the sheriff departments between West Salem and the International Peace Park in Montana.

"I appreciate your assistance very much, Judge, anything else I can do for you?"

"Well, I have two Glock pistols that are all legally registered, plus I have a concealed carry permit. Wade and I would like to do a little target practice. Can you suggest a good place for us to do that?"

"Sure can, Judge, we have a gun range at the rear of the building here. I'll call Deputy Mack Wilger and have him get things ready for you. Just take a minute," the Sheriff said.

An hour later, Wade and Thaddeus felt very comfortable using the Glocks. They had shredded several paper targets with their 9mm handguns and learned a few shooting tips from Deputy Wilger. The deputy also showed them how to quickly dismantle and clean their handguns and gave them fresh rounds to fill their clips. They now felt better prepared, but each prayed they wouldn't need to use them.

Chapter 22

Curly Algol sat in the green Honda Civic behind a billboard near Dickinson, North Dakota contemplating his past, present and future. His recent episode of maniacal mayhem at the convenient store near Mandan had resulted in his stealing nearly $600 in cash, plus a full tank of fuel and a five-gallon gas can that he filled. He also made off with a large sack filled with snacks, sandwiches and bottles of water.

Walloping the store manager was just a little extra entertainment for Curly who chuckled to himself when he recalled the manager begging not to be hurt. Curly nearly killed the poor feller just for the fun of it. He punched, kicked, elbowed, bit, kneed and stomped the man until he lay in a bloody heap. The manager would eventually recover but would never walk as well as he did before. Just one more victim for Curly's growing criminal resume.

Curly briefly thought back to when he was a kid on the farm with his parents and Luella. He resisted every positive memory that came to him. He didn't know why he felt so violently toward them, but it really didn't matter any more.

"Done is done, he said to himself; just move on."

He thought about his days at school and his reckless and aggressive behavior with the other kids on the playground.

"Fuck 'em," he said out loud. "They dang well learned not to mess with sweet little Curly.

And that high and mighty Judge Thaddeus Nathan sent me away to reform school all because prissy Lily Durham almost lost an eye when I crammed my finger in it. Hell, the other eye still worked okay… no biggie."

He thought about all of the stealing he had done, and recalled getting caught stealing from the church collection box by the minister.

"Yeah, he caught me red-handed alright, but I knew that damn pussy preacher wouldn't do nothing about it. Probably prayed for my soul," he chortled.

He thought back on running over that guy who objected to his stealing his car. He was dead when the police arrived. "He was my first kill. Just ran his ass over!

And once again, that high and mighty judge wanted to put me away in a cage, Curly ruminated. Jeez, breaking away from the cops was super stupid easy, and pushing the Judge's wife down the stairs was a bonus thrill. Just dumb bad luck that the guy I slashed on the lawn wasn't the Judge. Unfinished business."

He recalled his good ol' prison cellmate, Nerf McCabe, and his escape from the Federal Correctional Center at Russellville. "Whew, one bloody mess!

What a freakin' rube that Nerf was," he laughed. "I bet those Mexicans had a real fiesta with him. I couldn't believe he went for the plan. Adios Nerfy boy!"

Curly chomped on a sardine and mustard sandwich, and his fingertips turned a golden orange from the Cheetos he scarfed down. He stared out at the wheat field across the road and thought about hurting Luella. A brief glimmer of humanity told him he might have gone a little too far there. "Oh well, she'll live. Done is done; just move on."

And then his eyes grew dark and Curly's mind shifted to unfinished business.

"So where are you now, Judge?" Curly pondered. "Are you in front or behind me? It's like looking for a needle in a haystack, but no biggie. I got nothing better to do with my time, and I got gas, food and dough. I'm gonna git you, Judge. I just gotta keep looking for a black Land Cruiser.

I'm gonna git you, sure enough." He leered at himself in the rearview mirror and wiped Cheetos crumbs from his chin.

"I gotta see Salem Sue, Judge, it won't take but a minute and then I'd like to stop at the Dakota Dinosaur Museum, if you don't mind," Wade said. "I mean a 'selfie' with Salem Sue and some dinosaur bones would be great to send to mom."

"Sounds like a plan to me," Thaddeus said, "but then we should probably keep heading west after we see the dinosaur museum. I suggest we stop for the day near Medora, close to the South Unit of the Theodore Roosevelt National Park. Teddy Roosevelt sure deserves a lot of credit for helping to develop our national park system, and I'd like to see how we've thanked him with a park in his name."

"We can find lodging and check out restaurant possibilities, and you can go for that run you've been wanting. I wouldn't mind doing some exploring in the park while you're on your run. And, we need to phone your mom and Quentin sometime today too."

Wade agreed. They drove on and both laughed hysterically when they saw Salem Sue at the entrance to town. She really was enormous, but had a very sweet face. She looked like a contented cow.

"I guess every town wants to feel special in it's own way, plus have a reason for tourists to stop and spend money. A huge fiberglass cow is as good a mascot as anything I guess," the Judge offered.

They got out of the Land Cruiser and walked around Salem Sue, paying humorous homage to her magnificence. Wade found the whole cow thing very amusing and purchased a t-shirt as a remembrance of his visit with Salem Sue. The front of the shirt had a smiling portrait of Salem Sue with her name printed in a swirling script. The back of the shirt featured a large udder. Wade decided he'd only send his mom pictures of the front. Having had their fill of the world's largest fiberglass Holstein, they drove on I-94 to the town of Dickinson to check out the Dakota Dinosaur Museum.

The dinosaur museum included both an exhibit building and a large portion of the grounds displaying enormous skeletons. "It's hard to imagine that these enormous creatures populated our planet over sixty million years ago," the Judge said. "As humans, we're so accustomed to thinking in far briefer time spans. A dog or cat might live to be twenty at the very most, and people are lucky to make it to their late 80s, but the earth and planets and our universe has been around for billions of years, with billions of years yet to come.

I have always tried to keep our meager years on our planet in perspective," the Judge said. "We are born; live for a relatively brief time and then we are gone… stardust. Makes me think how important it is to make the best use of our time on planet earth.

People like Curly Algol never give this concept a second thought. You on the other hand, already know this, and you will know it even more as time passes. Everything and everyone eventually comes and goes. It's how we spend our time that defines who we are and gives promise to our species."

Wade listened carefully to the Judge's words. His father's death had already taught him about the impermanence of life. He promised himself that he would never forget, and that he would try to live his life in a way that benefitted humankind rather than victimizing it. "Everything and everyone comes and goes," he whispered to himself.

The dinosaur museum was very cool, and they both enjoyed the enormous exhibits. Wade and Thaddeus viewed the displays that showed that the dinosaurs were wiped out by an asteroid's impact. An extinction event. Wade thought again about how often we just take the night sky for granted; until something really big happens. Tough as they were, the dinosaurs didn't stand a chance.

Before they left, the Judge purchased a t-shirt that had the visage of a rather-toothy T-Rex that had a caption that read: "My T-Rex can beat up your third-grader on the honor roll." Despite his refined judicial bearing, Judge Nathan also had a very well-developed snarky sense of humor. Wade loved the shirt!

The drive along I-94 was picturesque. The grasslands were stunning in their subtle beauty, and both men knew that before too long, the rolling prairie of North Dakota would give way to the towering strength of Montana's mountains. Now, they were greeted by forests of cottonwood and junipers as they approached the south unit of Theodore Roosevelt National Park.

They arrived in Medora, ND in the late afternoon and checked into the Teddy Roosevelt Motel. It's sign bore the image of a grinning and bespectacled Theodore Roosevelt armed with an elephant gun hollering 'bully.'

Wade put on his Salem Sue t-shirt, and after stretching his leg muscles, he took off down a path that ran along the banks of the Little Missouri river. He thought back on his run along the banks of the Otter Tail and his seeing Curly Algol's Ford F-150. He shuddered and quickened his pace as if to outrun scary thoughts.

Breathe in; breathe out. One foot in front of the other. His body reacted well to years of disciplined cross-country training. His mind wandered to a cascade of memories and then thoughts about his future. He was excited about going to Duke and experiencing the world on a totally different level than Prindle County, and yet he was seeing a vast world out there, and he yearned to get to know it. So, he had a bit of a conundrum to deal with; some things to consider. Breathe in; breathe out.

While Wade was on his run, Thaddeus used the time to call and update Sheriff Noble Penrod about Curly Algol's latest travesties. He encouraged him to talk with his fellow sheriffs in Fergus Falls and Mandan. Next, the judge called Quentin to check on things back home.

"Evening Judge," came Quentin's cheery voice. "Everybody seems to doing okay here. Cassie has moved back to her house and is still very busy with her work for the college, and Luella has decided she wants to stay here at your house for a few days until she can get back on her feet. I think she's recovering okay, but given her brother's evil behavior, some horrors will probably never leave her."

Thaddeus sighed and expressed his sympathies for Luella. "You're a good man, Quentin Harp. Thanks for everything you're doing for her and Cassie and me. Wade and I are having a good adventure, but believe me, we're also keeping our eyes open for Curly and the green Honda Civic, as are all of the sheriffs' departments between us and the Canadian border. Don't know how he'd get across the border, but he might."

They talked a little bit longer and agreed to touch base around the same time tomorrow, barring questionable cell phone service as they approached the Rockies.

Chapter 23

THADDEUS DROVE THE **Land Cruiser** into the national park and stopped to talk with the ranger stationed at the entrance. He got a map of the park, and the ranger showed him some interesting spots not too far away. The ranger also alerted him that unless he had a permit for camping, the park closed at dark. Thaddeus thanked him and took the road along the Little Missouri River, but in the opposite direction that Wade had chosen for his run. As early evening approached, the park felt lush and cool and welcoming. Thaddeus thought Teddy Roosevelt would be pleased.

The river was stunning. Swift water, large boulders, a canopy of birch trees. He stopped at a meadow along the way and got out. He walked up to the stream which glowed both gold and silver in celestial light. The sun was warm on his face and the grasses were a soft russet tan. Thaddeus sat down on the grassy bank, leaned back against an inviting rock, closed his eyes and listened to the world around him.

He tried to clear his head from all thoughts, and to discern the different sounds that he heard. The loudest sound, of course, was the river. It maintained a steady, atonal rhythm, awash in sounds that only river rapids can make. It nearly masked out all of the other sounds, but Thaddeus focused on the "now" with his auditory senses and heard the calls of songbirds, the buzzing of insects and the wind in the birches. He heard the beating of his heart.

Before long, Thaddeus dozed off and dreamed again of being swept up by a comet and carried high into the sky to a point where he could clearly see the world around him, both the heavens and the earth. He felt a sense of calmness, as if he belonged here. He dreamed about his career as a judge and thought about the impact he had had on so many lives. He had devoted his life to making his small portion of the world a safer realm. He wondered if he could've done a better job rendering justice. He wondered what, if anything, he could've done to rid the world of evil people like Curly Algol. He believed he had done the best he could, but sometimes one's best efforts are just not enough. Regardless, he felt a cleansing sense of calm and rode the transcendental comet of his dreams.

And then he awoke and his thoughts returned, and Thaddeus realized how much he missed Ellie. For a brief moment, Thaddeus thought to himself that he could be content to die right here; right now; just pass away, next to this stream, listening to the sounds of… life.

Thaddeus sat like this for several more minutes, and then after he had spent enough time visiting his melancholy, he decided he had better get back to meet Wade at the motel. He took a final glance at the river and whispered "thank you."

The Judge drove back toward the park exit which was situated some fifty yards away from the entrance. As he began to pull away, he noticed a line of several cars waiting for the ranger to admit them. In the middle of the line was a green Honda Civic. He stared at the car and then his gaze fell on the driver who was staring right back at him, with a menacing leer on his face.

Thaddeus immediately pulled out his cell phone to call the sheriff, but realized he had no cellular service.

Curly tried pull his car out of the line to go after the Judge, but he had been hemmed in and only succeeded in causing a horn-honking, expletive-filled ruckus with the other drivers. By the time Curly managed to get his car out of line, Judge Thaddeus Nathan had vanished.

———

Thaddeus steered his black Toyota Land Cruiser in the direction of the motel and managed to reach the sheriff's office in Medora on the third attempt due to poor cell service. He introduced himself to the dispatcher and briefly explained the purpose of his call. He was immediately patched through.

Sheriff Marty Chandler had already been alerted by both Sheriff Rory South in Fergus Falls, MN and Sheriff Chris Bester near Mandan, ND to be on the lookout for a serial killer driving a green Honda Civic. Thirty seconds after taking the Judge's phone call, Thaddeus heard and then saw three police cruisers heading toward the national park entrance at a high rate of speed with lights flashing.

"We haven't had this much excitement around here since the pigs ate Damien Ypma's little brother," the Sheriff commented. Sheriff Chandler was running for re-election in a month, and he knew he'd have a lock on the job if he could nail this big criminal.

"This Algol man is no fool, Sheriff," Thaddeus warned. "He is an unrepentant killer with nothing to lose, so I advise your men to use extreme caution and shoot to kill if necessary. I wanted to go after him myself as soon as I spotted him, but I believed that innocent bystanders would've been harmed if I'd tried; so I decided it best to let the local law enforcement handle things."

"Good call, Judge. We may be a very small department, but we like to handle things our way around here. Any idea where he might be?" Sheriff Chandler asked.

"Not really," Thaddeus replied. "Seems like there'd be plenty of places for him to hole up around the park. Since he is after me and my traveling companion, Wade Henry, I might suggest you plant a couple of deputies near our motel and keep alert. I don't plan on running away from this bastard, Sheriff, and maybe using us as bait will draw him to us. We'll probably leave sometime tomorrow afternoon."

The Sheriff agreed it was a good idea and radioed two of his deputies to change into plain clothes and drive their personal vehicles to stake out the motel. Twenty-five minutes later, the officers were in place and Sheriff Chandler took an empty room at the motel as his command central.

If the situation with Curly weren't so serious, Thaddeus might've found the heroics of the Medora's sheriff's office a little amusing, but this was serious business, and Thaddeus planned on cooperating as much as possible.

Medora reported a population of 129 people and touted itself as North Dakota's #1 tourist destination. Thaddeus thought it was unusual for a town of only 129 citizens to have a police force of four individuals, but he was pleased to have a decent-sized law enforcement unit to count on.

When the Judge returned to the motel, Wade was sitting outside in an Adirondack chair taking in the sun and watching a college age girl over at the pool. He attempted to be cool and suave and pretend that he wasn't interested, but she was very pretty and filled her bikini nicely.

The Judge quietly approached Wade from behind and said, "Why don't you get the binoculars if you're that curious," he suggested.

Wade nearly fell out of the chair because he had been busted checking out the local talent and didn't even hear the Judge standing behind him.

"Er uh," Wade stammered. "I was just admiring the landscaping around the pool," and then realizing that he wasn't fooling the Judge, they both broke into laughter.

"Why don't you go for a dip, young Aquarius, maybe make a new friend, the Judge suggested. I think she'd be delighted to meet a handsome young feller like you. Nothing ventured, nothing gained, plus we have plenty of time before dinner," he added. Wade nodded his agreement and four minutes later he was in his bathing suit trying to contain his enthusiasm.

Thaddeus gave Wade a thumbs-up sign and said he wanted to rest up for a bit in his room and to give Quentin a call. He decided not to say anything to Wade yet about seeing Curly Algol because they could discuss it later, and he didn't want to dampen Wade's excitement at the swimming pool.

Thaddeus called Quentin when he got to his room and informed him about spotting Curly Algol at the park and notifying the local sheriff's office.

"Wow, this Algol guy doesn't give up easily," Quentin commented. "I would've thought he might have decided that the risk of chasing you wasn't worth the reward, but I reckon he doesn't think like normal people. What do you plan to do, Judge?"

"Well," the Judge began, "we certainly know that he doesn't think like normal people, but as I said before, I don't plan on running from this maniac. The sheriff's office is cooperating with a stakeout at our motel, and I plan on Wade and me trying to enjoy our trip on our terms; not Curly's. Having said that, we are keeping our eyes open, and we have some of our own firepower with us. I'd appreciate it if you didn't mention that to Cassie, unless she asks you specifically."

Quentin told him he would respect that request. Quentin then reported that everything at home seemed to be going well. My UPS boss even said I can take another week if I need it. He knows that I'm staying at your place, and well, he is still very appreciative of how you helped straighten out his son, Jared, when he had a drug problem. He knows you could've sent his son off to jail, but you didn't.

Also, Cassie and Luella went to town earlier today to stock up on some groceries and to get Luella her own clothes and toiletries. I think Luella is recovering pretty quickly actually, and she's really pitching in around your house and being a great help for Cassie too. It's also good having her company, and I think she and Cassie have begun to bond very well."

"Shared tragedy will often do that to folks," Thaddeus said. "I'm really pleased that everyone is getting along so well and that Luella is recovering. We've had some spotty cell phone service already; so don't be surprised if we can't always connect, okay. Wade is going to call his mom later this evening so she doesn't worry about him."

Thaddeus and Quentin hung up, and the Judge placed a call to Noble Penrod at Prindle County's sheriff's office and gave him a report about spotting Curly. Sheriff Penrod said he would contact the other sheriffs whose jurisdictions had been victimized by public enemy #1 to give them an update as well.

"Let me ask you a question, Noble," the Judge said. "I think you are aware that Wade and I have two 9mm Glock semi-automatics. Any chance you could connect with the Canadian authorities at the border and let them know that we're armed, and the reason that we're armed, and for them to permit our bringing our firearms into Canada?"

"Yeah, I can do that, Thad. Given the uniqueness of the situation, I don't think we should have any problem getting special dispensation for the Glocks, especially since you're still an officer of the court. I'll get right on it."

The Judge and Sheriff Penrod talked some more about the fiasco at the Russellville Correctional Center and Nerf McCabe's recovery. The sheriff also said he'd have Deputy Kristi Donovan swing by to see Cassie and Quentin and follow up on Luella's funeral arrangements for her parents now that the medical examiner had concluded his report.

After they hung up, Thaddeus stretched out on his bed and stared at the ceiling. He recalled his dream by the river, and cringed when he thought about making eye contact with Curly Algol. He actually did more than cringe though; he wanted to get this criminal once and for all and put him in a place where he'd never hurt another person ever again, preferably in a deep, dark, cold, unmarked grave.

Chapter 24

Kayla Lancaster lounged casually by the motel's pool, taking in the late afternoon sun and enjoying the quiet now that most of the other guests had already left for dinner. She was nineteen years old and had just completed her freshman year at Northwestern University in Evanston, Illinois.

Kayla had declared a double major in philosophy and biology, with a special focus on environmental issues. She thought about going to law school when she eventually graduated, but that was a decision she could put off for a while yet.

She and her mother, Bettina, had left her father, Stone, back in Indianapolis to tend to his medical practice, and they were enjoying a three-week girls' vacation across the northern plains states and several national parks.

Wade was excited that she had not left the pool area while he changed into his suit. He watched her from some thirty feet away as he entered the pool gate and was relieved to see that the only other guests by the pool were collecting their belongings and preparing to leave. Perfect timing, he thought.

A shadow fell across Kayla's eyes, and she looked up to see a handsome young man approaching her. She sat up and modestly pulled a beach towel to cover the lower part of her body.

"Excuse me miss," came Wade's polite but tentative voice. "I saw you sitting here by yourself and just wanted to say 'hello'. My name's Wade Henry, and I'm from Someday, Indiana in Prindle County."

"Hello Wade Henry, my name is Kayla Lancaster, and I'm from a little town called Indianapolis."

At that, they both smiled broadly recognizing that they were essentially neighbors, with Someday, Indiana being just an easy hour southwest of Indy.

"Small world, huh", were the only words that Wade could muster because he was immediately taken by how pretty Kayla was and how confident she seemed.

"You're welcome to pull up a chair and join me, Wade Henry. I've been traveling with my Mom, and it would be good to talk with someone closer to my age."

Wade did as she suggested and pulled a lounge chair alongside hers and couldn't help but notice that Kayla was really lovely, especially in her sweet, floral bikini. He guessed she was probably about 5'6" tall, and she had soft, shoulder-length honey blonde hair and a very spontaneous, warm smile. He also noticed that she seemed very fit, and he wondered what she did to stay in shape.

"So what to you do back in Someday, Indiana and what brings you to the booming metropolis of Medora, North Dakota?" Kayla asked.

Wade smiled and said, "I just graduated from high school and my friend and neighbor, Judge Thaddeus Nathan, and I are on a 'watch-about'. He noticed the quizzical look on her face.

"I mean," Wade continued, "that prior to my reporting for student orientation at Duke in August, the Judge and I decided to travel to Jasper, Alberta to do some sightseeing in the Canadian

Rockies and do a lot of stargazing with our telescope and binoculars. We made up the term 'watch-about' because we'd read about how the young Australian Aborigine males go into the outback to begin their journey to adulthood. So similarly, we're out to explore the world, but with a stargazing twist."

"You're kidding," Kayla said. "That's very cool. I guess my mom and I are on our own walkabout of sorts, traveling to wherever the spirit moves us. My dad is a surgeon, and he also loves astronomy. He's taken me with him a few times to the Link Observatory south of Mooresville, and I've enjoyed getting to know the night sky with him over the years."

"Wow," Wade said. "I've known you for all of two minutes and already we have some things in common. The Judge and I talked about doing some stargazing later tonight after dinner. If we do, maybe you and your mom would like to join us."

"That could be fun," Kayla said. "We'll see, okay? So, the judge is your neighbor? What about your folks?"

"Well, my mom's work at Kissinger College is keeping her really busy these days, and my dad died about a year ago. And so, the judge offered to take me on this trip to the Canadian Rockies as a graduation gift. He's retired from the bench, and he's also known some family tragedy. So, it's been a good way for both of us to heal, so to speak. You know; just two guys on the road dealing with whatever comes along.

"I'm very sorry about your dad, Wade. I think I know how devastated I would feel if I lost either of my parents, but I guess you never know until you're there."

"Yeah Kayla, I think it's one of those solitary journeys that you really can't imagine until you're there. I mean, sure, a lot of very kind and caring people have reached out to me and mom and the Judge, but in the end it's your own unique grief that you have to pass through, and honestly I doubt I'll ever be totally through it, and I've come to accept that that's okay too."

He smiled a little, and said, "But enough about me. Tell me more about who Kayla Lancaster is. You know, whatever you feel comfortable sharing."

"Well gee," she started and immediately blushed a little about whatever she was momentarily thinking. "I'm nineteen and getting ready to enter my sophomore year at Northwestern. My dad's a cardiovascular surgeon on staff at IU Medical Center in Indy. Mom's an artist and yoga instructor and keeps very busy with both passions. Dad built her a beautiful studio on our property, and she's been very successful with her artwork and has built a very popular yoga practice too. She's cool."

Kayla and Wade continued to talk for several minutes about all sorts of things: friends, school, music, short and long-range goals, the desire to travel and see different cultures. And, they both really enjoyed running and staying fit. Wade was surprised at how comfortable they were with the each other in just a very short time.

Before long, a woman came through the pool gate and waved to Kayla as she approached her and Wade.

"Hi Mom, come meet my friend Wade Henry. He's from Someday, Indiana."

Bettina Lancaster appeared to be in her early forties and had a warm smile on her face. She looked like a more mature version of Kayla; pretty, fit, and with a sparkle in her eyes. She reached out to shake Wade's hand and said, "Hello Wade Henry, what brings you to this part of the world?"

"Hello Mrs. Lancaster. My neighbor Judge Thaddeus Nathan and I are off on an adventure to Jasper, Alberta to hike, fish and stargaze at night. We just stopped here to visit the national park before we head on to Montana and then Alberta. We'll probably leave tomorrow afternoon sometime."

"Jasper National Park is an amazing part of the world. My husband, Stone, and I have been there twice, and particularly love

Maligne Canyon and the Valley of the Five Lakes. I envy you and Judge Nathan."

A moment later Thaddeus came through the pool gate and strolled up to Wade and the Lancaster ladies.

Wade used the same line that Kayla had used to introduce Wade to Bettina: "Hi Judge, come meet my new friends. Mrs. Lancaster and Kayla are from Indy!"

"Well, it is a pleasure to meet you both, I see that you are in very good company with my friend, Wade, here."

The four of them chatted for a while longer, and then Thaddeus said, "I don't know about you all, but I am one hungry Hoosier. Bettina and Kayla, unless you have other plans or prefer not to dine with strange fellows you meet at a motel, Wade and I would be very happy to continue our conversation with you over dinner as our guests."

There was a momentary pause in the conversation, and Bettina looked at her daughter who had a look on her smiling face that said "sure". Bettina was very good at sizing people up, and she felt reasonably certain that Thaddeus and Wade were men of character, and so she said, " Can we have thirty minutes to freshen up and meet you in the motel's dining room?"

Thaddeus said he would call and reserve a table.

Chapter 25

CURLY ALGOL WAS INSANE with rage and anticipation. He couldn't believe his luck in spotting that high and mighty Judge Thaddeus Nathan at the park, only to get hemmed in by other cars blocking his vehicle.

"Goddamit to hell, where are you, Judge?" "I didn't come this far to have you scamper away like some scared rabbit."

Curly knew that the park ranger would immediately call the cops after his tantrum in line; so he hid his Civic behind an old tool shed just as he heard, then saw the sheriff's cars come high-tailing it toward the park entrance.

"Just gotta keep looking and not get caught," Curly said out loud to himself. "Also gotta get a different car. This one's outlived its usefulness."

Curly laid low in his hidden car and then as nightfall approached, he eased his car from its hiding place and pulled back on to the highway heading back toward Medora. He drove into the Ferris grocery store parking lot, found an empty spot in a crowded area, killed the engine and watched for an opportunity.

A light knock came on the Judge's motel room door. Thaddeus opened it for Wade and asked him to come inside before they went to the dining room to meet Kayla and Bettina.

"Ah young Rigel, there you are, and look at how nicely you've cleaned up. You wouldn't be trying to impress someone would you?" he said with a twinkle in his eye. "We have a few minutes before dinner, and I need to talk with you about something."

"You're not going to give me the birds and bees talk, are you Judge, because mom and dad already laid that on me a few years ago."

"No Wade, no birds and bees talk, but I had an encounter earlier today in the park."

Hearing Thaddeus' words, Wade's blood went cold, and he dropped on to the edge of the bed bracing himself for the rest of the story. Thaddeus recounted how he and Curly Algol had spotted each other and how the Judge had called the local sheriff immediately thereafter.

"So," the Judge continued, "it would appear that our nemesis, Mr. Algol, isn't about to end this chase. Sheriff Chandler's men know who and what car to look for, but Curly is one crafty nutcase, and I wouldn't be surprised if he eludes them."

"What should we do, Judge? Should we skip dinner and just hit the road again?"

"I debated telling you about this, seeing how much you were enjoying yourself with Kayla, but we're equal partners on this trip, and you have every right to know," the Judge said. "But, we need to be smarter than Curly Algol, and as we discussed before, I want us to enjoy our trip on our terms as much as possible. Besides, the the sheriff has two plainclothes deputies outside the motel, and the sheriff is concealed in a room with a view of the lot. So, if you're okay with this, I suggest we head on up to meet our new friends for dinner."

Wade nodded "okay", but he was clearly shaken by this news. "Should we bring the Glocks with us?" he asked.

Thaddeus patted his jacket pocket as a sign that he was already armed. "We'll leave the other one in the car for now. And, let's just keep this our little secret, alright Wade. No sense in scaring the willies out of Bettina and Kayla". Again Wade nodded 'okay', but his earlier cheerful mood had been ratcheted back a few notches.

When Wade and the judge arrived at the restaurant, Kayla and Bettina were already there and had selected a table outside on the veranda. The evening sky was turning the world from daytime to nighttime, and the colors in the western sky were ablaze with magentas and oranges. Even so the night sky steadily pressed its darkness from overhead, and Venus came into dazzling view. Soon the bright colors would fade to grey and then slip into night.

"Good evening, ladies," came Judge Nathan's friendly greeting as he and Wade approached them. "You selected a great table for us, and thanks for arranging such a glorious sunset."

Wade and Thaddeus exchanged more greetings with the Lancasters and settled into their seats.

Kayla and Wade smiled at each other as he sat down beside her, and immediately his earlier anxiety about Curly lifted and drifted away on the wind. Kayla looked lovely. Her face had the stunning radiance that youth exudes. She had curled her light tan hair and wore only the slightest hint of lip gloss. He caught a brief whiff of her perfume that filled his senses. And, Wade couldn't help noticing how nicely her tanned skin looked with her pale yellow top and shorts.

"You look really nice," he said to Kayla, and then quickly added, "and you too Mrs. Lancaster." Thaddeus gave him a complimentary wink.

They ordered a pitcher of Margaritas and a hummus plate as an appetizer. Thaddeus knew that Wade and Kayla weren't technically of legal age to drink alcohol, but he and Bettina agreed it was a beautiful night and both kids were accustomed to occasionally drinking wine with their parents. The congenial restaurant manager just looked the other way.

"What shall we toast to?" Bettina asked as she lifted her glass. "How about a terrific trip to Canada for Wade and Thaddeus; and to new beginnings…"

"And," the Judge quickly added, "to new friends and star-filled nights!"

They all clicked glasses and proceeded to share an evening filled with surprisingly good food and even better fellowship. With some urging, Bettina talked about her art work which was rather unique. In addition to her award-winning photography, she wove intricate designs on hard-shell gourds that she grew. She also talked about her yoga practice to which she was totally devoted, as much for a way to keep fit as for the meditative aspects. She taught both at her art/yoga studio that her husband, Stone, had built for her on the grounds of their home near Broadripple.

Thaddeus gave a very brief sketch of his law career and his community involvement in Prindle County. He was tempted to go into a lot of detail, but decided that this should be a night for others to talk, so he modestly held back and listened attentively. He did talk, however, about his love affair with astronomy, and Bettina commented that he and Stone would have to meet since they both were totally infatuated with the night sky.

"And what about Mrs. Nathan?" Bettina asked, "Does she share your enthusiasm for stargazing?"

Wade gave the judge a quick glance, and heard him politely reply that Ellie had died about a year and a half ago, a few days after Wade's father, Ben, had died.

The levity of the dinner conversation momentarily slid into an awkward silence, and Kayla said, "We're so sorry for your loses. We didn't mean to pry."

"You're not prying, Kayla," the Judge offered. "Their deaths are a big reason why Wade and I wanted to take this trip. You know, to put some painful memories behind us and replace them with new adventures. And, I must say that meeting you two and sharing a lovely dinner and evening together is just what we needed, right Wade?!"

"Right Judge," Wade echoed, and he recognized the Judge's attempt to bring the dinner conversation back to a lighter mood. Wade stole a quick glance at Kayla to see her reaction and caught her looking at him with caring eyes. She realized that Wade was still grieving for his father.

As dinner came to an end, Thaddeus commented on what a delightful night it had been, but said he needed to make a call back home, and it was about time for him to turn in. Bettina was also feeling a bit tired too, but suggested that Kayla and Wade might want to pull out the binoculars the Judge had mentioned earlier and view the night sky for a while. Both Kayla and Wade were surprised at Bettina's suggestion and tried to contain their excitement at the thought of spending some more time together, unchaperoned.

"Yeah sure," they almost said in unison, and Wade suggested they take the Land Cruiser and try the bluff at the end of the service road. "It's flat and grassy, no trees."

"Have fun, you two," Thaddeus said. "The constellation Leo should be high in the southern sky, with Bootes to the east and Gemini in the west. And only a thin waxing crescent moon. Great night for viewing!"

"Thanks Judge, we'll take good care of the equipment. How about a later breakfast tomorrow, say around 8:30. I think I'd like to go for an early run, okay?"

The judge agreed, and he thought to himself, "methinks the lad may be using a 'run' as an excuse in case he stays out late with Kayla, exploring the universe."

Thaddeus walked Bettina to her door and said goodnight. She kissed him lightly on the cheek and told him how glad she was that she and Kayla had met them. Bettina suggested that they all get together again at her home later next month.

"I know that Stone will want to talk about astronomy with you, and I think you'd enjoy each others' company anyway. Plus, I'd like to meet Cassie too."

Thaddeus said that they would make it happen and that he looked forward to it. He said goodnight again and walked several yards away and entered his room. He stood for a few moments staring at himself in the mirror.

He sighed. "Oh Ellie, I wish you could be here…"

He straightened up a few items in his duffle bad and then placed a call to Sheriff Chandler to let him know where Wade and a friend were heading. He suggested that one of his deputies might want to tail them from a friendly distance, just in case Curly Algol is on the prowl for their black SUV. The sheriff was on it.

The bluff was just as Wade had described. It was basically a high grassy mesa, with very few trees, overlooking a broad valley below that was part of the Theodore Roosevelt National Park. Fortunately, Wade was able to drive the SUV right to where he thought the viewing would be the best. Kayla and Wade exited the vehicle and stood staring at the sky.

Full darkness was all around them. No city lights, no highway headlights, nothing but darkness. Kayla and Wade continued to look heavenward and allowed their eyes time to adjust. The Milky Way stretched above them in star-studded splendor, and the profile of Leo the Lion strode above them like a watchful guardian.

"It's stunning," said Kayla, "and I don't just mean in it's sheer beauty. The vastness literally stuns me sometimes when I try to understand what it all means. It's so easy to take it for granted because our minds and our technologies simply aren't adequately equipped to comprehend it all. My dad would love for me to be an astronomer, but I think my energies would be best used trying to protect planet Earth."

Wade turned on the power pack with the red night filter that allowed them to see without creating unnecessary light pollution. He and Kayla unloaded the Oberwerk 100 mm 45 degree binocular telescope and set it on the Jarrah wooden tripod.

Next he pulled out a small case containing the matched Tele Vue 27mm Panoptic eyepieces and inserted them into the scope. Almost ritualistically now, Wade turned the large binoculars toward Orion and focused on Alnilam, the huge center star in Orion's belt. Early on in his stargazing experiences, Wade became very familiar with the constellation, Orion, and so he automatically turned to his old friend when getting his celestial bearings. Tonight was no different.

Wade thought he would be able to impress Kayla with his knowledge of the "Hunter", but Kayla started rattling off names of the major stars like Betelgeuse, Bellatrix, Schaim, Rigel, Alnitak, Alnilam and Mintaka, and it was Wade who turned out to be mightily impressed.

"Wow, I guess I had better not try to out do you when it comes to identifying constellations," Wade cheerfully admitted. "I might end up embarrassing myself."

Kayla playfully chided him and said, "That's right, but I might take pity on you since you're six months younger than me and just a recent high school graduate."

They both laughed, and proceeded to spend the next hour taking turns slewing the binocular telescope to different objects and looking deep into the night sky.

Finally, Kayla unfurled a blanket and spread it on the ground, and pulled out a small cooler that the restaurant manager had given her right as they left.

"What's in the cooler?" Wade asked. "I was surprised when he gave it to you."

"I don't know," Kayla replied, "Let's take a break and see what surprises we have."

They sat down on the blanket, and Kayla pulled out two forks and styrofoam containers with pieces of cheesecake, and then two plastic wine glasses and a carafe of the Margaritas that they had enjoyed during dinner.

They both laughed with delight at their newly found bounty, and raised their glasses to toast the restauranteur.

"My goodness, Wade Henry, you sure know how to show a girl a good time."

They finished their dessert and lay back on the blanket staring up at the sky, wishing that this night would never end.

"So tell me, Wade Henry, what are your plans for the future?" she coaxed.

And at that, Wade leaned over and kissed Kayla softly on the lips, and to his relief, she did not pull away.

"My immediate goal for the future was to kiss you and see if you felt the same way."

"Well, I guess I did," Kayla said, and she leaned over and kissed him again.

They laid on the blanket under the stars, with Kayla's head resting on Wade's shoulder, listening to soft music on his iPhone. It was a perfect night.

"So, what are your goals, Wade Henry? Where do you go from here?" she inquired.

"That, Kayla Lancaster, is a great question," Wade replied. "After our trip to Jasper, I'll return home to Prindle County for about a month with mom and then head to Durham, North Carolina, to begin my freshman year at Duke."

"But ultimately," Kayla continued, "what would you like to do?"

"Actually, it's a bit of a tough question for me right now. All my life I was taught to work hard and do the right thing; to make a positive difference; and to become a man of character.

My parents are/were great, and I was fortunate to be raised by caring people who taught me by example. They convinced me that I could do anything to which I set my mind, and encouraged me to be the best I could be at whatever I chose to do. Sometimes, I'm still trying to figure out what that means, but I think that's okay."

They sat there on the blanket sipping their Margaritas and listening to music. Wade looked off into space and seemed distant for a moment.

"What?" Kayla asked. "Earth to Wade Henry."

"I promised myself I wasn't going to tell you this," Wade said, "but I want you to know something important, and I don't want it to frighten you."

Kayla turned toward him with concern in her eyes, and they became downright sorrowful as Wade shared the basic details of his father's and Ellie Nathan's murders.

Tears came to her eyes, and Wade pulled her close. They stayed like that for several minutes; then Wade lifted her chin to look in her eyes, and said "Thank you, Kayla. Thank you for being a friend, and for not freaking out when I told you."

Now they lay there, both looking up at the night sky. A shooting star crossed their lines of vision, and Wade said, "We're all becoming stardust someday. It's how we choose to live our lives between now and then that creates our legacies."

Kayla pushed a little closer to Wade's side, and said, "I'm gonna miss you, Wade Henry. Can we please keep in touch?" She kissed him again, and then again.

Finally around midnight, they loaded up the Land Cruiser and looked around to make sure they hadn't left anything. The drive back to the motel was brief; too brief for Wade and Kayla because they knew they were coming to the end of a special night.

Kayla told him they'd be leaving in the morning, heading back home to Indy, and Wade told her he and the Judge would likely be gone for another two weeks. They exchanged phone numbers and email addresses and promised to keep in touch. They already were missing each other. They kissed a final time, and then they said goodbye.

Chapter 26

URLY ALGOL SAT IN HIS purloined Honda Civic in the Ferris grocery store parking lot. He had dodged the Medora sheriff's men by hiding in plain view, but he knew his luck wouldn't last forever. He had to find another vehicle soon and keep moving west. He felt confident that he'd locate the Judge again, and this time he swore that nothing would stand in his way to exacting his revenge.

Curly had managed to get a couple of hours of sleep in the car and had hidden beneath a blanket that the car's rightful owner had left on the back seat. Now, he awoke refreshed, but hungry and anxious to get out of town before the cops closed in on him.

He looked around the parking lot for a car that he thought would be somewhat inconspicuous, but something he'd enjoy driving. Plus, being in a grocery store parking lot, he figured he'd be able to do a "twofer": steal a car and get someone's groceries. He looked around and then spotted a promising possibility.

An exotic-looking woman about forty years old pulled her sleek red Chevrolet Camaro into the parking lot a row down from his Civic and got out with two young boys. Curly knew it's color made it stand out more than he preferred, but he loved the car and really wanted it. He decided to wait for the mother, Katrina, and her boys to come back with their groceries and then make his move.

"Ivan and Jay," the mother called. "We need to move things along here. Your dad's working late again and will be home from work soon. He'll be tired and hungry."

Fifteen minutes later the young family emerged from the store with a half-loaded grocery cart and were putting their groceries in the trunk when a raspy voice called over to them.

"Pardon me, ma'am," Curly said as he suddenly appeared next to them, "but I'm almost out of gas and was wondering if you could spare a few bucks."

Katrina recoiled when she saw the strange, seedy-looking man standing near her car. The oldest boy, Ivan, was thirteen years old and didn't like the man's appearance one bit. He sidled between the stranger and his mom in a protective posture while his younger brother, Jay, put the rest of the groceries in the car.

"I'm sorry, sir," came the mother's reply, "but I just spent all of our money on groceries and don't have anything to give you."

Curly looked around the lot to see if anyone was watching and moved closer to the woman with a depraved leer on his face.

"Hey mister," Ivan said to him. "Mom told you we don't have any money to give you, and we have to leave now."

Curly shot the boy a menacing glare and told him to beat it.

At that, younger brother Jay came up to the stranger and kicked him in the shin. "You're a mean man, and we don't like you. Go away!"

Curly rubbed his leg where the kid had kicked him and swatted the boy away with the back of his hand. Now, Ivan joined in and kicked Curly's other leg and drove the shopping cart into his groin. Fearing for her children, Katrina dove into the fracas and begun throwing punches at Curly. Another shopper appeared at her car nearby and saw the brouhaha and started honking her horn to attract attention.

Curly couldn't believe that these two kids and the women had foiled his plan; so Curly did what Curly did best. He strode over to the woman honking her horn and punched her hard in the face. She went down hitting the pavement with an audible thud. The young mother collected her two sons and quickly got into their car, locked the doors and started honking her horn as well.

Curly grabbed the downed woman's purse and got her keys. He pushed her out of the way, kicked her hard in the ribs and lunged into her car. By now, other shoppers were aware of the brawl, and Curly heard someone shout, "call security!"

By the time the overweight and underpaid guard waddled out to the parking lot, Curly was gone, with Katrina offering assistance to the woman lying on the ground, and Ivan and Jay pointing to the exit where Curly had gone.

Curly laid rubber leaving the lot and steered his newly acquired silver Nissan Maxima in a westerly direction.

"Goddamit," Curly muttered. "I've killed me a bunch of people in my day, broke out of a federal prison and have cops from five states looking for me, and here these two punk-ass little kids and a couple of wimpy women beat me at my own game. I must be slipping." He absently rubbed his shin where Jay had kicked him and gently massaged his groin from where the shopping cart smacked into his jewels.

Curly spotted the ramp for I-94 west toward Billings, Montana and hit the gas. He glanced in the rearview mirror and gave Medora, North Dakota the finger.

Breathe in; breathe out. Wade had slept in until 7:00 AM when sounds in the parking lot outside his motel room stirred him from his reverie. He quickly washed up and did his usual warm-up stretching, and now he was running along the service road that he and Kayla had driven the night before.

He reached the grassy bluff where just a few hours earlier he had enjoyed one of the best nights he could remember. In the light of day, however, things looked different. Gone was the cocoon of darkness. Gone too were the stars, and sadly Kayla was no longer with him.

Wade walked around the bluff and saw the Land Cruiser's tire tracks and depressions in the grass from where he and Kayla had laid on their blanket. He knelt down and touched the area with the palm of his hand as if to resurrect the spirit of their time together. He knew it was silly to try, but it made him feel like they were connecting still, and he enjoyed the feeling.

He knew that Kayla and Bettina would likely be gone by the time he returned to the motel to have breakfast with the judge, but he promised himself that he would keep in touch with Kayla on his watch-about and contact her when he returned to Prindle County.

Breathe in; breathe out. Wade felt that his life had taken yet another decisive turn in meeting Kayla. He wasn't sure what it all meant, but he knew that his life was a little different now. High school seemed like it was light years behind him, and his future was shrouded in the unknown. He took a final look from his vantage point on the grassy bluff and began his run back to meet the judge.

"Ah there you are, Mr. Henry," Thaddeus cheerfully greeted him, as Wade returned to the motel. "Did you have a good run?"

"I did," Wade replied with a warm smile. "I'm starved; how about you?"

The two men enjoyed a leisurely breakfast and were joined by Sheriff Chandler who had spent the night on duty in the motel. He told Wade and Thaddeus that he'd received a report about a ruckus in the Ferris grocery store parking lot, and the description of the perpetrator and his Honda Civic made it clear that Curly Algol was still in the vicinity.

"My guess," Thaddeus offered, "is that he is long gone now, but I encourage your department to stay sharp and also alert your fellow officers along I-94 that Curly is likely in a silver Nissan Maxima.

Thaddeus and Wade took their time enjoying another cup of coffee and looked at the map of Montana.

"It's a huge state," Wade said, "nearly six hundred miles between Miles City in the east and Kalispell near Glacier National Park in the west. I don't see how Curly Algol can find us now, but I never would've imagined that he'd find us twice already."

"I agree, Wade", and pointing to the map, Thaddeus suggested their taking a different route instead of continuing on I-94. "What say we take highway 200S when we get to Glendive; then head north on route 13 until we come to Wolf Point. Then, we'll have a straight shot due west on US route 2 all the way to Glacier. We will by-pass several of the larger towns and maybe miss a few attractions, but hopefully we'll finally be able to shake Mr. Algol from our tails."

Sheriff Chandler concurred that their new route made a lot of sense. "There's not a lot to see up there, aside from gorgeous scenery, but I doubt our 'friend' will think to go that way. You might try to get as far as Havre. The sheriff there is a buddy of mine, and I'll ask him to arrange some good accommodations for you."

Both Wade and Thaddeus liked the change in plans. Forty minutes later Wade had showered, and they had the Land Cruiser packed and gassed up and were on their way toward Glendive, Montana.

Chapter 27

Back home in Indiana, Quentin was dutifully holding down the fort, and trying to be as helpful as possible to Cassie and Luella. In a very brief time the three of them managed to re-claim some semblance of normalcy in their lives.

The women had done some shopping together, and that went very well. Quentin's boss at UPS continued to be sympathetic to everyone's plight and told him to take the time he needed. They shared meals together when Cassie's work schedule permitted.

But total normalcy was still a long way off for Luella, in particular. She had lost her parents, her home and everything in her life, including her virginity. Earlier that day she buried her parents and arranged for a headstone to be installed when it was ready.

Then, she drove with Deputy Sheriff Kristi Donovan to inspect the ruins of her family's home. She could barely stand when she saw the total destruction. Here and there, bits of something she'd find would stir some memory, but the only home she had ever known was a total loss. She wept, and Deputy Donovan provided a steady arm.

The one and only bright aspect to her life now was having a friendship with Quentin and Cassie. Luella knew that she would soon need to find a job and a place to live, even though Quentin said she was welcome to stay with him, at least until the judge returned in a couple of weeks. And, Cassie had begun to look for a position for Luella at Kissinger College, and felt confident that something would open up.

Cassie's grant-writing for Kissinger College's capital campaign was continuing to be successful, but with each grant application that she got funded, the Campaign leadership committee was leaning on her for even more success. Cassie was very proud of her recent accomplishments and was also privately relieved that she had meaningful work to devote herself to instead of fretting about Wade and mourning Ben's death.

And so, this unlikely alliance of these three people from diverse backgrounds was coalescing very well, and each person was very grateful to have the others to lean on. Sometimes, necessity does indeed breed strange bedfellows.

"I didn't hear from Wade last night," Cassie said to Luella and Quentin. "Have you heard from Thaddeus?"

Quentin said that he didn't receive a call last night from the Judge, but Luella said that Deputy Donovan told her that Sheriff Penrod had. Apparently, the Judge told the sheriff that he'd spotted Curly in a park near Medora, North Dakota, and there was a report of a ruckus at a grocery store that the authorities attributed to good old Curly. But that's all the deputy knew.

That news sent a chill down Cassie's spine, and Quentin tried to be as re-assuring as he could, but he realized that Curly was still hell bent on causing trouble.

"The Judge told us they might have spotty cell phone service," Quentin reminded them, "so we just have to try to be patient with our communications."

Cassie's maternal instincts kicked in, and she wasn't quite as confident as Quentin.

"I'll tell you what," she said to Luella and Quentin, "if we don't hear from them soon, I might be tempted to fly out to Jasper."

"Now, now, Cassie, they can take care of themselves," but again, he wasn't quite as confident as his words made him sound. They'd just have to wait and see.

The drive from Medora, North Dakota to Glendive, Montana was quiet. Thaddeus was at the wheel of the Land Cruiser, and the two men occasionally commented on some aspect of scenery that they saw, but in the main, it was a time for reflection. Thaddeus sensed that Wade wanted to withdraw into himself and focus on what appeared to have been a special time for him and Kayla.

Wade eventually broke the silence. "Judge, do you believe you can feel a really close connection with someone even after a brief time together?"

Thaddeus looked over at Wade, and knew his young friend was really infatuated with Kayla. He smiled and was very happy for Wade.

"Yes, I suppose I do, came the Judge's encouraging reply, I mean, it takes time to nurture a truly close relationship with someone, but yes, I do think it's possible. It certainly was for Ellie and me, and my first impression of Kayla was very positive. I think your instincts about her are very good."

Wade nodded and put his ear buds back on. He went back to his music and watching the eastern Montana landscape roll by. Before too long they came to the bustling metropolis of Glendive, Montana whose motto is "Good People Surrounded by Badlands."

Glendive also boasted being the smallest television market as defined by Nielsen Media Research, with a population just under five thousand people. They stopped for lunch at the Almost Home diner and re-charged their bodies with buffalo burgers and Idaho waffle fries.

Wade pulled out the road atlas, and they spent time over lunch trying to see what upcoming attractions they wanted to visit. There certainly wasn't much between Glendive and Wolf Point. Mid-way between the cities is the town of Circle, Montana which has a population of six hundred and fifteen people. It is famous for being the furthest town from the nearest Starbucks in the lower forty-eight states. Everyone wants to be known for something.

After lunch Thaddeus suggested that they continue driving north along Route 13 to Wolf Point. Wade read out loud from Wikipedia that Wolf Point is the largest community on the Fort Peck Indian Reservation. It is situated on the high plains of Montana along the north bank of the Missouri River. It is best known as the home of the Wild Horse Stampede which is the oldest rodeo in Montana.

The two men looked at each other and starting smiling. For them it was a total hoot to be going to such small and wholesome locales. Sure, they both also appreciated visiting large, famous cities on vacation, but they also enjoyed the nuances and charm of small rural communities… not unlike Someday, Indiana.

Wade now took over the driving duties, and they cruised through the unincorporated villages of Lindsay and Vida until they reached Wolf Point.

Here, Wade noticed that both the land and the people took on different characteristics. Geographically, he knew they were getting closer to the mountains with each mile they drove across the northern plains, but they still had a long way to go through Montana. The grassy hills rolled on and on guiding them forward.

The land looked rugged and soft at the same time, and Wade thought about the thousands of years that native peoples dwelled and lived and died in these plains. Wade imagined their living off the land and looking upward into virtually the same night sky that he sees. He imagined how one generation of elders taught a younger generation about the stars. He wondered about the heroic tales that were told about the constellations, and how these tales were meant as models for young braves to follow.

In Wolf Point Wade began noticing many people with decidedly native American looking features. He recalled the photography book by Edward Curtis that the Judge had loaned him a while ago. The image entitled "Vanishing Race" was the most memorable to him because it harkened a heartbreaking destiny.

He recalled one particular portrait of an Indian chief whose visage conveyed a sad but noble wisdom. Wade recalled staring at the chief's eyes and felt deeply embarrassed by the history of how whites of European decent had mistreated the American Indians. And now, he had entered their land. He felt humbled by its history. He aimed to be a respectful guest.

It was the judge's turn to read out loud now. "The original inhabitants were from the tribes of Cheyenne, Crow, Sioux, Assiniboine, Gros Ventre, Blackfoot, Kootenai, Salish and Shoshoni. Later, when Europeans arrived in North America, the Chippewa and Cree tribes were driven into Montana."

"I don't understand why we treated the native Americans as badly as we did," Wade lamented. "We often referred to them as savages, but it seems to me that we white people were the ones acting savagely."

"Ah, my friend, that indeed is a question for the ages," the Judge said, "because it speaks to the nature of humankind. We are a magnificent species capable of great acts of kindness and creativity, but we're also capable of the worst crimes against our own kind. Greed and the need to belittle and control others often seems to trump any goodness that we have. Even after all of my years on the bench, I still struggle to understand our true nature."

Wade considered the Judge's words and knew he would have to find his own answers to his question. It was clear to him that even with the dogmas of religion and the code of behavior legislated by law, humans often acted in ways that contradicted the commandments of each. It was a mystery to Wade, and he wondered why an omniscient God would permit such travesties.

Thaddeus and Wade took time to stretch their travel-weary legs in Wolf Point. They got coffee and snacks and visited a few shops in the main business area.

Thaddeus stepped inside a bookstore and told Wade he'd be out in ten minutes. Wade stopped to read a sign about the history of the city and learned that the Lewis and Clark Expedition had passed by there in 1805. They were followed by fur trappers and traders and eventually steamboats coming up from St. Louis.

As Wade turned to continue his exploration of the town, he was immediately greeted by an elderly Indian man who blocked his path and stared at him. The ancient-looking man said, "You are the one."

Wade was surprised that he had not heard the man approach, and said "Excuse me, sir, but you must be mistaken. My friend and I just arrived in town an hour ago. Perhaps you are confusing me with someone else."

"You are the one," the elderly man said again. "Last night I had a dream that a young white man would come and eventually change the way we see the stars."

Wade did not know what to say, and looked steadily into the eyes of the elder and flashed back to the chief's portrait taken by Edward Curtis. They were the same.

A moment later Thaddeus stepped out of a shop to rejoin Wade. Wade turned to introduce him to the Indian elder, but just as quietly as he had appeared, the ancient one was gone.

"I just had the strangest experience," Wade told the Judge, and he explained what had just occurred. "I swear it felt like a waking dream. First, he appeared out of thin air, and tells me 'I'm the one,' whatever that means, and then he disappeared like smoke on the wind when you appeared."

Thaddeus listened closely, trying to divine his young friend's experience, and simply nodded. "Some things are just not meant to be totally understood, Wade, and it would appear that this gentleman believes he has seen your future.

After visiting a few more shops and stimulating the local economy by buying gifts for folks back home, they headed west on US route 2 along the Missouri River, then veered a little north with the goal of reaching the city of Havre in a few hours.

Chapter 28

CURLY ALGOL WANTED TO drive the Maxima like a bat out of hell on his way toward Billings, but what little common sense he had left told him to mind the speed limit. When he reached Glendive, Montana he slowly cruised through town to see if he could spot the black Land Cruiser, but seeing nothing, he continued driving west on I-94 along the Yellowstone River.

"So where the heck are you, Mr. High and Mighty? I saw you back there at that Teddy Roosevelt park, and I bet I'll find you again. Just gotta keep my eyes peeled and my shotgun handy."

Curly didn't mind talking to himself. He'd been doing it for years. Back in the prison at Russellville his old cellmate, Nerf McCabe, often wondered who the hell Curly was talking to. But knowing Curly, he thought it better not to ask.

"Hell," he said out loud. "The only good conversations I have are with myself."

He looked in the rearview mirror to see if anyone was sneaking up behind him, and then caught a view of himself in the mirror. He cringed.

"I guess I best get myself cleaned up so I don't scare no one," he admitted. "Besides I need to get some more cash, food and gas. I left my stuff back in the Civic when I 'borrowed' this sweet Maxima. So, I gotta do what I gotta do."

From Glendive Curly continued west on I-94 through the town of Terry, population six hundred and six, then on to Miles City. Here he saw something that really caught his fancy. The Range Riders Museum.

When he was a little boy, he saw some TV programs about these Range Rider guys, who acted all high and mighty and got to ride around the countryside whacking people. He thought he might like to do that when he grew up. So, here he was all grown up. Curly pulled into the parking lot and got out.

The first thing he saw was a large log building and a horse with an old buckboard. It looked just like TV-land to Curly. He could barely contain his excitement.

"Howdy there partner," said Curly to the volunteer on duty at the information desk. "I wanna sign up to be a Range Rider!"

"Well, I'm very sorry sir," Dillon Gerber said, "but there are no Range Riders anymore. However we do have some lovely exhibits if you care to pay the price of admission; or perhaps you may choose to become one of our Museum's members."

"What the fuck you sayin' there ain't no more Range Riders," Curly spewed. "I seen 'em on the TV. Now give me an application or a badge or something!"

Dillon Gerber literally started wetting himself and stammering a reply to this incredibly seedy-looking individual.

"But, but, we don't have an application and all of our badges are in the exhibits. Perhaps you may wish to purchase a toy sheriff star in our little gift nook."

Dillon had finished wetting himself at this point and was frantically looking for any other human being to please come and relieve him. He wasn't that lucky.

"I drove all the way from Indiana to join up with the Range Riders," Curly lied, "and now the only thing I get is a toy star!" He bellowed and verbally ravaged poor Dillon Gerber, and then he really got pissed.

He grabbed Dillon, soon to be ex-volunteer, and dragged him over to the exhibit that had a holding cell and shackles. Curly palmed Dillon very hard in the nose and his eyes rolled back in his head. His head smacked the floor with a sickening, wet thwack. Curly stripped the poor guy naked and attached shackles to his bare ankles. He then attached a strong lariat to the shackles and threw it over a stout ceiling timber.

"Upsie dazie!" Curly sang, and he hoisted unconscious, naked Dillon upside down into the air. He tied the rope off to a wall cleat and admired his handiwork.

"Well, I'd love to 'hang around' with you, but I got places to go and people to kill, I mean, see; so I think I'll just have to help myself to your cash box and be on my way. Poor Dillon Gerber was still unconscious, and at this point his other bowel proceeded to empty its contents on hapless Dillon. What a mess. Even Curly was grossed out.

"But before I go, sir, I think I need to properly recognize your meritorious service with an object of my un-appreciation." Curly reached over and grabbed a silver-colored metal star with a sharp spike attached at the rear and rammed it into Dillon Gerber's chest. It dug deep and then slowly a spigot of blood began to flow.

Chapter 29

THADDEUS WAS BACK at the wheel of the Land Cruiser, and they continued on their westerly journey. They passed through the city of Glasgow, and past the Sleeping Buffalo Hot Springs and the Nelson Reservoir. The miles kept coming and going.

"Wait Judge, I'm serious," Wade said. "That old Indian man in town just like came out of nowhere, and he spoke to me like he knew me. And his eyes, they were so intense and deep. I felt like he was peering into my very being. I mean I wasn't scared, but it happened so fast that it was a little surreal."

"Ah Wade," the Judge began, "I believe you may have chosen the perfect word, 'surreal'. From your classics studies, you may recall a quotation by Socrates who famously said, 'I only know that I know nothing.' "

"Seriously Judge! And how is that even remotely connected to my experience with this Indian elder?" Wade complained.

"Think about it," Thaddeus continued. "We are all filled with hubris; pride to us mere mortals. We think we are so smart, because humans can be very smart. We have built civilizations.

We have learned to control some aspects of nature for agriculture and the engineering of cities and roads. We have even cured many communicable diseases. So, it's easy to think that our species of Homo Sapiens has got life figured out.

Think again, my friend, Thaddeus cautioned. There are so many mysteries yet to be understood; so many ways of thinking that our western-educated minds can't even begin to grasp. It's true in medicine and has certainly proven true with many botanicals. Why couldn't it also be true spiritually? Who are we to believe that our way of thinking even comes close to reaching our potential?

Over the millennia," the Judge continued, "many native peoples have connected spiritually to things they did not understand. I'm not so sure that some of them didn't in fact attain a different level of spiritual enlightenment because they did understand. Your Indian chief comes to mind.

Maybe this experience you had was just a weird happenstance. Maybe. But, I encourage you to not forget this experience, including the way he looked; the intensity of his eyes; the sound of his voice, and what he said for your ears only."

Wade listened to the Judge very attentively. It was all so confusing, and while he didn't doubt that what the Judge was saying was true; it was just so hard to figure out what it all meant.

"Thank you, Judge, and I won't forget it. Something very powerful happened in Miles City, and I need to think about it some more."

Thaddeus and Wade continued driving west on US Route 2 and finally reached the city of Havre around 6:00 PM. They found the local sheriff's office and stopped in to see if the sheriff from Medora had connected with him and arranged comfortable accommodations for them. He had.

"So, you're the two gents that have this crazy maniac chasing after you," Sheriff Jake Clooney said. "Well, we don't like his sort around here; so out of respect to my friend Sheriff Chandler, we've got rooms for you at the motel, but I'd appreciate it if you didn't hang around my jurisdiction too long, understand?!"

Thaddeus was a bit annoyed by the Sheriff's brusque manner, but really couldn't blame the man for wanting to maintain tranquility in his little corner of the world.

"I assure you, Sheriff Clooney, my friend and I will be gone in the morning, and we certainly appreciate your assistance and your point of view," the Judge said.

Wade and Thaddeus checked into their rooms in Indian Pride motel, and Wade said he wanted to go for a run before dinner. Thaddeus told him he was going to take a brief nap and phone home to see how Quentin was getting along. He reminded Wade that he should call his mother when he returned. They agreed to hook up for dinner around 8:00 PM.

Breathe in; breathe out. Wade chose a dirt path leading to the Fort Assiniboine Historical Site. There was another path he could've chosen, but this one seemed more appropriate given his recent 'surreal' connection with the Indian elder.

Wade loved to run, and his long, lean 6'1" frame and musculature were well suited for it. Beyond the physical conditioning he got from running, he loved it because mentally he could let his mind wander and examine different thoughts and moods. It was his time alone. And boy, did he have a lot to think about. As if having a deranged murderer chasing after you and the Judge wasn't enough, he thought of his encounter with the Indian elder, and then on to sweet memories of Kayla.

Breathe in; breathe out. One foot in front of the other. One dilemma to ponder at a time, and then he felt a stab of guilt for not thinking more about his mom, or even about heading off to Duke in six weeks. Wade was learning to compartmentalize his thoughts, and he compared his running to dealing with issues: one foot in front of the other. Deal with each step as they come.

Wade arrived 30 minutes later at old Fort Assiniboine and saw the red brick parapets of the now defunct officers' quarters. He stopped in front of a bronze placard and read how the fort existed from 1879–1911 during the Cree Indian campaign. He also learned that General Black Jack Pershing, of WWI fame, had been stationed here early in his career.

Wade walked around the historical site, catching his breath and considered the history of the place. It was a well-kept public setting with a few visitors touring the grounds. Of all the people though, it was the native Americans there that captured his interest the most.

He saw a group of teenage Indian boys playing soccer, and he thought what similar games their ancestors might have played on these very grounds. He saw dour middle-aged women who were focused on various tedious chores: washing clothes and grinding corn meal. He saw four elderly men sitting in the shade, telling tales. Wade looked to see if the chief from Medora was among them, but he was not.

Wade casually walked near the group of elders to eavesdrop on their conversation. He didn't mean to be rude. He was just curious. He saw the men staring at him, and he sheepishly smiled and waved. The men went back to their conversation without further acknowledging his presence.

Wade was tempted to ask the teenagers if he could join their soccer game, but he knew he had to get back to the motel soon to call his mom and clean up for dinner with Thaddeus. Wade stretched his leg muscles for a few moments and then turned back toward the path.

"Young man," the voice of one of the older men called, and Wade turned to look at him. The elder pointed his finger toward Wade, then to his own eyes and then straight up into the sky. "Remember, you are the one," the old Indian said, and then he turned away.

Wade could barely contain himself. He wondered if he had heard the man correctly. He wanted to ask him what he meant, but the men stood up and left.

Wade's head was spinning. Had that really just happened? Had that old Indian really said, "remember, you are the one?" What on earth was going on… and why him? Wade returned to the path and ran like the wind, He couldn't wait to get back and tell the judge what had occurred, even if it did make him sound a little nutty. Breathe in; breathe out. One foot in front of the other. One dilemma at a time. He sprinted for home.

Meanwhile back at the motel, Thaddeus contacted Quentin who sounded a little relieved because neither he nor Cassie had heard from them for a couple of days.

"Everything's fine here, Judge, but I'm glad to hear from you," Quentin said. "Cassie's been pretty concerned because she hadn't heard from Wade, and she even said she's prepared to fly up to Jasper if she loses contact with you two; so FYI."

"We're doing fine, Quentin, and Wade is going to phone his mom when he gets back from his run. We've had some spotty internet and cell phone service, and I imagine it may get worse the closer we get to the mountains. Cassie's just being a good mom. By the way, how's Luella doing?"

"I think she's doing much better, Judge, but like I said last time, she's got a way to go. She's been enormously helpful around here. You wouldn't believe how clean the house is and how wonderful the gardens look. I think she poured herself into weeding the beds as a way to find some peace. Everyone's getting along really well; so you don't need to fret about anything here."

"Great! What about the mail?" Thaddeus asked. "Anything look like it might need immediate attention?"

"Well I haven't opened any of your mail, of course, but it looks like pretty routine stuff; you know, a few bills and catalogs, etc. It doesn't look like anything that can't wait until you get back."

"Well, okay then, Quentin, I just heard Wade return so I think I'll say adios until tomorrow or whenever we're able to connect. I'm going to call Sheriff Penrod after we hang up and bring him up to date about our dear misunderstood friend, Mr. Algol."

Chapter 30

AFTER SHOWERING AND TRYING unsuccessfully to reach his mom, Wade knocked on Thaddeus' door promptly at 7:59 PM. They drove over to a nearby family-style restaurant that looked somewhat promising and waited for a perky hostess to set a table for them. Thaddeus noticed that Wade seemed a little anxious, but he decided to wait until they were seated before he asked anything.

As soon as they were seated and the hostess left, Wade said, "It happened again, Judge."

"What happened again?" Thaddeus asked.

Wade proceeded to tell him every detail about his visit to the Fort Assiniboine Historical Site, and his encounter with another Indian elder who called him "the one."

"Judge, I'm feeling pretty spooked," Wade lamented. "I mean this really is a very surreal experience, and to have it happen twice now is beyond coincidental. Do you have any clue what they're talking about because I sure don't. These Indian elders make it sound like I am destined to do something with the stars."

Judge Thaddeus Nathan listened with the thoughtful solemnity of a seasoned judge.

"My honest answer is that I don't have a clue what it means, but if the elders think it means that you're destined to change the way we look at the stars, I could think of a lot worse callings to have."

The two of them talked more about the possible things it could mean, but reluctantly concluded it was a mystery beyond their abilities to solve.

"Try not to fret about it, Wade, but I have to admit that it does give one pause. Heck, these are some fascinating experiences you could share with Kayla. Everyone loves a mystery, and she may come to view you in a mystical way too. You might ask for her opinion. Perhaps she thinks you're 'the one' too."

They both smiled at that last comment and talked about what their itinerary showed coming up. They were an easy day's drive away from Glacier National Park and were excited to leave the plains behind. They hoped Curly stayed behind as well. After dinner Wade and Thaddeus decided to go out to the restaurant's veranda for a little dessert, and to watch the big Montana sky turn from day into night.

"I've been wondering," Wade said. "We know that many ancient peoples had their own unique stories and connections with the universe. I really enjoyed reading your book about Australian aboriginal astronomy, and I still clearly recall that dream I had being prepared by the tribal elders for a walkabout in the Australian outback. I remember being taught by the tribesmen to observe and listen to the songs of the land. And honestly, Judge, I have been trying to do just that here in Montana, but I don't think I'm very good at it yet.

Unfortunately," Wade continued, I don't know much about what our Native American tribes believed, and given my recent encounters with Indian elders, I'm thinking I need to be open and learn more. Do you know much about how the Indian cultures viewed the stars and planets, Judge?"

"That's a very good question, my friend. We often hear about what the early Egyptians and Greeks and Romans believed, but virtually all cultures tried to understand their worlds by looking to the heavens. The Native Americans were no different, but given that there were so many tribes spread over such vast areas, there were no single unifying practices among them. You'll recall that even the Australian aborigine tribes had creation stories that varied by tribes, and their 'dream time' accounts about creation became a form of tribal intellectual property."

The Judge continued: "Native American cultures sometimes used the movement of stars and heavenly bodies as the foundation for tribal governance, agricultural practices, and an attempt to understand the meaning of life."

Further he said, "The Pawnees referred to the stars forming the constellation, Corona Borealis, as the Council of Chiefs representing a form of governance to decide tribal matters, but they also used the stars to set agricultural times for planting and harvest. They referred to the North Star, Polaris, as the 'Chief Star.'

And, in New Mexico archaeologists found a cave painting that the Anasazi created 1000 years ago showing a supernova that may depict the Crab Nebula. While much remains unknown about the Anasazi culture, researchers found that they built a solar observatory suggesting that the sky was very important to their daily lives.

And the Navajo and Hopi peoples believe that there were worlds before this one, and that each world that existed before ours ended with the appearance of a blue star. It seems that what they saw may have led them to a belief in aliens.

And like our Australian aborigine friends, few myths extend beyond a single tribe. So, two things are very clear to me, Wade. First, many Native American peoples held very strong belief systems about the heavens; and secondly, that we really do not know enough about their mystical beliefs and practices. I wish I could offer more, but I think you're well on the path to understanding by at least asking the right questions."

The night sky was fully dark now with a waxing gibbous moon providing a warm clear glow. The lights on the veranda had been turned low so many stars were visible too. Wade and Thaddeus continued to talk about a lot of different topics; things back home, going to Duke, astronomy, Cassie, Kayla, Quentin and Luella. It had been a full and emotional day, and tomorrow they would be in the mountains.

Thaddeus and Wade decided it was time to pack it in. They had promised the sheriff they'd be gone in the morning, and so they said goodnight and headed to their respective rooms.

Wade lay in the dark thinking about everything that had transpired in his life in just the past few days. Between the two episodes with the Indian elders and his total infatuation with Kayla, his head was spinning. He tried to fall asleep immediately, but words and visions and thoughts kept his mind awake. Eventually he dreamed.

In his dream Wade found himself dressed in loin cloths made of animal skins and decorated with small bone beads and feathers. He was looking up into the night sky with his arms outstretched, beseeching the stars for an understanding of the meaning of life. He thought briefly that he was in the Australian outback again with the Aborigine elders until he saw that he was among a group of Native Americans. How similar he thought the two peoples were.

Wade saw the constellation Corona Borealis in the eastern sky and heard low humming and drumming sounds and saw his tribe seated around a campfire. The Judge and his father were there, as were the Indian elders he had seen recently. They chanted low tunes that vibrated with the sound of the drums whose musical notes drifted upwardly like the embers from the fire. He was being prepared for another walkabout, but this time he would be wandering the North American wilderness.

An elder stepped forward and placed a hand on Wade's shoulder and leaned his forehead against Wade's. Without speaking out loud, thoughts were transmitted to Wade about what he must undertake in order to attain his tribal manhood.

Wade stirred in his sleep from the power of the elder's thoughts. "You are the one. You will change the way we see the stars, but first you must overcome great adversity." Wade stirred more from the weight of the words and from his confusion about what was expected of him.

The dream shifted to a place in the far north that contained a deep gorge filled with rushing water. It was a beautiful setting, but he sensed an evil presence that he knew he must confront. The evil spirit was a man-beast that had sated its bloodlust on the bodies of innocents.

Wade cringed in his slumber; shaking his head trying to wake from this horribleness. He sensed he would meet this malignant presence soon, and he turned to the tribal elders for their counsel. He heard no words but saw the eyes of the tribal chief peering into his very being. They were timeless.

His dream shifted to a pastoral setting, high on a hill overlooking a milky river. He was seated next to a pretty maiden dressed in soft deer skin covering her loins and whose long auburn hair cascaded down her shoulders covering her youthful breasts.

She spoke to him in soft words telling him that there was a destiny that guided him and that she would be there for him when he returned from his walkabout. Wade stirred again in his sleep. He didn't want to leave her, but knew he must, and her presence drifted up into the night sky along with the fire's embers and the chants and drumbeats of his tribesmen.

Finally, Wade's dream led him to an ethereal place where his late father, Ben, stood shrouded in a celestial light. The two of them silently looked into each other's eyes, and tears of joy and disbelief flowed from Wade's. He rushed to hug his father, but his father held up his hand in a halting way, and said "My son, it is not yet your time to join the stardust. Listen to your elders and follow your heart. You have much to give and even more to learn." His father pointed to Wade, then to his own eyes, and then up into the sky. And then, he was gone.

When he awoke, it was morning. Wade lay in his bed for several minutes longer trying to resurrect the sequence and messages of his dream. He was confused by all of it but surprisingly at peace. He rose and felt prepared to meet the day, but he had no idea how he could possibly begin to explain a dream like this to the Judge.

Chapter 31

MEANWHILE ABOUT TWO HUNDRED AND fifty miles further south, Curly Algol cruised along I-94 still feeling a little depressed because he couldn't join the Range Riders. Even roughing up that dip-shit volunteer at the museum didn't feel as good as it used to. He figured he was just tired and needed to find a place to hole up, clean up and then giddyup.

But he also knew he had a long way to drive if he wanted to get to where that high and mighty Judge Thaddeus Nathan was heading. More than once today he wondered if getting the Judge was worth it, but in the end he leered at himself in the rearview mirror and said, "Hell yes it's worth it!" He stomped on the accelerator. "I'll hole up tomorrow in Kalispell."

The hours on the highway passed by slowly, but Curly stayed focused on his goal. He figured he had enough cash for food and gas, and probably enough for a cheap motel when he reached Kalispell.

He stared at himself in the mirror and cringed again at how badly he looked. He hadn't shaved, bathed, combed his hair or brushed his teeth in over two weeks, and he certainly hadn't had the benefit of deodorant. He was a mess, but he didn't care.

Curly drove slowly through Billings and Bozeman all the while keeping his eyes peeled for the Judge's black Land Cruiser. He stopped in Butte to gas up and stretch his legs, but he didn't see any sign of a black Toyota SUV here either.

He drove through the night reaching Missoula around 2:30 AM and turned north on to US Route 93. He actually enjoyed the sunrise over Flathead Lake and finally arrived at Kalispell a little after sunup. Curly felt wiped out after the long hours on the highway and pulled into the gravel parking lot of Lone Pine Motel.

The clerk at the front desk was a weary-looking, youngish woman named Yolanda Pigg. She recoiled when she saw Curly walk through the front door. It was very early in the morning, so thankfully no other guests were around.

"Need me a room with a shower and TV," he said as politely as Curly Algol was capable. "And I forgot my razor and stuff. You got anything I can use?"

Ms. Pigg pulled out a complimentary bag of toiletries that had a slight lavender scent and slide it across the desk so she wouldn't have to touch their new guest's hand.

She asked Curly for a credit card imprint for any incidentals that he might purchase but quickly relented when he told her he wasn't exactly the credit card type. She also found his leer rather creepy.

"Well then, may I please see some other form of identification, sir? It's motel policy. I'm sure you understand," Ms. Pigg stated.

Curly peeled off a $10 bill and held it in from of Yolanda. "Is this identification enough, Miss Piggy? I could even sweeten that a bit if you want to come by my room later on."

It was everything Yolanda Pigg could do to keep from upchucking her breakfast across the counter. This man was the grossest creature she had ever seen, and if she weren't already petrified, she might've dialed 911.

Her shift was scheduled to end in fifteen minutes, and she didn't want anything to get in the way of her getaway from Mr. Creepy. So, instead she took the easier route and slid a key in his direction and told him to keep the $10.

"We have a no-smoking policy here at the Lone Pine Motel, and our complimentary breakfast is from 7:00–9:00 AM," Yolanda informed him officiously, but Curly was already walking toward his room before she finished her sentence.

"Hell, everything in the joint is complimentary to me," he chuckled to himself. "I don't plan on paying for nuthin, and maybe that little chickie poo at the front desk might find out what a charmin' cuss I can be. My sissie Luella was my first poontang, but she won't be my last."

Curly opened the door to his room, kicked off his boots, ran to the bathroom, dropped his trousers and peed, then crashed on the double bed. A minute later he was asleep. Snorting.

———

It seemed like forever to Cassie since she had last spoken on the phone to Wade. She had missed two of his previous phone calls, but felt somewhat relieved from the cheery sound of his voice messages. Wade had told her that he and the Judge were having a great time, and that he had some very interesting and curious stories to share with her when he got back.

Cassie had tried to call him back a couple of times but hadn't been able to get through. Even though she knew Wade was with Thaddeus, she still fretted.

"Oh, don't make me come up there, Wade Henry," she said to herself.

On the evenings when Cassie didn't have to work late at Kissinger College, she often had dinner with Quentin and Luella.

The three of them continued to bond very comfortably, and with each passing day, it seemed that Luella was getting more and more emotionally stable.

While Quentin was on the phone with his boss in the Judge's study, Luella told Cassie that she had had her period earlier in the day and was so relieved that her dear old brother had not impregnated her with his evil seed.

"Please don't say anything to Quentin, okay Cassie? I just needed to tell someone, and well, I hope you know that I trust you. Plus, some men can get a little squirrelly at the mention of female bodily functions."

"That is great news, Luella, and I'm very relieved for you too. I didn't want to ask you because it's very personal, but I was keeping my fingers crossed that you weren't pregnant."

"And as for Quentin," Cassie continued, "my guess is that you could probably talk with him about most anything. I don't know if you've noticed, but he seems very devoted to you."

Luella blushed a bit and nodded that she had noticed that too.

"Both of you have been wonderful to me, and I am eternally grateful. Quentin is a dear, sweet man, and I feel fortunate to be able to stay with him here at Judge Nathan's, but I know I need to get a good job and a place of my own pretty soon.

I must admit he is pretty cute though," she blushed again. "And, thank you so much, Cassie, for keeping the period thing between us."

"And, as far as the job goes, Cassie said, I'm still looking into a promising possibility in the Admissions Office at the college. The Admissions Director has been away from campus on business, and she's due back in the office next week. We have a very good working relationship, and I've left a message asking her to call me when she returns.

And, I'm really glad you got those clothes when we went shopping the other day because you're going to look very professional and trendy when we get an interview set up for you. We can work on your resume too if you'd like and help you focus on your skill sets."

"That would be wonderful," Luella said. Both women were hugging when Quentin re-entered the room.

"Uh, did I miss something here?" he asked quizzically.

Both women walked over to Quentin and engulfed him in a group hug.

"Okay, okay," Quentin said. "Whatever it was will remain your little secret. Now who's hungry? I'm starved."

Chapter 32

"GOOD MORNING, WADE," came the Judge's cheerful greeting, "and how did you sleep last night?"

"Well, I'm not exactly sure," came Wade's cryptic reply. "I had a lot of confusing dreams. You and Dad were in them, as were Kayla and the Indian elders, and a sinister warning about an evil presence that I'm destined to encounter. How's that for one night's slumber?"

Wade then proceeded to give Thaddeus chapter and verse of everything he could recall from his dream. The two men sat there silently for a few moments sipping their coffee trying to understand Wade's dreams.

"It would appear that there is a lot going on with you here than we cannot easily explain," Thaddeus offered.

"I usually have trouble remembering my dreams," Wade admitted, "but these are still crystal clear. I'm tempted to go back over to Fort Assiniboine and look for the elders who I saw yesterday. Maybe they could shed some light on this. It's all so mysterious."

"Why don't we look for them on our way out of town? Thaddeus suggested. I'd be very curious to get their opinion too. Oh, and may I suggest that you try to reach your mother again. Quentin told me yesterday that she's starting to worry because she hasn't spoken with you. Plus, our cell service could be worse as we enter the mountains."

They agreed to meet at the car in thirty minutes and then head to Fort Assiniboine.

Wade packed his belongings and washed up quickly. While waiting for the Judge, he sat down by the car and composed an email to Kayla.

> *Good morning, Kayla, I hope you and your mom made it safely back to Indianapolis. The Judge and I are preparing to drive the rest of the way to Glacier National Park today and then to Jasper, Alberta a day or so later. We should be back in Prindle County in less than two weeks.*
>
> *We've had some very unusual experiences since I last saw you, and I'd like to tell you about them when I return home. Honestly, some of them have been a little spooky, and I'm afraid if I tell them to you in an email, you'll think I'm too weird.*
>
> *Anyway, I just wanted to connect with you and say that I miss you and have been thinking about you a lot. Let's get together when I get back, okay.*
>
> *My best, Wade.*

Wade re-read his email a couple of times before he hit the send key. It took longer than usual for the message to be sent, but it eventually went through. He wasn't sure how Kayla would take his message, and he didn't want to gush about her too much. He hoped he would hear back from her soon though, and that she would say some encouraging words.

A few minutes later Thaddeus came out to the Land Cruiser, and they looked at the map together. They drove over to the Fort Assiniboine Historic Site, but no one was around. Wade pointed to where he had seen the village elders seated, and they walked over there. No sign of anyone. Wade was discouraged because he really wanted the Judge to believe him.

As they turned to leave, Thaddeus said, "Hold on, Wade," and he pointed to the ground in front of a chair. There in the dirt was a scene that looked remarkably like the constellation, Corona Borealis. The two men looked at it and at each other. The mysteries just kept on coming. Next to it was an outline of two eyes with an arrow pointing up.

"It would appear," the Judge said half-jokingly, "that we are not alone in our appreciation of the night sky."

"I suppose so, Judge, but what's with the two eyes and the arrow pointing upward," Wade added.

The two men looked at the ground and then back at each. They both laughed a little nervously and shook their heads in disbelief.

"Let's go, Judge, before anything weirder starts to happen!"

"I'm with you, pal," Thaddeus said, and they both headed for the Land Cruiser.

The drive west from Havre on US Route 2 was fairly unremarkable. Small towns dotted the landscape with names like Kremlin, Gildford, Chester and Galata. They crossed over Willow Creek and past the city of Shelby at the junction of I-15.

They stopped for a quick lunch at a diner in the town of Cut Bank, near the banks of a rocky creek by the same name. While they were eating, Wade's phone chimed, and he saw that he had a reply from Kayla. He read a few lines and began to smile.

Dear Wade, I was wondering when I was going to hear from you. Mom and I got back to Indy last night. We had a really fun trip, but it's good to be home too. And yes, I've been thinking about you a lot too. We had a special time together. Stargazing may never be the same! So, please give me a call when you get back and we'll definitely do something. Oh, and please feel free to keep emailing me, okay. My best to you, Kayla

The Judge gently kidded him by saying, "Probably just some spam from a telemarketer, huh?" He knew better than to pry.

After lunch they continued driving west on Route 2 onto the Blackfeet reservation and stopped at the Museum of the Plains Indian in the town of Browning. They could see the mountains in the distance.

Thaddeus and Wade enjoyed the Museum's diverse collection of historic and contemporary art of the tribal people of the northern plains. They marveled at beadwork and textiles, pottery, paintings, stone carvings, quilts and masks from tribes including the Blackfeet, Shoshoni, Salish, Cree and many others.

"Growing up, it seemed that all we ever heard about Indians was their conflicts with the white settlers and the military," Wade said. "It's very reassuring and enlightening to see the arts and crafts that our native peoples created."

"It's fascinating to me," the Judge remarked, "that history is often highlighted by wars and treaties rather than the cultural aspects of different peoples. Go to virtually any museum in the world, and notice that humankind is often represented by two aspects of the human psyche: 'Man the Creator and Man the Destroyer'.

Look at virtually any aboriginal race," Thaddeus continued, "and all they really wanted was the same thing that we want: to raise our families in peace and prosperity, to contribute toward the greater good; to try to understand the natural world around us, and to pay homage to the great spirit."

Wade and Thaddeus left the museum with a deep abiding sense of respect for the Indian tribes of the northern plains. Wade now appreciated a fuller understanding that there are many ways that people can live their lives, and that the way of western civilization is only one of many.

An hour later they reached the town of Babb, Montana and the eastern escarpment of the Waterton — Glacier International Peace Park. The Canadian border was just a few miles north.

"I have a surprise for you, Wade," the Judge said. "Years ago when we were younger, Ellie and I visited the Many Glacier Hotel. We loved its rustic charm and always promised ourselves that we'd come back. Well, we unfortunately never made it, but I thought it would be a great place for us to spend some time. I phoned ahead and made reservations for us."

Just then they rounded a bend in the road, and Wade let out a low whistle when he saw the huge old wooden lodge. It was a sprawling historic Swiss-style chalet on the shores of Swiftcurrent Lake at the base of Mt. Grinnell.

"This is awesome," Wade gushed. "Are we really staying here?"

Thaddeus said, "Indeed we are, and I thought it would be a great place for us to pull out the 8" Celestron telescope at dark tonight and see what the night skies have in store for us."

Wade was thrilled, and after they parked and checked into their rooms, he changed into his running attire, grabbed his cell phone and told the judge he wanted to go for a run. What he didn't tell the Judge was that he wanted to email some pictures to Kayla, with a message saying "wish you were here."

Thaddeus took the time to walk around the hotel's grounds and get re-acquainted with the rustic, old structure. It didn't look much different from thirty-five years earlier, and Swiftcurrent Lake was as picturesque as ever.

Thaddeus tried to reach Quentin with his cell phone and then Cassie. Both calls were dropped due to poor reception in the mountains. He decided that he and Wade would try again later.

Chapter 33

Curly Algol awoke in the middle of the night in his room
at the Lone Pine Motel trying to recall where he was. He
peered out the window and saw his "borrowed" silver Maxima
in the parking lot and a dark outline of the Rocky Mountains to
the north and east. Now, he remembered where he was and what
his mission was.

"Gonna get you Judge Nathan," he mumbled.

After peeing again Curly wanted to get up and moving, but
breakfast wouldn't be ready for a few hours. The tribulations of
driving out west and whacking a few people along the way had
finally caught up with him though. He fell back into a deep sleep
and dreamed about a pristine land to the distant north.

His dream showed him a rugged place with large rock formations and rushing water where he and Judge Nathan would finally
come face to face. His dream showed him in an intense encounter,
but the outcome was veiled in mystery. He felt confident that he
could easily take the older man in fair fight; let alone a fight where
he cheated. Curly believed there was no such thing as a fair fight.

He awoke again around 7:00 AM feeling rested but annoyed that he hadn't seen the outcome of the struggle in his dream. For the first time in days, he washed his face and shaved; then brushed his yellow teeth and jumped into the shower. Fifteen minutes later Curly came out of the steamy bathroom looking more human than he had in weeks and feeling really hungry. His wet black hair was parted down the middle, and he smelled like lavender. He even whistled a little tune as he walked toward the lobby area for breakfast.

He looked around for Yolanda Pigg at the front desk but saw that her shift had ended, and he was greeted by a young, pimply faced guy who smiled at Curly as he walked by.

"Eat me, dickhead," was Curly's cheery reply to the friendly desk clerk.

Curly loaded up his plate with scrambled eggs, sausage, biscuits and gravy, and a cup of coffee. He found a plastic sack and filled it with apples, peanut butter cups and muffins. He watched CNN while he was eating and was disappointed that there were no news stories about his escapades. He'd have to change that soon.

He found a map of Glacier National Park in a lobby display, along with brochures touting areas of interest throughout the park. He perused the map looking for entry points across the border. With his shotgun in the car, he knew he'd have to be cautious where he tried to cross into Canada.

On the other hand, he figured one more whacked police officer would be fine with him if push came to shove. He just wanted the Judge dead, and then maybe he'd head down Mexico way to see the pretty senoritas.

Curly finished his breakfast and collected his meager sack of toilet articles that Yolanda Pigg had given him. He then bolted without paying his room bill and flipped the bird at the front desk clerk as he sashayed through the lobby to his car.

The clerk sputtered and stammered his objections at Curly's abrupt departure and would never really know how lucky he was that their guest had chosen to quickly bolt instead of creating a wet, bloody mess.

Curly sprayed gravel as he exited the parking lot and looked at his map when he was a few miles away. He decided his best and most entertaining route would be driving the Going to the Sun highway through the middle of park, over Logan Pass, toward the towns of St. Mary and Babb.

The night sky over Swiftcurrent Lake was unlike anything that Wade or the Judge had ever seen before. They stood outside enraptured by the night sky. There were so many stars that it felt like the heavens were pressing down on them. Seeing the stars of the Milky Way was breathtaking. No superlative adjective would come close to describing the magnificence of what they saw.

Upon learning of Thaddeus and Wade's interest in astronomy, the hotel manager arranged for them and their equipment to be transported to a large secluded canyon that would provide them with virtually no light pollution.

The manager, Jamie Waller, said "With my job I don't get the time I'd like with my telescope. When I do though, the canyon where you're going is the darkest place around. My son, Kent, will assist as needed. And, it's free of charge. I want Kent to sharpen his sky gazing and his hospitality skills. Have fun!"

The canyon was nearly fifteen miles away from the Many Glacier Hotel, and if you didn't recognize the entrance, it could be very easily missed, even in daylight. Kent Waller, who appeared to be around sixteen, knew exactly where he was going and drove the Hotel's Land Rover expertly.

They traveled another ten minutes through shallow creeks and along rock lined avenues that barely seemed wide enough to pass through. Kent kept moving without a hitch and before too long they came to a clearing at the end of the canyon. He turned off the headlights, and Wade reached for the 17amp power tank and turned on the red-filtered light for night viewing.

On the drive out, Thaddeus had already obtained the coordinates for their location. He and Wade worked as a well-coordinated team in setting up the sturdy steel tripod and mounting the 8" Celestron optical tube assembly and the Advanced VX equatorial mount on top. In a minute Thaddeus had the scope polar aligned and was ready for viewing using the Go To computer functions.

"Hey Wade, why don't you kill the red light for a bit and let's take a few minutes to let our eyes adjust," the Judge suggested.

Wade did and over the next few minutes the three of them sat in the dark peering up in the sky talking quietly among themselves. With each minute that passed, it seemed like the number of stars increased exponentially. Each person took a turn pointing out favorite constellations and their alpha stars.

Finally, the Judge trained the Celestron on the Orion Nebula low in the western sky. He solemnly stood trying to comprehend the incomprehensible. A moment later he stepped aside and invited Wade to take a look.

The silence was deafening. Wade had seen pictures and read books about the famed nebula. He had heard the judge talk about it as a nursery for stars, but seeing it with this magnification made it appear almost magical. Next Kent took his turn at the telescope and was as speechless as the two hotel guests.

For the next ninety minutes, they took turns looking through the telescope at different celestial objects. From time to time they just turned off the red light again and looked at the sky with their naked eyes. All three knew that what they were experiencing was very special, and when they finally succumbed to eye fatigue, Wade and Thaddeus thanked Kent warmly, and the Judge slipped him two crisp $100 bills. "One from each of us," the Judge said. "You've earned it."

Chapter 34

BACK IN PRINDLE COUNTY, Indiana life on Brick Chapel Road was progressing well. Quentin and Luella were working well as a team keeping Cassie's and Judge's properties in good order. Cassie was thrilled to have so much help from both of them and even happier to feel that she had friends that she could count on and vice vera.

Cassie had finally arranged an interview for Luella with Bernice Sweet, the college's director of admissions. Ms. Sweet was a sturdy, no nonsense individual who lived alone and whose sole purpose in life was to assure that the highest caliber of students graced the campus of Kissinger College. She worked tirelessly.

Cassie had spent a few hours working with Luella on her resume and coached her on how to answer tough questions. In the end Cassie thought that Luella would be a perfect fit as Bernice's assistant director, and believed that Bernice would come to a similar conclusion.

The hour of the interview with Ms. Sweet arrived, and Luella appeared promptly for her appointment at 3:00 PM. Bernice Sweet appeared to be in her mid 60s, and was beginning to show some fatigue from her nearly four decades of service to Kissinger College. Truth be known, she should have hired an assistant director years ago. No one in administration could deny her an additional staff position. She had done so much with so little for so long that she was entitled to help.

Bernice Sweet extended her hand and said, "Ms. Algol, I have the highest regard for my colleague, Cassie Henry, so I am pleased to meet you. Someone would have to live under a rock in Prindle County to not know the tragedies that you and your family endured. You have my sincere, heartfelt sympathy, Ms. Algol."

"Thank you, Ms. Sweet, I appreciate your kind words very much," Luella said, "but I know you are an extremely busy administrator, and I would like to speak with you about why I believe I am a strong candidate to work as your assistant."

Bernice Sweet smiled approvingly to herself. She appreciated that Luella Algol wanted to respect her time and get to the issue at hand, her new assistant's position.

For the next two hours, Bernice Sweet and Luella Algol discussed all manner of topics. They referred to the actual position description frequently but found that the discussion would often veer into other avenues further indicating Ms. Algol's strengths. Ms. Sweet knew that Luella was no stranger to hard work and long hours. Growing up on a farm, you learned how to work. You also learned how to solve problems because help wasn't always available.

No, it was very clear to Ms. Sweet. Luella totally understood the work ethic. Bernice was also pleased with how well Luella spoke and the diction that she used. Despite growing up in rural Prindle County, Luella was an educated woman who apparently wrote as well as she spoke.

Luella offered to prepare some written materials for Ms. Sweet to review such as a formal letter, design of admissions office materials, memoranda. Bernice Sweet thought that was an excellent idea, and it gave them an opportunity to work on an assignment together and get together again to discuss what she had prepared.

"Well, Ms. Algol, I believe our time has come to an end today, but I must say that I am most pleased to meet you and look forward to our getting together the end of the week. Shall we say Friday at 3:00 PM."

"That would be wonderful, Ms. Sweet, and please call me Luella."

They parted company, and Luella felt like she was floating on air. She was pleased with how the interview went, and how long it lasted. She was even excited to tackle the writing assignments that Ms. Sweet had given her. Thanks to Cassie and Quentin, things were really starting to look up.

Curly Algol had never seen mountains like these before, and he marveled at how big they were. He passed by the park headquarters and visitors center near the town of Apgar and drove northeast along Lake McDonald. Even a demented, nut case like Curly felt awe in seeing the natural wonder that surrounded him.

Before long he was driving on the Going to the Sun highway. Traffic was sparse and his Maxima was behind just one other vehicle that was cautiously traversing this section of road. The view was both breathtaking and frightening. One false move here, and it could be mean a swift and tragic fall off the side of the mountain. Curly idly sang as he drove, *"She'll be coming round the mountain when she comes…"*

An elderly couple in a Subaru Legacy were in front of him and taking their sweet time negotiating the hairpin turns while trying to catch glimpses of the dramatic landscape. Curly grew impatient with the elderly couple and began laying on his horn for them to speed up.

Aloysius and Roxanne LaViolette were both in their early eighties and could care less about the rude cuss in their rearview mirror. They were on vacation and were determined to enjoy the drive. Their car crawled along at a steady fifteen mph.

"Move over you freakin' fossils," Curly hollered out his window, but the aged couple couldn't hear his protestation. At one point Roxanne turned to look out the rear window to see what manner of rude individual was being so obnoxious. She was greeted by the sight of Curly giving her the finger.

Unfortunately there was no place for the couple to pull their car over to let this young whippersnapper pass, so they just plodded along at their octogenarian pace. Within a couple of minutes, Curly had had it with these slow pokes and honked his horn and bumped his car into the back of theirs.

Aloysius had never been involved in an accident before and had even received a gold certificate from his automobile insurance company for fifty years of safe driving. He pulled his car to a stop preparing to exit his vehicle to assess the damage, but Curly kept honking and pushing their car forward toward the edge.

Curly quickly scanned his surroundings to see if anyone was watching, and seeing no one, he gave the Maxima's engine one final roar and launched the LaViolette's Subaru over the side of the road. It teetered for a moment on the brink of oblivion and then careened down the side of the mountain. It tore through small trees and shrubbery, with the crunching sounds of metal and glass, and finally came to a stop against the girth of a large pine tree. Dust rose from a hundred yards below, and then it was deathly quiet.

"Oops," Curly guffawed, and then he went on his merry way singing a little ditty, *"They'll be crashing down the mountain when they come..."*

An hour later Curly ended his white-knuckle drive through Logan Pass and exited the park at the town of St. Mary. He drove slowly through the town and then through the town of Babb, all the while keeping his eyes peeled for the the black Land Cruiser. Seeing nothing, he plotted his course in a northerly direction toward the Canadian border. He sensed he was getting closer to finally finding that damn Judge.

Chapter 35

THE NEXT MORNING Wade and Thaddeus were still beaming with excitement from their stargazing adventure with Kent Waller the previous evening.

"That was one of the most awesome experiences I can ever remember," Wade gushed to the Judge. "I still can't believe how many stars we saw, and the Orion Nebula was everything you said it would be. I can't thank you enough for bringing us on this trip."

"You are quite welcome, my friend," Thaddeus said. "It was a very special experience for me too, and I can't wait to see what the night skies near Jasper look like. I've already checked us out of our rooms; so if you're ready, why don't we head north into Canada."

They both tried to phone home using their cell phones, but like before, the mountains were interfering with their cellular service.

"My mom's going to croak," Wade lamented, "because I haven't spoken with her in a couple of days now, and it doesn't seem that our cell service will get much better the further north we go."

"Well, we'll just have to keep trying, and we should have much better service when we get close to Calgary or Canmore and Banff," the Judge offered.

They bid adieu to Jamie Waller and the Many Glacier Hotel and thanked him profusely for the fine hospitality that he had shown the two of them. Then, with Wade at the wheel, he guided the Land Cruiser on to US Route 89 toward the US / Canadian border, and the next phase of their watch-about.

The drive toward the border was picturesque, but not nearly as breathtaking as the views they had seen in Glacier National Park. Before long, they came to the border and were greeted by a line of vehicles awaiting admittance into Canada.

"Good afternoon, folks," came the polite but reserved greeting from the border agent, Gene Allen, who asked to see their passports and the nature of their visit.

"Good afternoon to you too, officer," came Thaddeus's equally cordial reply. "We're heading to Jasper for a few days and hope to get through Calgary today, probably do some sightseeing around Moraine Lake and spend the night in Banff. We plan to be in Canada about a week before driving back home to Indiana."

Officer Allen looked at their passports and did a cursory look at their vehicle. He was about to send them through to the Canadian side, when out of nowhere an explosion tore through the window of the guard shack. The border agent was just as stupefied as Wade and Thaddeus and reacted too slowly to avoid the next blast. He was hit in the leg by a fusillade of buckshot and went down, alive but seriously wounded.

Wade and Thaddeus leaped from the car and pulled the officer into the safety of the Land Cruiser. Thaddeus looked up as Wade stomped on the accelerator and saw the frightening visage of Curly Algol staring at them and feverishly trying to reload his shotgun before they got away.

Thaddeus crawled over the seat and was doing his best to stem the flow of blood from Gene Allen's shredded leg. The agent was conscious but in shock. Thaddeus took his radio and the agent managed to instruct him how to call the attack in and where to drive for medical assistance and reinforcements.

A long fifteen minutes after his call, there came an armada of Canadian officers, with lights flashing and sirens wailing. They all pulled into the police post near Carway, Alberta, and two officers immediately began administering first aid. The agent was stabilized and airlifted thirty minutes later to the University of Calgary Medical Center. Fortunately he survived thanks to quick medical attention, but he lost his right leg below the knee. He faced pulling desk duty for the remainder of his career, but he was fortunate to be alive.

The other responding officers took off to secure the border, and to try to apprehend the perpetrator. When they arrived, Curly Algol was gone and no one saw what he was driving.

For the next four hours Judge Thaddeus Nathan and Wade Henry gave the provincial police a full accounting of Curly Algol's criminal history. Commander Lex Cobey managed to reach Sheriff Noble Penrod in Prindle County, Indiana and got the official version of Mr. Algol's history. Needless to say, none of the officers on either side of the border were pleased with what had transpired.

"Judge Nathan, first I want to thank you and Mr. Henry for your quick and decisive action. You likely saved officer Allen's life. Sheriff Penrod also informed me of the tragedies that both of you have endured at this maniac's hands, and if not for that, I'd likely be sending both of you back to the states. Having said that, I expect that you'll keep my office fully apprised of your itinerary while in our country, as well as any further episodes that might occur with the fugitive."

Thaddeus and Wade promised to comply in every way that Commander Cobey requested, and then informed him that they were bringing firearms into his country.

"Oh geez," Commander Cobey sighed. "You folks are full of little surprises, aren't you?" An hour later the Commander completed a thorough background check on both Americans and got a provincial judge to approve their bringing firearms into Canada. It had been one helluva morning.

Wade and Thaddeus were both quiet as they drove away from the police station.

When he did speak, the first words out of Wade's mouth were, "Judge, please don't tell mom about this."

Thaddeus nodded his understanding and said, "We'll figure something out, Wade."

Thaddeus took his turn at the wheel now as they cruised north on Route 2 through the towns of Macleod, Claresholm, High River, Okotoks and eventually entered the great western city of Calgary.

He was as stunned by Curly's sudden attack as Wade was, and he felt awful for the officer who had been wounded.

"You know, Wade, we should probably dump this car somewhere safe and rent something that Curly won't recognize," the Judge suggested.

Wade thought about it and said, "Judge, it's like you said a few days ago. We came on this trip to have an adventure, and like you, I'm tired of looking over my shoulder wondering where this bastard is. I vote we stay the course, and if he comes, he comes. Right now I almost welcome it."

The two men looked at each other with resolve in their eyes, and Thaddeus said, "You're a gutsy man, Wade Henry. We'll stay the course then, come what may." He patted the console of the Land Cruiser where the Glocks were stored.

"We also have backup, remember."

A few miles later, Wade said, "Why don't we stop at that diner up ahead and have dinner. I'm in the mood for breakfast."

"Me too," the Judge agreed. "A little comfort food would probably do us both some good. Then, if you're still in the mood for driving, we could make Banff in another hour or so, and I've reserved rooms in another great hotel for us."

Wade liked the idea, and they pulled into the parking lot of the Cattlemen's Diner.

"Goddamit to hell," Curly barked loudly. "That's the second time I let that high and mighty Judge Nathan get away. That's what I get for using a fifty-yard shotgun from sixty yards away. Well, I got the damn cop anyway."

After shooting up the border crossing, Curly beat a hasty escape on Route 6 to Pincher Creek and then worked his way west to Routes 93/95 north. He knew where the judge and that young feller were heading, and his current plan would allow him to sneak up the back way through towns like Skookumchuck, Invermere, and Spillimacheen; then turn east when he got to Golden and head toward Lake Louise. One way or the other, Curly Algol sensed that the end was near; up north in Jasper.

Chapter 36

CASSIE HENRY WAS CONCERNED. She hadn't spoken with Wade or Thaddeus in almost three days and neither had Quentin or Luella. She was actually more than concerned. Wade was the only family she had left, and with each hour of non-communication that passed, she grew more and more anxious. She knew all too well what a bestial person Curly Algol was, and she feared as only a mother can.

While making a presentation to the Kissinger College's Board about the status of her fundraising activities, it was clear that she was uncharacteristically distracted and upset. Her financial figures were very good, but her presentation was off.

After the meeting when the other board members had departed, Lucien Kindred approached her and asked if she'd like to have a cup of coffee. They found a quiet corner in the faculty lounge and sat down. Cassie tried to keep things as professional and normal as possible, but Lucien could see she was in real distress.

"Forgive me for saying so, Cassie, but you don't seem to be quite yourself today."

Cassie looked at him and sighed as if the weight of the world were on her shoulders.

"I'm sorry, Lucien," she said. "I have some family things I need to work through, but I'll keep it together. I promise my work for the college won't suffer."

Lucien Kindred smiled sympathetically and said, "Your work is fine, Cassie, no complaints from anyone. It's you that I'm concerned about."

She sighed again, and said, "Oh Lucien."

Lucien Kindred was a self-made man. He was Canadian by birth having grown up in Toronto. He had come from a very fine family, and while they were not a wealthy family, they were financially comfortable. Lucien's father was a highly regarded pediatrician, and with his dad as a mentor, he learned to contribute to the greater good of society rather than just selfishly grabbing at money.

Even from an early age, Lucien wanted to prove himself, whether it was on an athletic field or academically. He even declined his parents money for tuition to college and chose instead to seek scholarships and earn the rest through work.

Lucien was in his early fifties now; bright, tall, handsome, and quite wealthy. After college he went out west to Edmonton for a summer job in a lumber yard. He fell in love with the region and made it his home. Now, some thirty years later, he owned the lumberyard and nearly a half-million acres of pristine woodland from which he created an enormous, international timbering company. Lucien Kindred gained additional fame through his rigorous corporate practice of replacing every tree they felled with three new seedlings. His business model was world-renowned, as was his spirit of philanthropy.

He had never gone to Kissinger College, but when a position became open on the Kissinger board of trustees, the chairman, Brian Christopher, recruited him as quickly as he could. Brian had known Lucien through international cultural conferences that they both attended, and he thought Lucien would bring a unique perspective to Kissinger's board. Lucien exemplified the personal style and business philosophy that the college hoped would help foster similar attitudes among their students and perhaps inspire their faculty. Recruiting him for the college board was one of the best decisions the school ever made.

"I'm happy to listen, Cassie, if you need to talk," Lucien said.

Cassie closed her eyes and hesitated at first, and then she began talking about her concerns about Wade and Thaddeus. She told Lucien about Curly Algol and his vengeful pursuit of the Judge. Lucien knew that Cassie was not a hysterical personality and that her concerns were well founded. He gave her all the time she needed to express herself.

"I know that Wade is probably fine because he's with Judge Nathan," Cassie admitted, "but not hearing from him, and knowing this killer is chasing after them, has really gotten me terrified."

Lucien offered a suggestion to Cassie. "You know I live in Edmonton, and my corporate jet is over at Prindle County airport. With the board meeting being over now, I'm preparing to fly back. Why don't you fly to Edmonton with me, and then rent a car. Jasper is just a couple of hours due west. It would be an easy trip, and I'll be happy to join you if you feel like you need support."

Cassie sat there with her mouth open not knowing exactly how to respond.

"It sounds like a very good idea, Lucien, but I couldn't possibly prevail upon you like this, and besides my work here needs constant attention."

"Given your achievements this past year, Cassie, no one would begrudge you taking some time off. And, you have legitimate concerns about Wade and Judge Nathan. Plus, I kinda hate to say this, but given my recent financial commitment to the College's capital campaign, I seriously doubt that President Edberg is likely to say no to our going."

Cassie began to decline his invitation again, but the more she thought about it, the more she thought it made sense. It would certainly be more convenient and cheaper than taking a commercial flight to Edmonton or Calgary. She finally relented, and they agreed to meet at the county's airport in three hours after she had a chance to talk with her boss and staff; then pack and talk with Quentin and Luella about her travel plans. This could work out very well she thought.

Cassie met with her supervisor who understood and supported her need to go to Jasper. He really had hoped Cassie would continue to bring in major grants with the frequency she had been doing, but the fact that she was traveling with Lucien Kindred made it a moot point. He also knew that Cassie's staff was very much involved with the grant application process and could carry on quite respectably in her absence.

She arrived home an hour later and saw Quentin and Luella pruning the flower beds and shrubbery in the Judge's yard. She walked over and told them about her plans to go to Jasper to find Wade and the Judge.

"You know, of course, that Wade is going to be really ticked off if you show up there looking to mother him," Quentin said. "I know it's none of my business, but I'm just saying…"

"I hear you, Quentin. I really do, but I just can't sit here waiting for the phone to ring, and if it did, would it be Wade or Thaddeus or heaven forbid, some police department calling to give me horrible news. I'm going, period."

"All right then," Quentin said softly. "I'll get you the name and telephone number of the lodge where Wade and Thaddeus will be staying in Jasper. And Cassie, you know we'll be happy to collect your mail and look after your home while you're gone. We have a key and know the security system. Don't worry about anything here. We've got you covered. Please just be careful and keep us informed, okay."

Cassie thanked them both very much and wished Luella great luck with her second interview with Bernice Sweet on Friday. They went over a few more details and then Cassie hugged them both and hurried to get packed and head for the airport. She knew that Quentin was right in saying that Wade would be fit to be tied when she showed up, but her mind was set. She wasn't sure how Thaddeus would react to it either, but she believed in the adage "It's better to ask for forgiveness afterward, than for permission before."

Another hour later she and Lucien were aboard his jet and cleared for take-off. Destination: Edmonton, Alberta.

Chapter 37

THE DINNER AT THE CATTLEMEN'S DINER was pretty awesome, and the place was packed with casually dressed folks looking for good, wholesome home cooking. Wade ordered a western omelet that came with a short stack of buttermilk pancakes, home fries and sausage. Thaddeus opted for the steak and eggs and hash browns. Both men knew they were overdoing it with calories and fat, but neither really cared a whole lot after the experience they'd had at the border.

Thaddeus pulled out the road atlas, and they both examined it closely over coffee.

"As we head northwest from Calgary, we'll leave the northern plains behind," Thaddeus said. "In an hour we'll be at the continental divide and in the Bow River Valley."

Wade was excited. He knew the Canadian Rockies held a certain mystique for Thaddeus, and he hoped to experience some of that mystique too. He tried texting Kayla but the message couldn't get through. He tried calling his mom and then Quentin, but he had no cell service.

"The days Ellie and I spent here many years ago bring back very fond memories," Thaddeus said quietly. "I recall we spent two days in Canmore, and he pointed to the map. It was a charming town then, and from what I've read, it still is. I suggest that we bypass Canmore for now though and head to Banff. We can stay in Canmore on the way back if we'd like."

Wade was perfectly content following the Judge's suggestions. He had a feeling that it was all going to be spectacular no matter what.

After dinner, Thaddeus took the wheel of the Land Cruiser so Wade would be able to enjoy the changing scenery.

"It's only eighty miles, but it'll be pretty dark by the time we reach Banff," Thaddeus said. "So, we'll have to wait until tomorrow morning to get an eyeful of the real grandeur. With a thin waning crescent moon, though, we could see a ton of stars tonight."

Despite the failing sunlight, Wade was beginning to marvel at the way the land was changing. The Bow River was gorgeous as it swept through the land like a welcoming herd of horses leading them to the town of Banff. He saw signs for Mt. Assiniboine Provincial Park, and he reflected back on his experiences with the Indian elders at the Fort Assiniboine historic site. He wondered if the tribes from these two areas were related by blood and by culture. He wondered if he would have further surprises in the days ahead.

Before long, Wade could feel the dark looming shapes of the mountains engulf them. The crescent moon shone whatever little light it had on the Bow River. The palomino waters glowed in the moonlight.

Thirty minutes later, they arrived in the town of Banff, and drove over the charming bridge in the middle of town. They turned left when they reached Banff's stunning public gardens and headed up a steep road to the left. After a mile he pulled into the hotel's parking lot and turned off the engine at the hotel's entrance.

"Welcome to the Rimrock Hotel, gentlemen," came the greeting from a uniformed attendant. "Will you be joining us as guests?"

"Indeed we will," said Thaddeus with an air of playful nobility. "We'll take our bags, but would you please keep our car handy, sir. We may head out again to do some stargazing."

Several minutes later they checked into their rooms, washed up a bit and re-joined each other in the lobby.

"Wow, this is quite some place, said Wade. My room is awesome. Can't wait to see the view in the morning. I tried looking out the window, but it's too dark."

Thaddeus suggested that they use the hotel's business center to try to email Cassie and Quentin since their cell service still wasn't responding well. Thaddeus knew that Cassie would be getting concerned by now, and he hoped to waylay any fears she had.

When they arrived at the business center, an employee was working on the hotel's computer server and apologized profusely for the hotel's entire communications being down due to recent signal disruptions from unusually powerful solar flares.

"Well, what do you want to do, Wade?" Thaddeus asked. It's been a long day, but if you want to get the binoculars out, I'm game, or we can call it a night and start fresh in the morning. Your call." Wade caught Thaddeus in a yawn. Verdict in.

The next morning shone like nothing Wade had ever seen before. He woke around 7:15 AM; leaped from his bed and threw open the heavy curtains that covered his large picture windows. A celestial light poured through at 186,000 miles per second and nearly bowled Wade over with its brilliance. He felt radiant within the light and stood there with his eyes closed, feeling the sun's energy pour through him. When he re-opened his eyes, the jagged mountains towered around him like gigantic village elders, and the Bow River valley spread out beneath him like a buffet awaiting a hungry soul.

"So, this is what we've been traveling to see," he said quietly to himself. He felt humbled by the majesty of this natural wonder outside his window. The geology alone was magnificent, but when he also thought of the flora and fauna that had habituated this region for millennia, he felt even more awe.

The elk understood their role in this splendor; as did the trout and the ferns. The ground squirrels and the pine trees understood, and the bears and the dragonflies all felt connected in this primordial ecosystem called life.

And the native North Americans understood. Their spirit came from the land and the stars and eventually flowed back to its source. A cycle of life. How Wade admired those peoples who understood the nuances of life in the natural world.

Wade washed up and dressed in his running attire. He attempted to reach his mom again. Still, no luck. He heard a sharp rap on his door and opened it to a beaming Judge Thaddeus Nathan.

"Nice day, huh! I see you're ready for a run," the Judge said. "Why don't you join me in the restaurant for breakfast when you get back, and we'll plan our day. There's a lot to see between here and Lake Louise."

"Deal! I'll be gone ninety minutes," Wade called over his shoulder as he flew past the Judge. Then, he was gone.

Breathe in; breathe out. Wade bolted out the hotel entrance into the welcoming sunshine. His feet crunched gravel as he ran along the shoulder of the road until he found a foot path leading into the woods. Here the earth was firm but soft underfoot, and he felt like he was running on a cushion of mountain air. The early morning dew still clung to the ferns and low shrubs, and his shoes and lower legs were moist as if the natural world were washing away the impurities of man. Wade smiled as he considered this. He felt baptized.

Before long, Wade came to a small clearing in the woods. It was surrounded on three sides by large lichen-splattered boulders.

He bent over and leaned on an outcrop of pink granite and sucked in oxygen. Intellectually, he knew that higher altitudes created challenges in breathing, but Wade figured he was in great physical shape and he wouldn't be affected. He was wrong.

Wade stayed bent over a little longer than he usually did and felt his heart rate begin to ease. When he stood up, he saw a pretty little pond some fifty yards away, and he walked toward it. On the far side a deer was sipping cool water at the pond's edge and didn't appear concerned by Wade's presence. He watched quietly.

When the deer finally slaked its thirst, it looked up and both creatures looked knowingly into the other's eyes. Wade sensed a timeless sentience from the deer that surprised him. He felt a reverence toward the deer that deeply moved him. A moment later the deer snorted, slipped into the surrounding bush and was gone.

Wade stayed still a little longer hoping that the deer would return, but it did not, and Wade walked over to the place the deer had been. Hoof prints were imbedded in the soft sandy bank. Wade took out his cell phone and took some pictures he would send to Kayla and his mom once he regained cell service. He thought about "impressions" and briefly wondered how he would make his mark on the world. He was beginning to have a glimmer of a notion of how he wanted to live his life. Breathe in; breathe out. He returned to the foot path and his route to the future.

"Ah, there you are," the Judge said as Wade joined him in the Rimrock's dining room. "Did you have an eventful run?"

"I did," Wade confirmed, "and I had another unusual experience. I don't know if it means anything, but a deer and I communicated. Not with words, of course, but something transpired that I can't readily explain."

The Judge looked at Wade and smiled. "Your experiences are a bit of an enigma, my young friend. Are you sure you're not a Blackfeet Indian or an Australian Aborigine?"

"I don't think so," said Wade, "but I can't help but feel an unusual inter-connectedness with certain things and people since we've been on our watch-about. You know; the Indian elders, some dreams that I've had, and now with the deer; not to mention our unpleasant connection with Curly Algol. It's all very strange to me, Judge, and no telling what's coming next, huh. No telling at all."

"These are the mysteries of life, Wade, the Judge said solemnly, some things will become clear over time while others may be forever shrouded in the unknown. Perhaps one key to solving these mysteries lies in just being open to examining things in a way you haven't before. And, figuring out how to do that can be a mystery in and of itself."

"Oh gee, Judge, that makes everything clear as mud," Wade replied sarcastically.

"What say we pack our belongings and hit the road, Thaddeus suggested There are several places I want us to see, okay. How about we meet in the lobby in thirty minutes?"

Thirty minutes later they had checked out and were back in the Land Cruiser with Thaddeus driving through the heart of Banff. No more mysteries, so far.

They drove a few miles over to Johnson Lake, and Thaddeus told Wade how he and Ellie had hiked around the lake in their younger days. Thaddeus told him about an old cabin hidden in the forest he and Ellie had happened upon, and he hoped the two of them would find it again.

The two men got out and began walking through a mature hardwood forest. Within twenty feet, they were shaded by a glorious canopy of high leafy limbs. The sun streaked through the leaves casting dappled shadows on a vague earthen path. Wade nodded his head toward the path as if to say, "shall we". They followed it for a few hundred yards, seeing nothing but forest on either side.

They stopped to rest, and it was clear that the Judge was disappointed that they had not found the old hermit's cabin he remembered seeing with Ellie. Thaddeus scanned the perimeter for any sign of a man-made structure. He saw none. Then, he turned to face Wade, and he began to smile.

"What," Wade said. "Why are you smiling like that?"

"Sorry, my friend," the Judge said, "but I'm not smiling at you," and he pointed over Wade's shoulder.

Wade turned in that direction, and it took a moment for his mind to understand that the jumble of logs covered with moss and lichen was indeed the hermit's cabin. They both let out a triumphant hoop and trotted over to see it.

"Great eyes, Judge," Wade complimented. "I don't know if I would have recognized it as a cabin even if I was only ten feet away. Very cool."

Privately, Thaddeus was proud that he hadn't failed on this little adventure. And it was another way for him to keep Ellie's memory alive, plus it proved that his aging eyesight was still up to the task. Very cool indeed!

"I can't believe that it's still here," Thaddeus said softly. "The story goes that a man came to this place many years ago and built this cabin where he lived all alone. They say that he lived here for over thirty years, and no one knew. Eventually civilization encroached and the national parks people had to have known him. He's gone now, but his cabin still exists, sorta.

I wish I knew more about him, but I don't. Funny how some people choose to live their lives away from other people. He had to have had some form of companionship even if it were just the fox and squirrels; maybe a few Indians.

It reminds me," the Judge continued, "there are a lot of ways for people to choose to live their lives. I couldn't live like this, but I understand the desire to be off on one's own, testing oneself against the natural elements and seeing if you're still sane at the end of it. The long winters had to have been brutal, but he endured, and he became a legend. And here we are, two strangers that have stumbled upon his home."

Wade thought about the Judge's words and actually felt honored to be standing near this relic seeing the world as the hermit might've seen it. There was really nothing grand about the structure. The hermit had used stout logs from the forest and shaped cedar bark to create roof shingles. Now moss covered virtually every inch of the cabin, making it difficult to determine where a man-made structure began and the vegetation ended. No, there was really nothing grand about the structure, but in the dappled light, surrounded by a verdant forest, near a beautiful lake, it was one of the most glorious structures Wade had ever seen.

Thaddeus and Wade peered in through the pane-less windows and saw nothing of note except a hearth for cooking and an old wooden platform that might've served as a bed. Wade noticed that the hermit had carved various symbols on the interior log walls. He saw images of a fish and mountains. He saw trees and what appeared to be a bear. And on the wall by the sleeping platform, he saw gouged out stars, with the outlines of two eyes and an arrow pointing up.

"Judge," Wade said, and then again, "Judge, please tell me I'm not seeing this," and he pointed to the wall.

Thaddeus came over and began to shake his head in disbelief at what he saw.

"My dear, Mr. Henry, there has to be a logical explanation for this. This is just too coincidental. Perhaps these same symbols of the stars and the eyes and the upward-pointing arrow are part of a widely-known myth that we're just not familiar with. That's got to be it; otherwise this is just getting too spooky for words."

The two of them looked at the symbols some more and then reluctantly decided it was time to move on. They slowly circumnavigated the rest of the gorgeous lake in an hour and then drove away wondering what would last longer; the cabin itself or the memory of it.

Chapter 38

AFTER FOUR HOURS IN THE AIR, Lucien Kindred's corporate jet landed smoothly at a private air field on the western edge of Edmonton, Alberta. They were greeted by Lucien's right-hand assistant, Gordy Fontaine, who led him to a small office at the air field to handle some corporate business that required his immediate attention.

During their flight, Lucien had radioed ahead and requested that his Cadillac Escalade be available upon their arrival and a duffle packed with outdoor clothes. He also instructed Gordy to contact the police in Jasper about Curly Algol, and to let them know that Judge Nathan and Wade Henry would be staying at the Chalet Village. They were more than happy to oblige Mr. Kindred. And finally, Lucien asked Gordy to stow his Kimber .45 caliber handgun in his gear with extra clips. Gordy had everything ready when they arrived.

"Hey boss," Gordy said. "I packed everything you requested. Any idea how long you might be gone? I'm sure I don't have to remind you we have the deadline coming up in two weeks on the Swan Hills timber acquisition."

"Trust me, my loyal friend, that is not something that I'll let lapse. We have an opportunity to make some dough but more importantly," Lucien said, "we can protect that land from other companies and eventually donate it as a provincial park."

Gordy Fontaine had worked for Lucien for twenty-five years, and even though he occasionally called him 'boss', it was a term of endearment and respect rather than one that defined their relationship. They were almost like brothers.

"So, who's the pretty lady?" Gordy inquired.

Lucien proceeded to tell Gordy about Cassie's position at Kissinger College, and what he knew of the violence that had befallen Cassie and Wade Henry and their neighbor, Judge Nathan. Normally Gordy was never at a loss for words, but he closed his eyes and shook his head in sympathy. He knew Lucien wanted to help.

"I need you to keep a close eye on the business while I'm gone," Lucien said. "Should be only a couple of days, but like you said, the Swan Hills deal is very important to us and to the ecological future of our region. I'm just a call away."

"Don't worry, Lucien, go do what you need to do. I've got this end covered." Lucien returned to his car and saw Cassie anxiously walking about.

"I just tried calling Wade again, Lucien, and I still can't get through," Cassie lamented. "Something just isn't right. It's not like Wade to be out of touch, and definitely not like the Judge."

"C'mon Cassie, let's go find them," Lucien said, and they climbed inside the Escalade which Gordy had stocked with beverages, salads and sandwiches for their four-hour drive to Jasper.

Curly Algol was growing weary. It had been a very long drive from Indiana, and he had failed in his two opportunities to kill Judge Nathan. He stopped in the town of Golden, British Columbia to gas up the Maxima and get some lunch. He actually liked the little town, mainly because it was in the middle of nowhere.

"Soon," he thought, "very soon and I'll be in Jasper and that high and mighty Judge Nathan won't escape this time. Then, maybe I'll go see those pretty señoritas down Mexico way."

The drive east, over the continental divide, to the town of Field was breathtaking, even to a deranged nut case like Curly. The town was a charming little spot nestled in the middle of Yoho National Park. Curly pulled up to the old telegraph station at the entrance to town and got out of the car to stretch his legs and glance at his map. Soon; very soon, he thought.

It took Curly all of two minutes to drive through the town. After seeing such highlights as the water tower and the Truffle Pig Inn, he decided he had better keep moving north.

He decided to avoid the area around Lake Louise because of all the tourists but thought he might stop at the Athabasca Glacier along the Columbia Icefield parkway. He had never seen a glacier before, and he thought he ought to pay it a visit before all that global warming stuff occurred and melted it into a big crick. He drove on and couldn't believe the mountains and streams that he saw. Soon; very soon!

"Sure don't look like the cornfields back home," he mumbled to himself. And then he remembered he had no home.

<hr>

Thaddeus and Wade continued driving north along Route 93 and stopped for lunch at Chateau Lake Louise, one of the truly grand hotels in all of Canada. They sat on the patio outside of the main dining room and marveled at the turquoise-colored lake and the snow capped peaks.

"Oh Ellie," the Judge whispered to himself. "It's been a long time since we were here." He stared off into the mountains, and Wade noticed a small tear form at the corner of his eye.

Wade took pictures of the lake and mountains and tried sending them to Kayla.

"I can't believe how crummy the cell service is up here," Wade grumped out loud.

"Believe me," the Judge countered, "there will be plenty of times in your life when you'll be thrilled to be 'non-communicato' with the outside world. Try to enjoy the grandeur all around us. You'll be back in touch with the world soon enough."

Wade nodded his understanding, but he still wanted to connect with Kayla and show her the beauty he was seeing.

They left Lake Louise and continued their adventure, stopping at Kicking Horse and Takakkaw Falls; then on to the Athabasca Glacier.

"This glacier is one of the premier night sky viewing spots in all of North America," Thaddeus said. "I'm eager to get to Jasper, but maybe we can stop here on the way home."

They drove past Mt. Columbia, Mt. Alberta and Mt. Edith Cavell, all of which were over eleven thousand feet in elevation. An hour later they finally arrived at their destination… Jasper, Alberta. They were two thousand miles from home.

Wade tried one more time to text Kayla. His message was brief. "We made it!" He hit the send key, and a moment later saw that his message had been delivered.

Thaddeus drove the Land Cruiser to the center of town, parallel to the railroad tracks. They parked and decided to walk around Jasper to visit some shops and stop into the visitors' information center to get a map of the area.

"Look here, Wade," Thaddeus pointed. "That's the shop where Ellie and I got you the soapstone polar bear sculpture." They went inside and marveled at the fine native artifacts that they saw.

Thaddeus told the manager that he and his wife had visited the shop some twenty years earlier, and he asked if they still carried work by the artist, Shytoo Muckpah. He was delighted when the manager pointed out some of her recent work. Thaddeus bought a lovely soapstone sculpture of an Inuit Indian in a kayak for Quentin. He also purchased a lovely bracelet for Luella for helping watch his home. Wade bought beaded earrings for his mom and a pretty little stone pendant for Kayla.

They made a quick stop in the visitors center and had a helpful conversation with a volunteer on duty. The three of them looked at a map together showcasing some of the nearby major highlights like Maligne Canyon. Thaddeus was excited that he and Wade would be going there tomorrow.

After their walking tour of Jasper, they got their bearings and retraced their way back to the southern entrance to town and finally pulled into the lot of the Chalet Village, just across the road from the roiling, milky waters of the Athabasca River.

The village was one of the prettiest places that Wade had ever seen. All of the cabins were beautifully crafted and the grounds were carefully attended to.

"Greetings gentlemen," came the bright voice of Marly Hilton, the owner of the village. "How may we help you?"

Thaddeus said, "I'm Thaddeus Nathan, and this fine young man is Wade Henry, and I believe we have reservations in one of your cabins for the next three days."

As Marly checked her computer to confirm their reservations, Thaddeus couldn't help but notice how lovely she was with her honey blonde hair, petite figure and engaging smile. He guessed she was in her early sixties. He felt a pang of guilt for admiring her loveliness and managed to contain his appreciation.

"You sure do," she said. "We have you in cabin # 8 just around the corner here. I believe the room has already been prepared for your arrival."

She took an imprint of Thaddeus' credit card and his vehicle information and handed them two door keys. Marly encouraged them to let her know if there was anything she could do to help make their visit enjoyable. The men thanked her and drove the Land Cruiser to #8. An elk and her calf were grazing on their front lawn.

"Wow," Wade exclaimed. "This place is awesome, Judge! Everything about it is perfect!"

He snapped a few quick photos of the Elk and proceeded to email them to Kayla; and then in a separate email he sent them to his mom and Quentin.

Thaddeus was delighted that Wade was so pleased and shared his excitement.

They quietly unpacked their gear and walked past the grazing elk who could've cared less that they were being joined by humans.

After stowing their gear inside and checking out the cabin's amenities, Wade said he wanted to go for a run and pointed to the path that ran along the banks of the Athabasca River. A few minutes later, he had changed into his running gear, stretched his travel-stiff legs and was off on another running adventure.

Breathe in; Breathe out. Wade's legs felt stiff at first, but after the first hundred yards, he felt like he was hitting his stride. The path was fairly flat and the ground underneath his feet was sandy but firm. And his view was spectacular.

The Athabasca River was unlike any waterway he'd ever seen close-up, and now he was running beside it, trying to keep pace. The color of the water looked like milk, and Thaddeus had explained earlier to him that the milkiness was the result of being glacially fed. The river was low and broad and scattered with scores of submerged boulders that made the water look like a rolling herd of white stallions charging alongside him. It was a powerful yet visually-appealing scene, and he loved being a part of it.

Beyond the river were the Canadian Rockies, and everywhere he glanced the scene looked like something out of a travel brochure. The skies were a deep blue, with an occasional puffy white cloud. The trees were so lush in their verdant foliage, pines, oaks, maples; on and on for miles upon miles extending far north to the tundra. But it was the mountains that attracted his attention. They were enormous and endless and solemnly commanded the landscape like cathedrals of nature.

Breathe in; Breathe out. Wade kept a steady pace until he came to the bridge near the entrance to Tekkara Lodge. Here he slowed to a brisk walk to catch his breath. Wade really was thrilled that the Judge brought him on this trip. It was a perfect way to have some separation from Wade Henry the high school kid to Wade Henry the ________. The "what?!"

For the first time in maybe forever Wade began to question what he wanted to do with his life; not just in college, but for a career, for marrying and raising a family. These were all big, tough adult issues, and he wasn't sure of anything right now.

At first, these thoughts were distressing to him, but then as he looked around the grand landscape, and he thought about his recent experiences with the Indians, and definitely Curly, he became more comfortable with the concept of taking his time to make decisions that felt right for him.

"Too much thinking," Wade said out loud to himself. "It's like running, remember? One foot in front of the other. Tackle one issue at a time." Breathe in; breathe out.

Wade reversed his course, running with the Athabasca River now on his left side. The herd of white river stallions were now rushing toward him instead of with him. He welcomed their forceful motion and the challenge of going against the flow.

When Wade returned to the Chalet Village, Thaddeus was sitting in one of the Adirondack chairs by the river's edge watching the swift milky waters flow by.

Wade joined him, and the two men sat quietly for several minutes taking in the natural beauty all around them.

"It's like life, isn't it," Wade said. "I mean the river keeps flowing on and on, seeking its own path."

"Yes," the Judge agreed, "until such time that it flows no more… and then even the river will eventually vaporize and become stardust."

Wade considered Thaddeus' perspective. Here he was a young man with ostensibly a lifetime of experiences in front of him, and the Judge was an older man, certainly not decrepit, but old enough to know that there was an inescapable end point out there. The two men were looking at the same river, but saw it in uniquely personal ways.

"I'm starting to get hungry," the Judge said. "Why don't we head in to the grocery store in town and pick up enough food for the next couple of days. We've spent over a week eating in restaurants, and it was be nice to prepare a home-cooked meal."

"Then," Wade suggested, "maybe we can pull out the binoculars and set them up over by the Adirondack chairs. The skies are clear, and it could be a great night for viewing; especially with the sounds of the river for accompaniment."

With dinner over and the dishes cleaned and put away, Thaddeus and Wade pulled out their pairs of Oberwerk binoculars. The sun had dipped below the western mountains, and a purple and rose-colored hue stretched over the darkening land.

The chairs and the river were just on the other side of the road from the Chalet Village which made it very convenient for hauling and setting up their gear. They sat by the river for about twenty minutes waiting for the skies to darken more and for their eyes to adjust.

It was a perfect night outside with the air temperature hovering around sixty-eight degrees and very little wind. Wade and Thaddeus had been outdoors for about forty-five minutes looking at various constellations and their major stars when they heard someone crossing the road to join them.

"I thought you fellas might like some beverages while you're out here enjoying the universe," Marly Hilton said. "Thought maybe a couple of pitchers of Sangria might hit the spot."

"Well, you certainly run a full-service operation here," Thaddeus gently teased, "but in all seriousness that's very kind of you to bring us some libations. Why don't you join us, Marly?"

Marly set the pitcher on a small table and asked what they were looking at. Wade proceeded to tell her about the constellation Leo the Lion that was facing downward in the southwestern sky.

"Oh," Marly said. "That's the constellation that has Regulus at the lion's heart, Algieba above it near the sickle, and Denebola at the tip of Leo's tail."

Both men looked at each other in total disbelief and then stared at her in shock.

"How do you know so much about Leo?" Wade asked.

"My husband passed away a dozen years ago, but he was a dedicated amateur astronomer, and we spent many a night together under the stars looking up into the heavens. I wasn't as enthused about it as he was, but you know, over time you just pick up on things. Leo is so grand, and it's always been a favorite of mine."

Thaddeus shook his head in amazement and thought to himself, "Hmm, very pretty and smart as a whip too." They spent the next two hours taking turns looking through the binoculars, drinking Sangria and getting acquainted. A perfect night.

Chapter 39

Back home in Indiana, Quentin and Luella continued to settle into their lifestyle together.

"I called my boss earlier," Quentin said, "and he told me he needed me back on the job on Monday. He's really been terrific allowing me to take the time off, but it's time that I became a working stiff again."

Luella had really grown to enjoy their time together and had felt like she and Quentin worked really well sharing responsibilities in keeping the Judge's and Cassie's homes in great shape. Plus, he wasn't bossy. If anything, Quentin made a genuine effort to ask her opinion of things, and it became clear to Luella that he liked her a lot. Happily, she felt the same way too.

"Well, you knew they'd need the best UPS driver in Indiana before too long," Luella complimented. "I can keep an eye on both places while you're at work. I have my second interview with Bernice Sweet in Kissinger's admissions office tomorrow at 3:00. If I get the job as her assistant, I think Ms. Sweet will want me to start fairly soon. But even if both of us are working, Quentin, we'll manage."

For the first time since Luella had stumbled down Brick Chapel Road and into his life, Quentin pulled her close and gently kissed her on the lips. Luella kissed back.

Curly drove north on Route 93 along the spine of the Canadian Rockies and passed by the same mountains that Thaddeus and Wade had passed earlier in the day. He was planning to stop at the Athabasca Glacier and go for a tourist ride on the ice, but once he saw it from the visitors parking lot, he thought the glacier was over-rated. Just a bunch of snow and ice coming off a mountain.

"Hell, I've seen more snow on Waterworks Hill back home in Prindle County," he said smugly. And then he remembered again that he no longer had a home in Prindle County. He leered at himself in the car's rearview mirror, but a brief flash of sadness overtook him, and his leer faded to a boyish frown.

Curly continued driving north and an hour later he entered the town of Jasper, Alberta. He had arrived. Now all he had to do was find Judge Nathan and finish the job. But where to look?

He pulled the Maxima over to the side of the main street through town and sat there watching a very long train inch its way along. He turned his gaze to look at the people on the other side of the street, and he noticed the Jasper visitor information center.

"Ah, now if I was new in town and didn't know my way around these parts, I might just stop in this joint and get me a map and some touristy type information. I wonder if the Judge and that kid with him would do that. One way to find out, I reckon."

Curly exited the Maxima and crossed the busy street, flipping the bird at motorists.

"Now be cool," he said to himself. "Don't go causing no ruckus. Just want to ask a few friendly questions is all. Just looking for my buddies," Curly rehearsed to himself.

Curly entered the information center and saw two volunteers on duty. One volunteer was helping another tourist; so Curly approached the other man behind the counter. There was no one else in the room, but he reminded himself to be cool; no ruckus.

"Say, I just got into town," Curly said, "and I'm supposed to hook up with some buddies, but I lost my phone and don't know how to call them. I don't suppose you saw an older man and a teenage boy come in from Indiana earlier today; maybe yesterday."

"Sorry sir, but I don't recall seeing anyone who fits that description today, and I didn't work yesterday."

Curly was disappointed and turned to leave when he heard the other volunteer say, "Older fellow with a younger man, yeah, they came in earlier. Said they had driven all the way from Indiana to do some hiking and stargazing. They got some maps and brochures, and we talked about some points of interest."

"Oh, thank you very much," Curly said as politely as he was able. "Don't suppose they said which places they'd be visiting. Sure would like to hook back up with them."

"Seems I recall they were excited about seeing Maligne Canyon. The older gent said he'd been there many years ago with his wife and wanted his young friend to see it. I remember they talked about going tomorrow actually. Here's one of the Canyon's brochures," the volunteer said, and he plucked one from the rack on the wall.

Curly damn near peed his pants with excitement. He could not believe his luck. Now, all he had to do was find the place, wait for the Judge and blast him.

The sun was beginning to get lower in the west as Lucien and Cassie began their drive toward Jasper. Cassie was exhausted from the travel and her anxiety about Wade. She checked her phone for cell service again but had no luck. Her dread worsened. She closed her eyes and before long she somehow drifted off to sleep and then began to dream.

In her dream, Cassie was in a beautifully wild setting with large rock formations and swift water cascading through a deep gorge. She was walking alone in this rugged place, calling out Wade's and Thaddeus' names. The only sound she heard back was the deafening sound of the fast water hitting rocks.

Lucien saw that Cassie was in a deep, fitful sleep and thought of gently touching her shoulder to rouse her but decided to leave her alone. She needed the rest.

"No, no!" Lucien heard her mumble in her dream state. "Wade, be careful," he heard her say. Then, she grew quiet again.

A few minutes later Cassie woke up and looked over at Lucien who offered her a supportive smile. "How was your nap?" he asked. "You looked like you were dreaming."

"I was. I just had an unsettling dream about trying to find Wade in a very unusual place. I guess it's because I haven't been able to connect with him by phone. I'm sorry Lucien, but I don't think I'll be able to totally relax until I finally see him."

Lucien nodded at her and said, "We'll be in Jasper in less than three hours. I suggest we head straight for the Chalet Village. I suspect their office may be closed by the time we arrive, so we may have to be flexible about accommodations."

They saw a highway sign giving mileage for the towns of Edson and Hinton. Then for Jasper. One hundred and forty miles ahead.

Chapter 40

THE NEXT MORNING'S SUNLIGHT came streaming through the cabin's windows with a golden glow that appeared almost celestial. Wade pulled his pillow over his head to block the light, but then he remembered where he was and bolted upright to look out his bedroom window.

He smiled when he saw the elk calf on their front lawn calmly grazing on tender shoots. He figured the Judge was still in his room sleeping off the residual effects of Marly's pitchers of Sangria. Wade quietly crept from his room so as not to disturb Thaddeus and slipped out the front door.

The elk calf looked up and casually snorted when she saw Wade; then went back to grazing. The calf's mama was in the next yard happily grazing too. She was equally as unperturbed by Wade's presence. Wade took a few photos of the mother and calf with his cell phone and emailed them to Kayla, his mom and Quentin.

Wade decided to walk up to the Chalet Village office and get two cups of coffee in the lobby for Thaddeus and him. A young woman was on duty at the front desk, but Marly came into the lobby when she heard Wade's voice.

"That was a lot of fun last night," she said to Wade. "It brought back many fond memories when my husband and I would stay out late enjoying the night sky. So, what are your plans for today?"

"Not entirely sure yet," Wade replied, "but I know the Judge really wants us to see Maligne Canyon; so I guess that'll be first on our list. You're welcome to join us if you'd like, Marly."

"As much as I would love to do that, Wade, I have a bunch of things I really need to take care of around here this morning. Maybe later this afternoon, the three of us could drive to the Valley of the Five Lakes. Each lake is a different color. It's not far, and the hiking is pretty easy."

"That sounds very cool," Wade said. "I'll suggest it to the Judge, and we'll let you know, okay. We'll probably head for the canyon after we have breakfast."

When Wade got back to the cabin, Thaddeus was dressed and sitting on the cabin's front steps tossing pieces of apple and celery to the mama elk and calf.

"Ah, there you are," came the Judge's greeting as Wade returned, "and I see you've brought coffee. Bless you!" He pointed to the two elk and said, Our woodland friends here seem to have had their breakfast already. Are you ready for some bacon and eggs and toast?"

The two men dawdled over their breakfast and enjoyed second cups of coffee that Wade brewed as Thaddeus prepared their meal. The elk had apparently enjoyed enough of their human entertainment and casually wandered off into the woods.

After cleaning up the breakfast dishes, the two men took turns showering and straightened up their belongings. They drove up to the Village office, and while Thaddeus went inside to say hello to Marly and confirm directions to Maligne Canyon, Wade walked over to see the classic red pickup truck and admired the terrific restoration work someone had done to it.

"G'morning, Marly," Thaddeus said as he entered the lobby. "Looks like another glorious day!"

"Morning Thaddeus, came Marly's friendly reply. "It is a glorious day indeed, and it's nice to hear you finally call me by my first name instead of Ms. Hilton."

"We sure had fun last night," Thaddeus said, "and it was really nice of you to join us, though I must admit that I'm feeling a little fuzzy around the edges from your great Sangria."

"Well, I might've cheated a little by putting in some white rum. My own recipe," she confided playfully.

"So Thaddeus," Marly asked. "What's on your agenda today? Wade said you and he would probably go to Maligne Canyon. It's one of my favorite places for hiking."

"Yeah, it's been many years since I was there last. My late wife, Ellie, and I fell in love with the canyon's geology, and I recall they have a nice little restaurant there too."

"They call it a 'tea house', and a friend of mine manages it. Tell Bekka that I sent you, and she'll take good care of you. You guys really should plan to see the Valley of the Five Lakes too. It's beautiful, and if I'm free by then, I'd like to join you."

"Sounds like a fine idea," Thaddeus said, and the two of them held each other's gaze for a few moments longer. Then feeling slightly embarrassed, the Judge said, "Well, I guess we best be on our way to the canyon. We'll plan to see you later this afternoon then, okay?"

Thaddeus walked out of the Villager office feeling like an adolescent schoolboy. He called over for Wade, who was still admiring the red pickup truck, to join him at the Land Cruiser. They got in, buckled up and took off down the road.

"If I'm not mistaken," Wade said as he was looking at the brochure for Maligne Canyon, 'maligne' means evil or bad. That sounds rather ominous to me."

"You're correct," Thaddeus confirmed. "Odd that such a beautiful place would have such a forbidding name."

After flying nearly two-thirds of the way across north america and then driving another couple of hours west, Cassie and Lucien decided to book two rooms in a motel in Pocahontas, Alberta. They figured the Chalet Village would be closed by the time they arrived, so they decided to get a good night's rest and drive the remainder of the way in the morning.

They got up early the next day, had a quick breakfast and arrived in Jasper an hour later.

About thirty minutes after Wade and Thaddeus left for Maligne Canyon, Marly looked up from the front desk and saw a couple in a Cadillac Escalade pull into the Chalet Village parking lot. The couple got out, stretched their travel-weary limbs and entered the lobby.

"Good morning, folks, welcome to the Chalet Village," Marly said cheerfully. "How may I help you?"

Cassie spoke first and said, "Good morning, I'm Cassie Henry and this is my friend, Lucien Kindred. We were hoping to speak with the owner or the manager please."

Marly sensed a tone of urgency in Cassie's voice, and she said, "I'm Marly Hilton, and I'm the owner of the Chalet Village." Again she said, "How can I help you?"

"First," Cassie said, please tell me my son, Wade Henry, is staying here with Judge Nathan, and that they're both okay."

"Cassie, I can see that you're very concerned about something, and that's certainly your personal business, but I can tell you they were both doing very well last night when the three of us did some stargazing across the road for a couple of hours. And, they were fine this morning when I spoke with both of them about thirty minutes ago. So, I'm a little confused by your concern."

Just then Marly's assistant, Jacquelyn, entered the lobby, and Marly asked her to take over the front desk while the two new guests joined Marly in her personal office. She motioned for Cassie and Lucien to follow her.

Once seated in Marly's office, Lucien looked over at Cassie and spoke for the first time.

"Marly, we have a rather unique and sensitive situation that we'd like to share with you, and we'd also like to rent a cabin with two bedrooms if you have lodging available. And, I want to assure you that we are not cranks, and we wouldn't be speaking with you now unless it was very important."

"Mr. Kindred," Marly said, "everyone in Canada knows who you are, and it's an honor to have you stay with us. First things first though, what's going on?"

Cassie took the lead again and sensed that it was okay to share personal details with Marly about Curly Algol's history of murder, including Wade's father and Thaddeus' wife, Ellie. She informed Marly about Curly's trail of murder and mayhem across multiple states and his goal to get revenge on Judge Nathan.

Cassie explained how important the Judge was to her and Wade, and how they all wanted this trip to be a special graduation gift for Wade, and a time for the two of them to go off on their own walkabout. Cassie told Marly that she hadn't spoken with Wade in four days now and was extremely concerned.

She went on to explain her position at Kissinger College and Lucien's role on the board of directors. She told Marly how grateful she was to Lucien for helping her get to Jasper and to help look for Wade and the Judge. Now, all she wanted to do was make sure they were safe.

Marly listened intently as Cassie and Lucien continued to fill in details. She was spellbound and stunned by what she was hearing.

"I am so sorry, Cassie, that you've had to endure any of this, and Lucien, you're a good man for helping her out this way. Thaddeus and Wade hadn't shared any of this with me, which is totally understandable, and honestly they seem to be doing just fine. They left here less than an hour ago to hike Maligne Canyon which is only about twenty minutes from us."

Marly buzzed Jacquelyn in the lobby, and asked her to re-arrange her schedule to handle the front desk until she returned in a couple of hours.

Then, she said to Cassie and Lucien, "C'mon, let's go to the canyon and find them. We can look for them at the tea house by the entrance to the park."

Cassie breathed a huge sigh of relief. They all climbed into the Escalade, with Lucien behind the wheel and Marly serving as navigator.

Curly Algol had spent the night in his car in a campground on the outskirts of Jasper. He was stiff from sleeping in the Maxima and hadn't shaved or bathed since his stay at the Lone Pine motel near Kalispell. He looked awful and smelled worse. He went to a rest room at the campground and tried his best to clean up his act, but his clothes smelled as badly as he did. A young boy took one look at Curly as he entered the rest room and ran screaming for his mommy.

After jimmying the vending machine for his breakfast consisting of Cheetos and Mountain Dew, Curly got back in the car and drove over to the parking lot at Maligne Canyon.

"Be cool now, Curly boy," he cooed to himself. "I got a feeling that today's the day for final justice with that high and mighty Judge Thaddeus Nathan."

He slumped down in the driver's seat, pulled his ball cap low over his eyes and scoped out the people who arrived at the park. No sight of the Judge yet. He reached behind him and lugged his daddy's shotgun up to the front seat with him. He had four shotgun shells left, and he aimed to make good use of them.

Chapter 41

DURING THE DRIVE TO Maligne Canyon, Wade read out loud to the Judge about the canyon's unique features.

"Says here in the Parks Canada brochure that Maligne Canyon is the deepest gorge in the Canadian Rockies. At some points it's only six feet across but 160 feet deep. It's carved out of the Palliser Formation which is a layer of limestone deposited in a shallow sea by lime-secreting plankton about 365 million years ago. There are four bridges across the gorge which features waterfalls, fossils, potholes and underground stream outlets."

"Sounds very interesting," the Judge said, "but as you know, 'one picture is worth a thousand words.' Wait till you see the place. The geology is a little like our Turkey Run State Park in Indiana but even more dramatic."

When Wade and Thaddeus arrived at the entrance to the park, there were only a few visitors strolling from the lot to the canyon. Thaddeus pulled the Land Cruiser into the parking lot, and concealed the telescope and binoculars under a tarp. He reached into the car's console and pulled out one of the Glocks and slipped it securely into the waistband of his jeans and pulled out his shirt tails to hide it.

Wade watched as Thaddeus hid the firearm and asked, "Expecting trouble, Judge?"

"Not necessarily, Wade, but forewarned is forearmed, and I don't plan on our being too casual with Curly on the loose." Wade thought about taking the other Glock and then decided he'd rather let the Judge do any shooting that needed to be done.

"C'mon," Thaddeus said. "Let's fill our water bottles at the tea house and say hello to Marly's friend, Bekka, if she's around."

Bekka Dillard was a stout woman, about sixty years old, who had a jolly demeanor and could easily be mistaken for Santa Claus' wife. She became even jollier when Wade and Thaddeus introduced themselves and told her that Marly Hilton said they should stop in to say hello.

"When you guys get back from your hike, stop in the tea house, and I'll make sure you're well taken care of. Marly and I go way back, and any friends of hers are friends of mine. She's a smart, sharp lady, and treats everyone graciously. The men thanked Bekka and set off walking down a verdant path into the waiting maw of Maligne Canyon.

Within fifty feet of entering the canyon, their world was totally transformed. Gone from sight were the huge mountains that surrounded Maligne Canyon in all directions. Gone too were the big skies above and the distant vistas beyond. And thankfully, the unnatural din of motorized vehicles was gone as well.

Here, within the canyon they were in a different ecosystem, with a broad canopy of trees overhead, occasional sub-tropical vegetation, massive stone limestone walls and soft pine needles underfoot.

But the feature they noticed the most was the sound of rushing water cascading onto rocks.

Thaddeus stopped walking and closed his eyes. He breathed in the humid air, and absorbed his surroundings.

"Listen," he whispered to Wade. "Listen to the sound of the water."

Wade closed his eyes too and did as the Judge suggested. He held this pose for several pensive moments, and it was an almost mystical experience. In those very brief moments he flashed back on the Indian elders he had encountered along the way and the deer he saw by the pond near the Rimrock. He breathed in the canyon air and felt a certain connection with all of his surroundings that he couldn't explain. He felt comfortable with that too. Perhaps he was part Blackfeet Indian after all.

When he opened his eyes, Thaddeus was smiling at him in a paternal way.

"Well, my friend, we made it, didn't we? Despite driving two thousand miles and dodging one crazy lunatic the entire way, not to mention having more than a few spooky experiences, we made it."

"We sure have," Wade offered, "and it's been a terrific trip so far. I know my dad would've loved seeing this part of the world; mom too. I can't thank you enough, Judge, for making this all possible."

"My pleasure, Wade," Thaddeus softly added. "It's been very special for me too. What say we keep going. I wanted us to stop here and listen to the water. Sort of like centering ourselves spiritually while paying homage to the spirit of the land."

Curly was growing very impatient sitting in the car. The sun was well up in the sky, and he was getting hot and grumpy, plus he needed to pee.

He got up to use the port-o-let, and as he was walking back he noticed a black Toyota Land Cruiser parked on the other side of a large recreational vehicle. It was only about ten spaces away from where he was parked, but he hadn't seen it because the RV blocked his view. Curly looked around cautiously and then walked over to the Land Cruiser. It had Indiana license plates.

"I'll be damned," Curly muttered to himself. "Been sitting here all this time, wondering where those two pricks are, and they've been here all along."

He walked back to the Maxima, grabbed the shotgun, loaded two shells and put the other two shells in his pocket.

He leered at himself in the car's rearview mirror and proclaimed, "Time to do me some hunting!"

Twenty minutes after leaving the Chalet Village, Marly showed Lucien where to park the Escalade in the Maligne Canyon's parking lot. The three of them got out and began walking toward the tea house when Cassie pulled up short and said, "That's Thaddeus' car. See, it's got Indiana license plates. They're here."

It was a short walk to the lovely tea house, and Marly led the way. Bekka saw them enter and strolled over to welcome Marly and her friends.

"Well, if it's not one of my favorite people in the whole world," Bekka called out to Marly. "Where have you been, girl?"

"Working hard; same as you," Marly replied. "You're looking good!"

"Aw! Oh, and those two nice gentlemen stopped by a bit ago to send your good wishes. Fine men, both. I told them to stop back after their hike, and we'd take care of some lunch for them. So, I guess maybe two hours from now they'd be back, give or take."

Marly introduced her friends, Cassie and Lucien, and said they were hoping to connect with Wade and Thaddeus sooner than two hours. They needed a plan.

Bekka excused herself to assist a customer and Cassie, Marly and Lucien moved over to a corner to talk among themselves.

"I say we split up," Cassie said. "I recommend that since Marly knows the lay of the land in the canyon that she goes in there to look for them.

Lucien, how about you stay with your car in the parking lot and keep a really close eye on Thaddeus' Land Cruiser? That way we'd have it covered if they returned straight to their car; or if we needed a ride in a hurry. I can keep watch by the entrance to the tea room."

When Cassie finished with her recommendations, Marly and Lucien looked at each other with raised eyebrows. They were both impressed.

"I think your plan makes a lot of sense," Lucien said, and I'm fine with it if you are, Marly."

Marly knew Maligne Canyon like it was her own backyard. She couldn't begin to tell you how many times she had been here over the years. She knew it very well; both its beauty and its dangers.

"Okay," Marly said, "but remember we're not going to have cell phone coverage here, so our ability to communicate with each other is going to be severely compromised."

"There's one more important point that we haven't discussed," Lucien stated. "There's this Curly Algol person that we have to factor in. We don't know exactly where he is right now, but we should be equally on the lookout for him."

All three of them nodded their understanding, and Marly took off at a brisk pace into Maligne Canyon.

"Lucien, I am so sorry to have dragged you into this mess. It's very unprofessional, and heavens knows, you have more important things to be doing than roaming around the countryside helping all of us. It must come off as pretty darn nutty at best and down-right scary at worst."

"Cassie, we'll get together with Wade and Thaddeus very soon," he comforted her, "In the meantime, let's follow your plan and get into position."

"Oh, and Cassie," he continued, "I must say I've never experienced an adventure quite like this before. Later on maybe you can tell me what you have planned for an encore."

They both laughed a little and Cassie thanked Lucien very much again. Then, they went to their positions.

Chapter 42

CURLY ALGOL STRODE INTO Maligne Canyon like a man on a malignant mission. He felt like a shark who smelled blood in the water. He reckoned there couldn't be too many ways in an out of this place, so he'd just 'be cool' and keep his eyes peeled. His double-barreled shotgun dangled from his arm.

"Now, where are you, Judge?" he whispered to himself.

As he got further into the canyon, he came to a wooden bridge that traversed the gorge. A group of six college-age students were on the bridge enjoying the canyon's beauty and taking photographs. Curly kept up his forceful stride as he approached the bridge, and the students spread out like Moses parting the Red Sea when Curly came barreling through.

"Hey, can't you say you're sorry?" one of the male students hollered.

Curly kept walking.

"Asshole!" came a second confrontation from the student.

Curly's pace slowed and then he stopped. He turned around and looked at the kid.

"Hey, can't you say you're sorry for the way you busted through us like that," the kid said more apprehensively when he saw that Curly was armed.

Curly thought about the words the kid had just uttered, "Can't you say you're sorry?" Curly knew the answer. He couldn't say it. Not for his ma, not his pa, nor Luella, nor for a whole bunch of people. He existed in a psychological abyss from which he'd never return. And he certainly wasn't going to say he was sorry to these snooty-ass college pukes.

Curly leered at the kids and pointed his shotgun straight up in the air.

"Seems to me you ought to be the ones apologizing for blocking the bridge that way," Curly reprimanded.

"Gee mister, we're sorry, but we were here first," came the same boy's lame reply.

"Well maybe 'sorry' isn't good enough," Curly lectured again, and he lowered the shotgun in the boy's direction.

With that, all six kids took off running in the opposite direction, back toward the entrance to the canyon, and hopefully to safety.

Curly laughed at the spectacle of their hightailing it. He pointed the shotgun straight up in the air again and pulled the trigger. Kaboom!

"That'll teach them to mess with good old Curly," he chortled to himself.

The sound of the shotgun blast echoed all throughout Maligne Canyon. Marly stopped dead in her tracks when she heard the blast and a minute later she was passed by six terror-stricken students. The boy who had confronted Curly was the last to reach her, and she grabbed him by the shirtsleeve and asked him what happened.

"There's a crazy man down by the first bridge with a shotgun." Then he took off running again to catch up with his friends.

Marly debated on whether to go back to the tea house and get help, but she figured the kids and anyone else who heard the blast would call the police. She forged ahead deeper into Maligne Canyon. She didn't know what she would do if she ran into the crazy man, but given what Cassie and Lucien had told her about Curly, she wanted to help Thaddeus and Wade if it was him. She quickened her pace.

Cassie had also heard the shotgun blast up by the tea house and her blood went cold with fear for Wade and Thaddeus, and Marly too. She went inside the tea house and found Bekka who immediately placed a call to the police station and to her supervisor at the Parks Canada office.

Lucien also heard the unmistakable shotgun discharge while seated in the Escalade. He debated about whether he should hustle up to the tea house to join Cassie, but he re-considered in case the Judge and Wade made a bee line for the Land Cruiser. Lucien instinctively patted his lap to confirm that his Kimber pistol was still where he had placed it. He wanted to be ready for anything.

Curly broke into a fast trot along the trail. He suspected that Judge Nathan and that kid were ahead of him, and he wanted to get his revenge and escape into the forest before the cops showed up.

Thaddeus and Wade were standing near a waterfall by the second bridge when they also heard what they thought was a shotgun blast.

Wade turned to Thaddeus and nervously asked, "Did that sound like a shotgun to you, Judge?"

"Sure did, Wade. Even with the noise from the waterfall, I'd know that distinct sound anywhere. C'mon, let's go see what's going on… and be careful."

They took off following the path back toward the first bridge. No other people were around now, and there were no sounds from birds or other wildlife. The only sounds they heard were their footsteps and their breathing and the rush of flowing water.

The trail back was slightly uphill, and Wade was soon several yards ahead of the Judge. When Thaddeus came around a corner, he saw that Wade had stopped on the trail with his back to the edge of a fifteen-foot drop into the gorge. Then, he saw why Wade had stopped. Curly Algol was standing twenty yards away with his shotgun pointed at him. He had a menacing leer on his face.

Thaddeus slowly walked up beside Wade and looked into the eyes of his long-time nemesis.

"Put up the shotgun, Mr. Algol," the Judge commanded. "There's no reason for there to be any more bloodshed. Besides, I'm the one you want."

"Well, well, if it isn't that high and mighty Judge Thaddeus Nathan," Curly said victoriously, and he aimed the shotgun at the judge. "So, I finally get to settle the score with you. Maybe shoot this little prick kid, too. How's that sound, Judge?"

"Fuck you, Algol," came Wade's uncensored response. You murdered Mrs. Nathan. You murdered my dad. You even slaughtered your own parents. You're like a rabid animal, and you don't deserve to live."

"Is that so, hotshot!" Curly sneered, and he pointed the shotgun in Wade's direction. "Say adios, kid," and just as he pulled the trigger, Thaddeus leaped in front of Wade and took a partial blast from the shotgun on the right side of his body. Thaddeus stumbled backward and a moment later he fell off the ledge, into the swirling waters below and was swept away.

"Judge!" came Wade's frantic cry, but Thaddeus had disappeared from view.

Curly trained his double-barreled shotgun on Wade now and pulled the trigger again. Nothing happened. He had forgotten to re-load when he'd scared off the kids with his blast on the bridge. He reached into his pocket for his remaining two shells and began to re-load both barrels.

Wade didn't wait around. He sprinted away as fast as he could, dodging and weaving as he ran, trying to remain a moving target. He ran in the direction that the fast moving water in the gorge had carried the Judge. He had to get to him. He knew he was wounded, and he'd never forgive himself if Thaddeus died trying to save him. Breathe in; breathe out. Wade ran like the wind, with Curly in hot pursuit.

Marly heard the second shotgun blast and quickened her pace. She had no idea what she'd find when she caught up to Thaddeus and Wade, but she was determined to offer whatever help she could. She suspected that Cassie had also heard the gun blast and knew that she and additional help would be on their way soon.

A minute later she arrived at the edge of the gorge and saw where the horrible confrontation had occurred. She saw blood sprayed on the ground and groaned, "Oh no!" She continued running along the path. She prayed for Wade and Thaddeus' safety.

Even carrying the shotgun, Curly was fast, but not nearly as fast as Wade Henry. The gorge continued its steep downward trend for another two hundred yards, and then transitioned into a hilly, woodland terrain. The rushing water abated its mad rush and finally pooled into a broad, shallow pond created by a logjam of fallen trees and brush.

Wade saw the pool of water and began frantically looking for any sign of the Judge. There was vegetation everywhere, and it was difficult doing an adequate search while also constantly looking over his shoulder for Curly Algol.

Finally, Wade focused on a place where the rushing waters entered the pool, and he carefully watched the way the current shifted dramatically and carried surface flotsam to the far left side of the pool.

"Go with the flow," he thought, and he went over to examine that area of the pond.

Wade examined the logjam here very closely, but couldn't see anything. He peered into the shallow water around him in case the judge was caught somehow. No luck. Wade knew that time was critical now if he was to save Thaddeus. He intensified his search. He looked under brushy banks. He dove underwater to see if he could see anything. He didn't. He saw another large jam of fallen trees and ran over to it. He pulled up short. Curly Algol was standing fifteen feet away.

"You know, kid, I'm getting a little tired of this running around the woods shit. What say we put an end to our little Canadian adventure here. I reckon even if the Judge did survive the 12 gauge blast, he'd have likely drowned in the gorge. Hell, falling off the cliff probably broke his freakin' neck. Anyway, it's been real fun, kid, but you gotta go!"

Curly aimed the shotgun at a despondent Wade Henry, and the sound of a gunshot echoed throughout Maligne Canyon. A moment later Curly Algol's body went rigid, and he fell to the ground, dead, with a 9mm bullet hole through his neck.

Wade stood there totally stunned. He saw Curly's body laying face down in the mud, saturated in blood. He cringed and reveled at the sight. Then, he looked over to the direction from which the shot had come, and he saw a battered and bloodied Thaddeus Nathan lying on his back on the bank of the pond with his Glock in his hand.

Wade rushed over and dropped to the ground next to the judge and prayed that he was still conscious.

"Judge," he cried out anxiously. "Judge, can you hear me? It's Wade. Please don't leave me." Wade's chest heaved and tears started pouring from his eyes.

Thaddeus' eyes fluttered open and he saw his tearful friend cradling his head.

"Oooh, that really hurt." He winced. "Did I get him? Did I get Curly Algol?"

Wade was never so happy to see anyone in his entire life. He pointed to where Curly's lifeless body lay in the mud and said, "You sure did, Judge, you got him good."

The Judge tried to give Wade a little smile, but he'd been severely injured, and it was a miracle he was even alive. He winced a little more instead.

A few moments later, Marly burst through the underbrush and fell alongside Wade and Thaddeus. She saw there wasn't much she could do, so she immediately ran back to meet any others on the trail so they could get medical attention for Thaddeus.

The first person she saw was Cassie, who came running at full tilt, followed shortly thereafter by two EMTs and three police officers. Bekka's earlier phone call to the police had gotten immediate action and was likely responsible for saving the Judge's life. They all followed Marly who began leading them back down the trail to where Thaddeus and Wade were.

Wade was basically unhurt, with the exception of some abrasions and symptoms of mild shock. Thaddeus' injuries were far more serious. He suffered trauma mostly to the upper right torso area of his body. A large area of skin had been shredded away by the shotgun blast. Most of the bleeding had stopped, aided by the cold water temperature, but infection would be an immediate concern for the medical personnel.

Wade sat wearily on the bank of the pond, holding Thaddeus' head, and stared into space waiting for help to arrive. His mind drifted to different people in his life… his mom, his dad, even the Indian elders.

He briefly wondered if Kayla would ever want to be with a guy who led such a violent life. He couldn't blame her if she didn't. He told himself he'd cross that bridge when he came to it.

He remained seated on the bank of the pond holding the Judge when he heard, "Wade, Wade honey!" He turned and was in even further shock when he saw his mom running toward him.

"What..." was about the only word Wade could utter before Cassie engulfed him in an enormous mother-hug. She held on to him tightly; then she held him at arms' length so she could look at him.

She then kneeled down to look closely at Thaddeus as the EMTs began assessing his injuries and stabilizing him for transport. Thaddeus briefly opened his bleary eyes and saw Cassie crying and smiling at him. He gave her a weak smile back.

"Sorry, ma'am, but we have to go," said one of the EMTs. "We have a medical helicopter meeting us at the top of that ridge; so we have to take the patient on a little uphill hike first. Don't worry. He'll be okay. We've got him!"

Wade and Cassie watched as four very strong-looking men carried Thaddeus in a litter up the side of a steep ridge. Two minutes after they reached the summit, the helicopter was airborne en route to Jasper Regional Medical Center.

Marly joined Cassie and Wade, and together the three of them slowly walked back up the canyon trail and finally came to rest at the tea house where Lucien and Bekka were waiting for them. They were emotionally and physically exhausted.

"Mom, I am shocked to see you here," Wade said when they were inside the tea house. "I mean I'm really glad to see you, but this is a total mind blow. You're actually here in Jasper! When did you get here? How did you get here?"

"I know, Wade, and please don't be cross with me. I'll explain it all to you later. I just got so worried because I hadn't heard from you for a few days, and I knew that crazy Algol man was stalking you guys. I am just so glad that you're okay and pray that the Judge pulls through."

"Mom, the Judge saved my life twice! He got shot for me, and he shot that killer to protect me. I can't believe how brave he was, and I'm just so grateful to him for everything he did. He was incredible, Mom."

Cassie cried when she heard Wade share this. She was so thankful to Thaddeus and couldn't believe his bravery either.

"I don't know what I would do if anything ever happened to either of you. That's the real reason why I came up here. Please forgive a caring mother."

They hugged again and then went to join the others. Cassie introduced Wade to Lucien Kindred and explained how helpful Lucien had been in flying her out to Edmonton after the Kissinger board meeting and then accompanying her to Jasper.

"Lucien's been a friend, Wade. I wouldn't have managed as well without him."

Wade thanked Lucien very much for helping his mom and apologized for Lucien's getting dragged into such a tragic situation. They agreed they'd talk more once things calmed down.

After the police secured the park and took initial reports from Cassie, Wade, Marly, and Lucien, they all returned to the Chalet Village to recuperate. It had been an ordeal, the likes of which none of them ever wanted to experience again.

Chapter 43

THE DAYS THAT FOLLOWED were a bit of a challenge for every-one. Each person had to find their own way to process all that had occurred at Maligne Canyon. Once Lucien was convinced that Cassie and Wade were safe in Jasper, he returned to Edmonton to oversee his pressing business operations. Cassie promised to keep him apprised of developments as they occurred. Their trip to Jasper together had forged a bond between them that they would carry forever.

Cassie also contacted president Charles Edberg at the college to share details, and to request a leave of absence. Lucien followed up with his own calls to President Edberg and board chair, Brian Christopher. They all agreed that Cassie could take as much time as she needed.

Thaddeus slept for the first thirty-six hours in the hospital's ICU. He was watched round the clock and then listed in stable but guarded condition once all threat of infection had been elimi-nated. Despite being medicated for pain, he was reasonably alert and hospital staff moved him into a private room where he was permitted visitors.

But the physical wounds weren't the only medical consideration. He was depressed. He had never killed a man before, and even though he believed that Curly Algol deserved to die, he never expected that he would be the executioner.

"Hey there, handsome," Marly warmly said as she entered Thaddeus' hospital room. "Want to go for a hike in Maligne Canyon?" she gently teased.

Thaddeus was very pleased to see her smiling face. "Maybe tomorrow," he replied. "I may need a shoulder to lean on though."

The two of them talked quietly, with Marly doing most of the talking and Thaddeus nodding as needed.

"Wade and Cassie will be coming along shortly, but I wanted to see you and make sure you hadn't totally given up on Jasper hospitality."

"I understand from Doctor Provine," she continued, "that you may be released in a few days. He thinks you may need a rehab facility for a couple of weeks though. I told him that you are welcome to stay with us at the Chalet Village, and I'd be happy to dust off some of my old caregiver skills and keep a close eye on you."

"That's very generous of you, Marly, but I feel like I've brought enough hardship on you folks as it is," Thaddeus sighed. "I don't want to be an imposition. Thank you though."

"Thaddeus, why don't you let me worry about the imposition part," Marly countered. "Besides, I think Cassie and Wade would feel a lot more comfortable knowing that I was looking after you rather than some short-term facility where nobody knows you."

"Well, I suppose you're right," the Judge relented. "Thank you very much for your kindness and your concern. I won't forget it, Marly."

Cassie and Wade appeared in his doorway a few minutes later. Cassie held a bright bouquet of flowers, and Wade looked like he was carrying the weight of the world on his shoulders. The sight of the bandages covering Thaddeus' torso made Wade sad, and he teared up when he saw his friend and mentor lying in the hospital bed.

Marly sensed that the three of them needed to re-connect, so she politely excused herself and told Thaddeus she'd be back tomorrow.

"Well, it's not exactly as comfortable a place as your kitchen, Cassiopeia, and I'm sure the food's not nearly as good, but I guess it'll have to do for a few days anyway," Thaddeus said.

"Oh Thaddeus, how can we ever thank you for everything you've done?" Cassie cried. "We just want you to heal and come home. I called Quentin and Luella yesterday and told them everything that's happened. Quentin said he'd be happy to stay on at your place until you're ready to come home. Luella didn't shed a tear over her brother.

I also called Sheriff Penrod," Cassie continued, "to tell him about Curly, but he told me the Jasper police had already contacted him and all the other police departments whose jurisdictions Curly Algol had terrorized."

"Sounds like you two have things pretty much under control," Thaddeus remarked. "When do you think you'll be heading back to Indiana?"

She told him that Lucien Kindred had to return to Kissinger College in two days for another board meeting, and that he offered to fly them back.

"So, we'll leave tomorrow afternoon, but I hate the thought of leaving you here," Cassie lamented.

Thaddeus nodded his understanding. "Marly's offered to put me up till I mend, and I think I'm going to take her up on that."

The trip hadn't turned out exactly like Thaddeus and Wade had planned, but he knew it could easily have been far worse.

"Mind if I talk with my traveling partner here for a few minutes, Cassie? We could probably both use a little closure on our episode in Maligne Canyon."

Cassie kissed Thaddeus gingerly on the forehead and told them to take their time. She'd be waiting in the lobby.

"I hate leaving you like this," Wade said. "You saved my life, twice, and I feel like I'm walking out on you." He began to weep.

The two men sat quietly in Thaddeus' softly lit room, and then Thaddeus spoke.

"We had one heck of a watch-about didn't we, Wade? Well, aside from that last part in the canyon. I suspect we'll always remember our adventure. I know I will."

Wade managed a little smile. "Yeah, me too, Judge."

"As I've gotten older," the Judge began again, "I've come to understand that some things in life you just can't control, no matter how well you've planned. Curly Algol was hellbent on death and destruction, and it was only through sheer luck and our determination to stick together that we managed to stay off his list of trophies."

"It might've been sheer luck," Wade added, "but I'll never forget how you jumped in front of me when he pulled the shotgun trigger. No sir, that was the bravest thing I've ever seen."

The two of them spent several more minutes recounting some of the episodes from their journey... the visits to see Salem Sue, the Dakota Dinosaur Museum, the Rough Riders Museum and many other stops along the way; not to mention Wade's excitement from meeting Kayla. They chose not to dwell too long on the murder and mayhem wrought by Curly's hands. Those tragedies were not something they wanted to think about right now. They were preparing to say goodbye for now, and it was hard for both of them.

"I still don't understand how the messages from the Indian elders figures into all of this. It's still such a mystery."

"Ah, my dear friend, welcome to Life. It's all a mystery, but the journey's been worth it to me. The best part for me was traveling with you, Wade; being able to see life through a smart young man's eyes. And now it's time for you to continue on your own. You have got so much to look forward to, Wade Henry, and I've never been prouder to call anyone my friend."

Wade teared up again. "Oh Thaddeus, thank you," was the only thing he was able to say.

"I'll be back home in a few weeks," the Judge added. "I know that you and your mom and Quentin and Luella have things well in hand. And don't fret about me. I've got a feeling that Marly will help me on my road to recovery, and besides, I'm not ready to become stardust yet."

As Wade turned to leave the Judge's side and meet Cassie in the lobby, Thaddeus looked at him directly in the eyes and spoke one last time.

"And remember, my young friend, you are the one who will change the way we see the stars." He pointed to Wade; then to his own eyes and then straight up toward the sky.

Chapter 44

AFTER THE TERRIBLE EVENTS at Maligne Canyon, Thaddeus had been hospitalized in Jasper for a week. Then, under Marly's tender care, he convalesced at the Chalet Village for a few more weeks and found himself feeling very comfortable there. He knew he would have to return to Indiana sometime soon, but knowing that Quentin had things under control, he decided to take his time and heal.

He wasn't quite as physically robust as he had been prior to the death-struggle with Curly Algol in the canyon, but he managed to improve with each week that passed.

Marly didn't exactly dote on Thaddeus since she was so busy running the Chalet Village, but she was definitely in tune with his needs, and she and her staff kept a watchful eye on him. Truth was, Marly really enjoyed having Thaddeus as a guest at the village. She appreciated many of the Judge's qualities and was very impressed by Thaddeus' youthful spirit and his passion for justice. More than anything though, she was attracted to his kindness. He was a fine gentleman, and she admired that.

She had set him up in a lovely cabin next to hers, and they enjoyed several dinners together, and of course did some occasional stargazing as the night skies permitted. Marly was cautious to give Thaddeus all the space he needed, but as time went on they spent virtually every day together and grew very close.

Thaddeus returned to his home on Brick Chapel Road about a month after leaving the hospital. He wanted his return to be a bit of a surprise, but Marly had spilled the beans to Cassie and Wade, and they held a small welcome home party for him.

"I don't suppose it would be possible to plan something as simple as coming home, and not have the whole county know about it," Thaddeus mused when he saw everyone waiting on his patio with signs and balloons.

He was actually very touched by their show of affection but covered his emotions by giving his friends and neighbors a little guff. It was a small gathering. Wade and Cassie of course were there, and Kayla had driven over from Indianapolis to be with Wade. Quentin and Luella had the house spotless and ready for the Judge's return.

Quentin introduced Thaddeus to Luella, and the Judge offered his heartfelt condolences to her on the death of her parents and the loss of her home. He also thanked her very much for everything she did to help Quentin take care of his and the Henrys' properties.

At first Luella felt a little insecure meeting Judge Nathan because he was such a highly-regarded legend in Prindle County, and because of all of the tragedies that the Judge had suffered at her brother's hands.

Thaddeus sensed her insecurity, and said, "Luella, you were not your brother's keeper, and you are welcome to stay here as long as you choose. You too, Quentin. We can talk about it more tomorrow."

"And you sir!" Thaddeus said warmly to Quentin as he scanned his property. "The place is looking mighty good. I can't thank you enough for the peace of mind you provided us when Wade and I were galavanting across the northern plains.

Seriously Quentin," the Judge solemnly added, "you and Luella have shown a lot of character, and I am eternally grateful to you both."

Quentin replied graciously and said he'd be happy to give the Judge a little tour of things after the party was over. But the party didn't end early that night. No one was in a hurry to leave.

Cassie was supposed to have an early meeting at Kissinger College the next day, but she texted her assistant and said she'd be in the office mid-morning instead.

Around 12:30 AM Quentin and Luella began cleaning up the patio and kitchen and Kayla said it was time for her to head back home Wade walked Kayla to her car and said, "There are obviously some important things I haven't told you yet, about our experiences after we left you and your mom in North Dakota. I promise I'll fill you in later if that's okay with you." She nodded yes and kissed him goodnight.

Cassie and Wade talked for several minutes more with the Judge, and Cassie said, "I can't believe that just a few weeks ago we were all here talking about your taking your trip to Canada, and now here were are again. Hard to believe everything that's happened in the interim."

Cassie went into the kitchen to help with final clean-up and then bid everyone a fond goodnight. Quentin and Luella retired to their guest room, and Wade and Thaddeus sat on the patio, under the stars, talking about their futures.

Wade surprised Thaddeus by telling him that he had been in touch with the administration office at Duke University and had requested that they delay his admission until the following fall. The university agreed.

Wade felt like he was recovering well enough from their ordeal, but he wanted to see some more of the world before committing to furthering his education. He thought that once his college career began, he could have trouble finding free time again.

Wade also nurtured his close relationship with Kayla who respected Wade's decision to put off starting college. She was particularly excited when he told her where he planned to travel. Chile. She planned on staying in close contact with him and visiting him in Chile during her semester breaks at Northwestern.

"Chile!" Thaddeus exclaimed. "Why Chile, and how does your mom feel about this?" And then when Wade pointed up to the sky, Thaddeus knew and he smiled.

"I think Mom's fine with my decision since she knows my time away is part of my education too," Wade said. "And besides, Judge, it's all your fault," Wade teased. "If you hadn't gotten me hooked on astronomy, I wouldn't be going."

Wade explained how he had written to the administrator at Chile's famed Atacama Large Millimeter Array observatory requesting an entry-level position. He was elated when they wrote back and said they would be happy to have him serve an internship studying star birth formation during the early universe.

Thaddeus shook his head in amazement at how much his young friend had grown intellectually and emotionally in just a few short weeks. He couldn't help but feel that their walkabout together had achieved some of the results he was hoping for.

"As for me," Thaddeus said when Wade was finished explaining his plans, "I think I have some unfinished business in Canada that I need to settle. I may be gone for a while too."

Wade wasn't entirely sure what the Judge meant by this, but he had total faith in any decision that Thaddeus might make.

"I promise I'll keep in close touch with you and your mom, and I need to speak with Quentin and Luella about staying on here at the house for a while longer."

After Wade went back home, Thaddeus sat in his familiar chair in his study and looked around the room. He turned the lights low, poured himself a glass of Glenmorangie scotch and looked around the room. His eyes fell on Ellie's photograph, and he sighed deeply at her memory.

"Oh Ellie, I'll always love you, honey, but I need your permission to move on with my life."

Ellie's image smiled back at him as if to say she understood. Thaddeus knew his late wife would never begrudge him his opportunity for happiness, but he felt pangs of guilt too. He quietly said, "Thank you, darling." After several minutes he picked up his phone to call Marly at the Chalet Village.

"Well, good evening Thaddeus," came Marly's warm greeting. "How was the party?"

"It was really nice," Thaddeus replied. "Everything looks and feels pretty much the same, and yet I can't help but feel that my future lies elsewhere. Any chance you'd be willing to put up with my old sorry self for a while longer, Marly?"

"Come home to me here, Thaddeus, we can build a beautiful life together."

The next morning Quentin found the Judge sleeping in his chair in the study. He gently placed a comforter over him, but Thaddeus awoke in the process.

"Quentin, I have something I want to discuss with you," he quietly said. "I haven't shared this with anyone else yet, but I'll be returning to Jasper soon for an extended stay, and I'd really like it if you and Luella would consider making this your permanent home."

Quentin was bowled over by Thaddeus' generosity and stammered, "But this is your house, and well, I love it here, but this is your home."

"Not anymore, my friend. Everything and everyone comes and goes, and it's time for me to move on. And financially, don't worry,

I'll set up a special bank account before I leave that will handle all of your household expenses, including taxes, insurance, utilities and maintenance. Please accept this as my way of thanking you for your friendship and perhaps helping you get started on the next phase of your life."

Quentin was humbled by the Judge's kindness and generosity. He hugged Thaddeus and said, "It will always be your home, Judge, and I promise you that Luella and I will take good care of it for you."

During the next two days Thaddeus Nathan made what would be his last visit to familiar haunts in Prindle County. He visited with a few long-time friends and made specific arrangements with his financial advisor and legal counsel.

The day before he left for his return to Jasper, he made a special point of bringing Cassie with him to talk with Lyndon Tweedy at Kissinger College's Von Timm Observatory.

"Lyndon, I've been doing some talking with Cassie, and I've got a suggestion that could be a win-win for everyone concerned."

He proceeded to share his intention of making a major seven-figure endowment gift that would put the college's fundraising campaign over it's financial goal.

In consideration of Thaddeus' generosity, Cassie announced that board chair Brian Christopher and president Edberg recommended creation of the "Eleanor and Thaddeus Nathan Professorship in Astrophysics.

Lyndon knew what this meant to the future stability of his astronomy program and the Von Timm observatory. He was humbled and deeply grateful to his long-time friend and colleague for his generosity.

"You honor us, sir," came Lyndon's emotional reply. "I and my successors will be proud to sit in the Nathan Chair in perpetuity."

That evening Thaddeus enjoyed a final quiet dinner at Cassie's table surrounded by Wade, Cassie, Quentin and Luella. Their love brought closure for the Judge.

The next morning, Thaddeus was gone.

Epilogue

~ Twenty Years Later ~

Y EARS PASSED, and the adage that "time heals all wounds" proved to be mostly true. Regardless, none of the people who had been touched by the ugliness of the Curly Algol saga would ever be quite the same again.

The good news was that goodness had indeed triumphed over evil. The bad news was the terrible price that too many people had paid along the way.

Quentin and Luella married a year after Thaddeus returned to Jasper to be with Marly. Another year later, they had twin sons that they named Nathan and Henry after the two families they had come to love and admire. They lived in the Judge's home on Brick Chapel Road for another fifty plus years.

Luella had indeed earned the position as Bernice Sweet's assistant in the college's admissions office. She and Bernice worked very closely together as a coordinated team for five years, and upon Bernice's retirement, Luella stepped into her role as director of admissions and continued in that capacity for many years to come.

Quentin Harp continued to drive for UPS for three more years, and then his supervisor took him off the road and had him learn the operations of the UPS distribution center in their hometown of Someday, Indiana. Upon his boss' retirement, Quentin was tapped to fill his shoes. He performed admirably in that position until his own retirement many years later.

Cassie Henry resided in Prindle County for the duration of her days, but she and Lucien Kindred remained very close friends. She seriously considered marrying Lucien at one point and moving to Edmonton, but she couldn't bring herself to leave the Midwest and her work at the college. It wasn't that she didn't care deeply for Lucien. She did, but she also knew her heart would always belong to Wade's late father, Ben. As serendipity would have it, Kissinger College's President Edberg asked her to fill Ben's previous position as director of the Stanley Institute for Ethics. Under her direction, the Institute's reputation grew in international fame.

She and Quentin and Luella grew even closer over time, and their presence helped soften the loneliness she felt from Wade's absence.

Kayla graduated from Northwestern University with a bachelors degree in Biology. She then followed in her father's footsteps and became a highly regarded physician. Her medical school studies, internship and residency at the University of Chicago kept her enormously busy, but not too busy to cultivate an enduring love for Wade Benjamin Henry.

They had married on a mountaintop in Chile on Wade's thirty-third birthday and finally ended their fifteen year, long-distance courtship. They remained married for nearly sixty years, and had two beautiful children, a son named Thaddeus and a daughter named Cassiopeia.

Wade's walkabout with the Judge paid a lifetime of dividends for him. Upon graduation from Duke University in International Studies, Wade earned his MBA from Duke's renowned Fuqua School of Business. The combination of these two degrees was further enhanced by Wade's ongoing association with the astronomy teams at the Chilean observatories.

Along the way, Wade also cultivated close professional friendships with several prominent administrators and researchers at NASA. Before long, MIT came knocking on Wade's door and recruited him as a doctoral candidate in astrophysics.

During this time Wade and Kayla enjoyed living in Cambridge, Massachusettes with their young children, and Kayla enhanced her medical career further on the faculty of Harvard University and Massachusettes General Hospital. Cassie visited them regularly to dote on her adorable grandchildren, and Wade and Kayla returned to Indiana as often as their busy schedules allowed.

Over the years Wade kept in regular touch with Thaddeus and Marly. Thaddeus was constantly sending articles to Wade about new astronomical discoveries, as well as clippings about Wade's latest achievements. No man could ever have been prouder of another than Thaddeus was of Wade.

Thaddeus Nathan had indeed moved to Jasper where he and Marly married, and he spent his remaining years helping Marly look after the Chalet Village. He loved the Canadian Rockies and became an expert on the geology, flora and fauna of his newly adopted home.

He also became a principal figure in the establishment of the Jasper Dark Sky Preserve, and he was recognized as its international goodwill ambassador. The Preserve's logo bore the image of the Corona Borealis with the outline of two eyes and an arrow pointing upward.

On a frosty evening in mid-October, Lucien Kindred's corporate jet landed on a runway at Jasper's international airport. The plane's passengers disembarked and climbed into two waiting vehicles. One was driven by Lucien, and the second by his life-long friend, and now business partner, Gordy Fontaine. They drove the short distance to the Chalet Village, and Marly met them at the entrance to her cabin.

"He's out here," Marly said to everyone who had come to pay respects to the Judge. Cassie, Wade and Kayla, Quentin and Luella, and Lucien all followed her out onto their large deck. The Judge was now ten days shy of his ninetieth birthday, and he sat in a large chair covered in blankets cradling a small pair of binoculars.

His health had been failing recently, and Marly wanted to be sure that all of the special people in Thaddeus' life had a chance to say goodbye before it was too late. The end was coming very soon.

"Thaddeus," Marly softly said, "you have company, dear."

Thaddeus turned his head and saw who was gathered around.

"Oh, my goodness" he cried out. "It's my family!" he exclaimed. He reached out to touch everyone in turn, and then he smiled at Marly and simply said, "Thank you. Thank you for everything."

Wade kissed Thaddeus on the top of his head and knelt in front of him so they could be eye to eye. Wade told the Judge about his most recent assignment as the new director of project development for the Giant Magellan Telescope. It would be built on a mountaintop in Chile, and when operational, it would see deeper into the universe than anything ever before. It was the opportunity of a lifetime.

Wade had been selected because of his unique resume. The financiers behind the billion dollar project were delighted to find a candidate of Wade's caliber who understood international relations, finance, politics and astrophysics.

Thaddeus patted Wade's hand, and said, "See, the Indian elders were right. You are the one who will change the way we see the stars."

They remained together for a while longer, and then Marly suggested that Thaddeus needed his rest. Each took a tearful turn saying personal things to Thaddeus, and then they departed.

After Wade left the cabin, he walked across the road to where years ago he and Marly and the Judge had peered into the night sky drinking Sangria. The Athabasca River continued its endless, rolling flow, and above him the Milky Way displayed its celestial wonder.

Wade looked back across the road to Thaddeus' cabin a final time and then glanced heavenward. He saw a shooting star streak across the sky, and then it was gone.